THE SAWT(

A CASE LEE NOVEL

Book 10

By Vince Milam

WANT TO JOIN MY READERS CLUB WITH INSIGHTS, UPDATES, AN INSIDER'S LOOK AT STORY DEVELOPMENT, AND OTHER FUN ITEMS?
Go to: www.vincemilam.com

Other Case Lee adventures (click for **Vince Milam's Amazon Author Page**)
The Suriname Job: A Case Lee Novel Book 1
The New Guinea Job: A Case Lee Novel Book 2
The Caribbean Job: A Case Lee Novel Book 3
The Amazon Job: A Case Lee Novel Book 4
The Hawaii Job: A Case Lee Novel Book 5
The Orcas Island Job: A Case Lee Novel Book 6
The Nevada Job: A Case Lee Novel Book 7
The DC Job: A Case Lee Novel Book 8
The Texas Job: A Case Lee Novel Book 9
The Sawtooth Job: A Case Lee Novel Book 10

Acknowledgments:
Editor—David Antrobus at BeWriteThere - bewritethere.com
Cover Design by Rick Holland at Vision Press – *myvisionpress.com*.

As always, Vicki for her love and patience. And Mimi, Linda, and Bob for their unceasing support and encouragement.

Contents

Chapter 1

It started with mystery and misdirection and shadowland fog. It ended with terminal actions and lies and a murky affirmation I'd done the right thing.

"We are not alone, my Georgia peach."

Bo's statement slapped bad news across the immediate setting. When Bo made such a claim, you took it to the bank. I pulled the Glock from my jacket pocket, turned, and began asking for elaboration. He had gone, disappeared. Typical. Our former special ops spearhead, Bo could pull the cloak of invisibility routine in a heartbeat. I took comfort in that. But a third party joining us left comfort far down the table.

A late weekday afternoon, and we stood inside Bart and Ruth Hall's house in Palo Alto, California. Dr. Bartholomew Hall, PhD—engineering physics, and Dr. Ruth Hall, PhD—biomedical science. I sought Ruth, although Bart had hightailed it somewhere as well. Late to the game, the situation—the unwanted third party included—came as no surprise. Jules of the Clubhouse had warned me, and she would know.

Back against a disheveled bookcase, Glock in hand, I waited for either the third party's appearance or a sign Bo had flushed and captured the quarry. Smart money would bet on the latter. The neighborhood, dead quiet. The house, ransacked. My adrenaline meter, low. I couldn't fathom an OK Corral shootout within the current environment.

The unmistakable sound as a body hit wooden floor, a loud grunt, and an explosive expletive rang from the kitchen area. The expletive, Hebrew. I scooted along the wall-length bookcase, led with the Glock, and peered into the kitchen. Bo straddled a fit-looking midsized man and applied his weird hand grip along the guy's jawline, focused on nerve endings. The victim's left arm and leg twitched. Bo looked up and smiled.

"That's a spook you've got there, Bo."

"What flavor?"

"Mossad."

Bo leaned into the man's left ear and said, "Do not be frightened, and do not be dismayed."

"Romans?" I asked.

"Joshua. This is an Old Testament gentleman."

"I don't think this cat's up for an ecumenical discussion right now, bud, but keep your hold while I take a gander."

I rifled through the spook's clothing and pulled a passport, wallet, small high-end camera, and phone. Along with a small Beretta semiautomatic pistol chambered in .22 LR, for up close bullet-to-the-head work. I didn't believe whacking us was this guy's intent, but you never knew. His Israeli passport claimed "David Levy"—high odds a BS name. Mossad agents were top-notch, with deep cover a standard operating procedure. His phone remained locked, but his camera wasn't. A half dozen pictures contained close-ups of me and Bo. Damn, Sam.

I'd traveled under a false ID with accompanying false-name credit cards from a Cayman Island bank. Dollars to doughnuts this guy sent those photos to Tel Aviv and, within minutes, received a Case Lee dossier courtesy of facial recognition software at Mossad headquarters. A limited dossier, but one that entailed past dealings with them. A few false friendly encounters, others somewhat benign. One encounter, not included in my dossier, involved having a hand in offing one of their agents, which remained unknown on their end. Thank God.

"Okay, let him up, Bo."

Levy stood, stretched his neck, worked his jaw, adjusted his clothing, cast a stone-cold stare toward Bo, and addressed me.

"I expected a friendlier reception, Lee."

There it was. Sometimes high tech sucked, and Levy's use of my name tossed any discussions onto thin ice.

"We failed to hear your hail-fellow-well-met Mossad greeting. My apologies."

"Who's your partner?"

A good sign—Bo remained off Mossad's radar. And database.

"Ask him."

He turned and addressed Bo. The Mossad agent was in his midthirties, fit as a fiddle, with close-cropped blond hair.

"That's a slick grip you applied. I'm starting to get feeling back in my left side. Do you have a name?"

The spook's accent—midwestern US, Indiana flat. Not surprising. A good-looking guy, he'd blend in anywhere in the States. A man with a ready smile, ingratiating personality, and prepared to put a bullet in your head without remorse.

"I'm a fellow wayfarer," Bo said, smiling. "Riding, as do you, universal currents. We should acknowledge common ground, you and I. An affinity for arid lands and ancient souls binds us."

Levy stared, blinked once, nodded, and turned back my way.

"Who is your client on this one, Lee?"

"Maybe you guys."

True enough. A shadowy outfit in Zurich, Switzerland, named Global Resolutions offered up my gigs. They acted as an anonymity buffer between me and whoever contacted them with requests. I seldom knew their client's identity, and on the flip side my identity remained undisclosed. Unless spookville entered the picture, which pushed all bets off the table and made my response to Levy hold water. Mossad may have contacted Global Resolutions and asked for me. A possibility, and one not lessened with Levy's question—a casual enquiry that could have acted as cover for misdirection. Welcome to freakin' spookville.

"Let's say it was Mossad." He rotated his shoulder and stretched his neck again, countering the aftereffects of Bo's ministrations. "Feel free to tell me what you've found."

"The Halls are lousy housekeepers."

"Perhaps it reflects their genius."

"Perhaps because every spy outfit on the planet has already trooped through here."

"Starting with your government."

Fair enough. The Company—the CIA—might have worked with the FBI and Homeland Security chasing down *Where's Waldo?* clues. Might, because the Company remained restricted to foreign operations only. This stricture—a codified law—was often ignored for a variety of reasons, the foremost being the Company could get away with it. Laws for thee, not for me.

As for other spook outfits, I'd bet good money Mossad, Britain's MI6, and China's MSS—along with several other alphabet soup names— had rummaged through the Halls' lifestyle detritus like ragpickers working a garbage pile. The FBI, or the Company, first grabbed the good stuff, anything related to the Halls' work. That pile sat in a locked room somewhere in DC while forensic experts crawled over it like ants. Same with whatever they found in the Halls' Stanford offices, our next stop.

The swarming activity pointed toward a solid reality, flaring neon bright. The Halls (or at least Ruth Hall) were still missing. Hence my contract. I was late to the game and held little hope of success but would give it the old college try.

"Regarding your government," Levy continued, "there's an FBI agent parked on the street several houses down."

"Do tell."

"Don't say I've never done you a solid."

Bo and I had hopped the back fence for house entrance, the same as Levy, so it appeared the FBI weren't too concerned with who meandered in at this point. One guy out front kept tabs on things and signaled that little remained discoverable at the Halls' residence. High odds we'd wandered in while Levy picked through the house's interior. He, too, appeared late to the game. Maybe. You just never knew, and I wouldn't burn too many mental calories backdooring spook rationales.

"Here's the deal, Levy. Go hang in the backyard while my partner and I have a look-see."

"My possessions?"

"I'll leave them on the kitchen table. By the time you retrieve your peashooter, we'll be too far away for it to have any effect."

"I'm happy to oblige, but consider this: we're both after the same thing, and for all the right reasons. We should cooperate."

A fruitless pitch, and he knew it, but his training mandated the offer.

"I'll mull it over. Now get your ass out the door."

He did, taking a seat on a back deck rattan chair. Bo smiled my way with an eyebrow lift and tapped his left ear, gently pointing out major screwup number one on my part. The house could have bugs planted all over it. Listening devices from multiple outfits, which now added another layer of vital concern. Levy and I had bantered each other's name about. No big deal for him as his was fake, although I'd mentioned Mossad. Which may have served his needs. But his spouting out my last name could have sent analysts from Beijing to London scurrying for connectivity. Great. If the FBI guy down the street also listened in, he'd forward everything to DC. Just freakin' great.

We split up and scoured the house, a 1950s Eichler construction. It had a Frank Lloyd Wright look and feel, with an open floorplan. At about fifteen hundred square feet, it would run for a cool two million plus in Palo Alto due to housing demand from Google and Facebook employees. The same house in Amarillo or Des Moines would go for a hundred grand. Go figure. The Halls had lived there for thirty years, and what spookville considered old and irrelevant intel now lay scattered about on bookshelves, floors, and tabletops.

I scoured the living area, Bo the kitchen. Books, books, and more books lay scattered about—some esoteric, others plain vanilla. Clandestine services had scooped up all the inevitable science-related publications, leaving books on the fall of Rome, chronicles on Leonardo da Vinci, house construction techniques, political thrillers, noir mysteries, hot springs in the western US, best buy automobiles from 1998, *Joy of Cooking* (1975 edition), famous Irish farm breeds. Plus two large coffee table books—one on impressionist painters, the other Hudson River artists. Mixed with the reading material, their pieces scattered: jigsaw puzzles. Large ones.

Their bedroom held little other than a small clothes closet, half full, and minimal jewelry or other adornments. A broken picture frame had held a photo, now on the floor, of Ruth and Bart. They both stood wrapped in oversized beach towels, the background a rocky slope. Both in their early sixties, bodies toward the camera with heads turned, smiling at each other and holding hands. She was thin as a rail with short, wet gray hair, a head taller than her husband's roundish body. Their towels—hers with Minnie Mouse in assorted poses against a white background, his blue-and-white striped—were wrapped tight just under their armpits. Bart showed almost bald, and what little Friar Tuck hair he had lay plastered wet against his head. Both their sets of eyeglasses displayed fogged-over lenses, Ruth's frames retro cat-eye, his owlish round.

The photo struck a poignant note, warm and touching. Two genius scientists, clearly in love, goofy mannerisms evident, with a total lack of concern how they might look to others. Most folks would only frame a more posed photo, one both parties approved. The Halls' picture hollered goofballs, two goobers standing together, in love. I thought it was great.

I took the photo, although I had plenty others downloaded from their Stanford profiles and scientific conventions where they'd given speeches. Bo met me at the bedroom door and held up a half-eaten box of chocolate treats. I raised one eyebrow and he pointed at the chocolate's source: Belgium. I showed him the photo.

"Two as one." He whispered with gravity, nodding. "Sealed, bonded, and supporting each other on their mutual path. Right and tight."

"I thought so as well," I said, also whispering. "What's with the chocolate?"

"European."

"So?"

"We gather gleanings, the reapers having passed through. The confection's origin may hold meaning."

I sighed and said, "Yeah, maybe. It's a picked-clean environment, bud."

We both checked the lone bathroom. Not a single personal possession remained—no toothbrushes, no soap, no pills—with DNA collection and medical data already harvested.

I gave another long sigh and head-pointed toward the back door. On the back deck, Levy sat, one leg crossed, and raised a single eyebrow my way.

"Well?" he asked, regarding collecting his personal items.

"On the kitchen table."

"Any interesting finds?" he asked, rising.

"They're both in Nome, Alaska. It's a tad chilly up there this time of year, but if you hustle you can beat the competition."

"Thanks for sharing."

"Don't say I've never done you a solid."

He headed for the back door, stopped, and said, "I may text you down the road and see how things are going."

Mossad knew my number from past dealings.

"Don't bother."

"We could help each other, Lee."

Variants of the same line—delivered over the years from the CIA, MI6, Mossad, China's MSS, and Russia's SVR—held a common thread. Bullshit.

"Let us maintain cosmic connectivity," Bo said with a smile. "Free flow, unencumbered by technical machinations."

Levy stared Bo's way for several moments, shook his head, shot me a last glance, and entered the house. Bo and I climbed the back cedar fence and headed through the neighborhood toward my parked SUV armed with flotsam and jetsam intel—Rome's fall, beef bourguignon recipes, a photo of two towel-wrapped scientists, a quick refresher on Monet, and a small box of half-eaten Belgian chocolate.

THE SAWTOOTH JOB

Chapter 2

The job offer came in while I reloaded the firepit on Jess's back courtyard. Jessica Rossi, my girlfriend and former Charlotte PD detective and current private investigator. She engaged with classic sleuthing jobs that often involved infighting within high-net-worth families. Jess's niece, Lily, helped me with the firepit.

"It's not that cold," Lily said.

"No, it's not. But Jess likes a fire. I do too."

"I kinda like getting one started. Pops showed me how."

Pops—Jess's dad.

"Then you can fire this one up. Watch out for splinters."

"I know," she said with an early teen eye roll.

I smiled and acknowledged Lily's perspective toward me as a brand-new incursion into her challenged family structure. And acknowledged my status as older than dirt in her inexperienced eyes. Not as old as Pops, but high odds she deemed anyone over thirty as nigh on ancient.

Jess and I had returned from Portland, Oregon, several weeks earlier. We'd attended Catch's wedding—a blood brother from Delta Force days—where Jess had met my family and other Delta brothers. The event had triggered an honest opening in our relationship that had, until then, teetered on a pass/fail fulcrum. The relationship, and wedding, passed with flying colors, and the honest exposure included Jess's home situation.

Her sister, Betts, was a heroin addict. A reality Jess had kept hidden during our monthslong relationship. The reveal wasn't a showstopper—

drug addiction affected hundreds of thousands of families across the US, and I expressed as much, along with sympathy and admiration for Jess stepping up to the plate regarding Lily. Betts had good days and bad days, good weeks and awful weeks. During grim periods, Jess would take Lily into her place. When on a job, Pops, who I'd yet to meet, would substitute as best he could. A lousy situation, but one handled with aplomb by all parties. In particular, Lily. She accepted the situation as part of her life, appreciated and loved Jess, and rolled with the punches. A great kid.

"Watch your fingers," I said.

Lily wielded a small hatchet, creating kindling.

"What would you do if I chop off a finger?"

She spoke toward the firewood chunk she worked on.

"I suppose haul you to the hospital. If reconnecting the finger proved unsuccessful, break out the steak seasoning."

"What?"

She halted her work and looked my way.

"We'll take advantage of the extra meat, and fire-roast an appetizer. Silver linings, Lily. Silver linings."

"Gross."

It came with an exaggerated eye roll, but when she focused again on the task at hand, she wore a wide grin. Jess strolled from the kitchen, through the double french doors, handed me a Grey Goose on the rocks, delivered a quick kiss, and said, "Lil, when you get the fire started, come help in the kitchen, please."

I enjoyed shared kitchen time with Jess, but she'd explained when Lily lived with her, their time together during meal prep opened locked conversational doors. I got it, and remained on the courtyard, scooted my chair closer to the fire, flipped open my laptop, and captured the dark web message from Global Resolutions.

Find Ruth Hall, PhD, Stanford.

The timing was right. Jess would take off in a few days for her new contract in New Hampshire. Something about stolen and hidden money from a family trust. A multimillion-dollar trust. I'd left the *Ace of Spades* in Charleston and driven the three-plus hours to Charlotte, staying with Jess for five days—our longest together time. The first few days involved a conscious tiptoe around my first encounter with Lily, which disappeared once we became acquainted. But time for a new gig, my wounds healed from the last job in Texas, and the usual antsy factor began its encroachment on my downtime.

First, a Ruth Hall perusal. Renowned scientist, working at a Stanford research center with a focus on biomedical science. Which revealed diddly-squat for me. I'd visited Stanford years earlier and had a cursory grip on the Bay Area's look and feel, remembering it seldom dipped below freezing. A biggie this time of year with winter encroaching. Case Lee Inc.'s lone employee didn't handle cold weather well.

A solid gig, with no violent earmarks. A missing scientist. Can do easy—well, it was never easy, but compared to previous requests this one sounded like a slam dunk. Ruth Hall's husband also worked at the research center. I'd start with him after meeting with Jules of the Clubhouse—standard protocol before a new job's kickoff.

I'd make the five-hour Chesapeake, Virginia, drive, meet with Jules, and head west, young man. Well, not so young anymore. A reality aided and abetted with semi-healed bullet, knife, and fragment wounds. But I didn't tote an ounce of self-pity and was blessed with a marvelous girlfriend, a loving family, and three blood brothers. Any way you cut it, I sat in high cotton on life's prairie, and expressed as much toward the big one upstairs every morning.

I shot a reply to Global Resolutions and committed, jumping right on it.

Accepted.

I sent Jules a meeting request for the next afternoon, again via the dark web.

Ruth Hall, PhD Stanford, missing. Meeting tomorrow afternoon?

She replied with her usual succinct manner.

Two o'clock.

Done and done. An abrupt departure, but I'd played a disruptor role with Jess and Lily, and an early departure allowed those two private time for several days without my presence in the mix. Laptop closed, another firewood chunk tossed on the firepit, and I joined the kitchen crowd.

"Got a new gig," I said, pouring Jess and me a red wine blend from Virginia. "Good timing, with you on your New Hampshire job in a few days."

Jess stopped stirring and looked up.

"When does it start?"

"I'd like to get on it tomorrow."

She returned an indecipherable stare for several seconds before returning to her pasta sauce prep. It was clear I'd screwed up somehow. And not grasping the somehow plopped me smack dab in relationship-dumbass territory—not my first visit there. But we'd work it out.

"What's the job?" Lily asked as she chopped salad components.

"Find a missing scientist. She's a PhD in biomedical science. Don't ask me what that means."

"Jess told me you do dangerous jobs."

"Never on purpose. Things turn out that way sometimes."

Jess and I exchanged looks. Our relational reset at Catch's wedding included her acceptance that my jobs often went sideways. She didn't like it and alluded to such tight spots as fulfillment for a hang-it-on-the-edge slice of my psyche. She was right. And she also made it clear in the long term, such endeavors would have to fade. I got it.

Supper conversation ran the gamut from an English assignment at school due Friday to favorite foods to books and movies. Casual exchanges mixed with light laughter and gentle teasing. We never mentioned Lily's mom. Afterward, I cleaned the dishes while they reviewed more schoolwork. Then Jess asked Lily to shower and hit the sack. She and Jess hugged and kissed goodnight. No physical exchanges between Lily and me, expected, although she tossed a "Be careful on your job" my way. Good enough and a solid start. I genuinely liked her.

Jess and I gathered around the outdoor firepit, its warmth now welcomed, with cognacs in hand.

"She's a good kid," I said. "And lucky to have you in her life."

"It's a tough situation for her and, to a lesser degree, all of us. But she takes things in stride, which, I guess, is about all I can ask for. Lily knows she's loved without condition, and Pops and I will always be there for her."

We sat in comfortable silence for a while as the fire crackled, scooting chairs to avoid the smoke, and settled close together. Jess slipped off her shoes and laid her lower legs across my lap, the starter signal for a foot rub. Fine by me.

"So, starting the job tomorrow?"

"Yeah, I figured it would remove me from the personal dynamics so you two could have Case-free time."

"Well, here's the deal, bub. We're partners, right?"

"Yep."

"In the future we should discuss personal logistics together." She groaned as I worked her toes. "I would have liked you hanging out here another day or two."

"Sorry. I can change plans."

"No. You've lit the adrenaline fuse and would spend the time moping."

"I don't mope."

"So says the guy who lives on an old boat cruising up and down the Ditch. A brooding element might sit in *that* mix."

The *Ace of Spades*. My home. An old wooden cruiser transporting me up and down the Intracoastal Waterway, or the Ditch as fellow travelers called it, from Virginia to Florida with direction and destinations often dependent upon the weather.

"Reflection and meditation, madam. A far cry from brooding over slings and arrows."

"You're edging away from the matter at hand. In the future, can we discuss things affecting us both without unilateral decisions?"

"You're right and I'm sorry and I'll work on it."

"I would appreciate it. Although you've gained several brownie points with the massage. On to the heels, please."

"How would one cash in those points?"

"On our next rendezvous, bub. Lily is in the house. Besides, afternoon delights while she's at school have rung the register, have they not?"

"Yes, ma'am. Big time."

We laughed, sipped cognac, and stared at the crackling fire.

"Should I worry about shadowy players or flying bullets on this job?" she asked, her voice now low and filled with concern.

"Kinda doubt it, Jess."

A cavalier statement meant to ease her angst. Hard reality and past experiences pointed toward another gig with the ever present possibility of going sideways. You just never knew.

THE SAWTOOTH JOB

Chapter 3

A blustery day in a seedy section of Chesapeake as wind whipped and rain threatened. I nestled within an abandoned shop's doorway and checked my back trail. A parked car in front of a nearby liquor store halted a plastic grocery bag's tumbling progress along the street as an old man stepped from a ramshackle bar four doors down, lighting a smoke. Past the liquor store, a two-story brick building displayed a dry cleaner sign. Filipino operated, the dry cleaners occupied the lower floor. Above, ensconced within steel walls, sat Jules of the Clubhouse.

The Clubhouse was a blue-collar version of the CIA. Its clientele included run-of-the-mill operators like me, other clandestine services, industrial spies, and a wide array of information collectors. Unlike the other clandestine services with their focus on digital surveillance, Jules relied on human assets. Assets spread across the world. They included smugglers, fixers, chatty government bureaucrats, corrupt politicians, political staffers, black-market dealers, thieves, killers, revolutionaries, and general ne'er-do-wells of all stripes and colors. Her spiderweb tendrils extended into the shadow world's dark nooks and crannies, and her intel had saved my butt more than once.

The old man finished his smoke and returned inside, and my back trail showed no danger signs, so I crossed the street as my jacket fabric billowed with the wind. A brass bell hung from the dry cleaners' inside doorknob clanged while hooded Filipino eyes greeted me. I placed the Glock and cell phone and jacket on the wooden counter as an old woman covered them with dropped-off clothing. Jules didn't allow Clubhouse entry with such items. Through a discreet doorway, up squeaky wooden stairs, and a tap on the steel door. The door lock, electronically activated, clacked open.

Then the usual. I stepped in, greeted with a double-barreled shotgun's business end, wielded by a small older woman. Her one eye squinted as she aimed at my midsection.

"Enter, dear boy, and allow me perusal."

Translation: pull jean pockets out and perform a slow turn. I did, one hand holding an index card, the other with a wad of Benjamins. Satisfied, she used the weapon's barrel as a pointer, indicating I should sit in one of two uncomfortable wooden chairs across from her ancient desk. The door closed at my back, the lock engaged, and I sat.

"How are you, Jules?"

"Comme ci, comme ça. This withered creature before you, wracked with worry, celebrates your return from the borderlands. Tell me everything and leave nothing out."

She referenced my last job in Texas. As I provided a detailed overview, she leaned back, fished for a kitchen match in her work shirt pocket, and fired up a dead cigar resting at the desk's edge. Her black eyepatch, the band lost within her short DIY haircut, forced a focus on her good eye, which observed, eaglelike, as I told my tale. She waited until I'd finished for commentary.

"I shall repeat an admonition, too often ignored. You, and your compadres, are no longer spring chickens, and such endeavors as performed in Texas bring you, and them, far too close to the precipice."

"No other options, Jules."

"There are always other options. You, dear heart, are my favorite client. It wears on me knowing you muck about in the world under such perilous conditions."

I slid the index card across the table with the hope it would change the conversational direction. It didn't.

"You choose to avoid sound advice. Fine. But do remember you have saddled me with the painful task of informing your loved ones of your demise. I am not sanguine about such a burden. A load lessened if you behaved with greater caution."

"The ugly stuff finds me. I don't seek it."

"So you have said. Repeatedly. And yet, once again, you resided within the maelstrom while exhibiting, I can safely assume, a glint in your eye."

I made another attempt at an off-ramp.

"The index card contains a list of names. The ones with contact information still walk among us."

She puffed the cigar and stared at me before assessing my artifact.

"The Company asset?" she asked, perusing the list that contained, among the living, a CIA operator and a French Interpol cop.

"Low level."

"The Frenchman?"

"Interpol."

She accessed her accounting system, an old abacus, and lifted it at an angle. The black balls slid downward.

"Items with limited value," she said, now all business.

She slid the index card into a desk drawer and extended a bony finger, shifting a single ball along its rail.

"I know. But my backstory contained a few goodies."

"Hmm."

The backstory held, for her, no financial benefit. The abacus remained unadjusted. Hell, she might have known the Texas job's shadow machinations long before I did.

"Speaking of maelstroms, shall we discuss the Halls?" she asked.

"Helluva lousy lead-in, Jules."

"Would you prefer I prevaricate and speak about unicorns and rainbows?"

"No. But finding Ruth Hall didn't sound like, at least on the surface, ugly business."

She delivered a heavy sigh and slow headshake.

"Once again, you have ignored the one big thing."

The one big thing—nothing was ever as it seemed. And yeah, I'd ignored her golden rule.

"How bad is it?" I asked.

"Bad is relative."

"Relative to what?"

"You claim, dear boy, an aversion to wading in murky waters. Waters containing clandestine sharks. Yet here you sit, innocent and unassuming and unaware the bell tolls for donning your wetsuit."

Damn, Sam. I hadn't seen this coming. But on the upside, her descriptive proved, once again, Clubhouse value. Without Jules, I'd be screwed, blued, and tattooed.

"I've already accepted the job. And I've never pulled away from one. So, what's the gnarly factor?"

She shot me a wry grin and said, "You shall join a legion of fellow seekers. None benign, several imbued with terminal certitude. Perhaps, brave Ulysses, the time has arrived for declining an engagement."

"Let's talk context before I pull that trigger."

She leaned forward, elbows on desk, and blew smoke toward the ceiling.

"Clubhouse renumeration is required regardless of your in-or-out decision."

"Understood."

I didn't blame her. She'd spill whatever beans she had available, valued intel, and I'd pay for it. Fair enough and no hard feelings. The business items dispensed with, she leaned back, puffed the cigar, and delivered.

"You seek both husband and wife."

"That's not what the contract said."

"Oh, to live in such a world as yours. Taking events at face value as you mantle yourself with an innocent waif's perspective, choosing to ignore my repeated exhortations."

"Does listing my shortcomings cost as well? If so, let's skip that part."

"You pay for revelations. Revelation one—you seek both husband and wife."

"Okay. Let's play that one out."

"Both are missing."

I mulled over her statement for a few seconds. Possibility doors flung open, more questions than answers presented.

"Alright. Help a poor boy out, Jules. They're both professors at Stanford, right?"

"More or less."

"I take it clarity isn't on the menu."

She cackled and smiled.

"They are researchers, dear boy. Working together."

"Okay."

"Ruth, it would appear, brings biomedical science to the proverbial table. Bartholomew focuses on engineering physics. Together, they make an interesting amalgam. Which leads, Poirot, to the rumors and innuendos."

"Pins and needles, Jules."

"A tool, a device, which has more than piqued the Pentagon's interest, and the interest of other military entities."

"A weapon?"

She wafted a hand and stared at the ceiling.

"Who can say?" She lowered her head and delivered a hard stare. "What the Clubhouse *can* say is they both went missing at the same time."

My turn to stare at the ceiling with a frown, scratching a recent but healed shoulder wound. Item one—spooks would crawl all over this gig seeking the Halls, which made it a given I'd rub shoulders with a few. Nothing new there. Distasteful, but not new. But mutual pursuit presented a less dangerous format than having a target on my back. Hound dogs unleashed, the baying muted. I could navigate those waters. But a contractual request for finding half the team raised unknowns out the wazoo.

"Why only Ruth Hall, then? Find one, find them both?"

"I doubt your client seeks a bargain, dear. However, I'd suggest your client's identity may hold answers."

Global Resolutions wouldn't reveal the paying client. Nor reveal me to them. A clean relationship. Do a job, deliver a report, and confirm payment into my Swiss bank account.

"Client ID is a dead end."

"Make of it what you will." She slid open a desk drawer, retrieved an index card, and slid it across the table. "Our scientists' home address and their campus office locations."

"Great starting points. Thanks."

"Welcome to academia, Aristotle. You might consider a nighttime campus visit. A gentleman with your look and demeanor would strike some as incongruous in broad daylight." She chuckled and puffed the cigar. "You will also note the cell phone numbers of our two PhDs. Neither will answer, of course, but you may find the contact information handy at some point."

As I memorized the card's information—Clubhouse artifacts never left the premises—wooden abacus balls clacked.

"Two thousand, dear."

I peeled off Benjamins and asked, "Do you think the Pentagon already has Bart Hall in hand? Which would make them my paying client."

"You fish in brackish waters, and the Clubhouse does not deal in roll-of-the-dice speculation. Seek, my favorite Argonaut, and perhaps you shall find."

She chuckled again, the door lock clacked open at my back, our meeting over. At the door, she added, "Do bear in mind, pursuing a peek behind the curtain could place you in greater peril. Tread softly, dear boy. And do not hesitate to reach out. I am here for you."

Chapter 4

JJ called as I prepped for the Palo Alto trip. Julie Johnson. An Albuquerque-based FBI agent and Bo's partner, proving opposites attract. JJ was focused, dedicated, and very much lived in the cut-and-dried realm. Bo, much less so. But they loved each other and made it work.

JJ had received a serious wound during a Texas border shoot-out, and now worked a very limited schedule at the FBI, deskbound. I'd continued checking on her since her release from the hospital and her call, filled to the brim with a plea, didn't surprise.

"Hey," she said, voice low, indicating she called from their home. "What are you up to?"

"Heading for the Bay Area."

"Take Bo."

I smiled. It was the polar opposite of her long-standing position regarding Bo's engagement with my endeavors. She'd crawled my butt more than a few times over his participation. However, a small crack in her concrete stand had recently appeared when she fessed up a recognition, an acceptance, of Bo's internal thrill switch. The same switch within me that I skirted with dubious side glances when in an introspective mood. But a direct request to take him with me—a first, big time.

"Not such a good idea, JJ. You still require looking after."

"I'm fine, all systems are go, and you don't understand."

"Oh, I bet I do."

My smile widened. Bo had taken personal responsibility for JJ's injury, which, while untrue, kept him focused laserlike on her mental and physical condition. He was mad about her and considered recovery oversight his immediate life mission.

"He creates these elaborate meals every evening with candles and placemats and his strange Andean flute music playing in the background. I can only eat a quarter of what he serves me, but he doesn't care. Every evening it's rinse, repeat."

"Sounds like he makes a fine nursemaid."

"Oh, yeah?" she asked as her quiet voice rose and became more strident. "Have you ever had chicken feet?"

"Can't say I have."

"Well, they're gross to look at. And they have a gelatinous texture when you gnaw on them. He claims they're good for the immune system. And have good-for-the-skin collagen. Which is another thing. He's always rubbing his homemade ointments, several of which smell like a skunk's butt, on my wound scars. Take him with you to California."

I couldn't help but chuckle at the situation. Without doubt, my best friend hovered over her every waking minute.

"He may be right with the immune system and collagen stuff."

"Is that right? Then why is haggis on the menu tomorrow night? What the hell does *that* help fix?"

"Maybe he intends to soothe your Scottish yearnings."

JJ had explained her lineage when we first met. Hispanic, Apache, and English. Scottish wasn't in the mix.

"Maybe you should call him now and express an urgent need for help. Guess what he's working on at this moment?"

"Tell me."

I'd fulfill her request, both for her and me. Bo's addition on any job upped the success odds.

"A Balinese puppet show. Just for me. As the evening's entertainment."

"I understand the music accompaniment for those can be pretty doggone stunning."

"Shut up and please call him."

"He loves you, JJ."

"And I love him, which doesn't deflect my pending mental breakdown."

I laughed out loud. Couldn't help it.

"I'll ask him to join me. Promise."

An audible sigh of relief returned.

"Thank you. A few days or a week would make me more than relieved."

"I'll try."

"Now make me feel a little better about the coming guilt over sending him off. Your contract doesn't involve car chases with military-grade weapons through San Francisco neighborhoods, does it?"

"You overestimate my life's excitement factor. I just talked with a guy who'll replace a water pump on the *Ace* while I'm gone."

"I'm well aware what kind of life you lead, and you're still prohibited from having Bo join you overseas. At least in the States I can provide him backup."

"Gotcha."

"What is this job?"

Shaky ground. I'd remained off US law enforcement's radar throughout my career. A concerted effort driven by having littered expired bad guys across the US landscape. Opening the kimono with JJ about this gig also opened the potential for some guy named Case Lee to appear on law enforcement databases. Not good.

"I'm chasing down a missing scientist from Stanford."

She paused, wheels turning, and said, "I remember something about that on a daily briefing report. As I recall, we parked it as clutter. The DIA is handling it."

The DIA—Defense Intelligence Agency. A federal outfit specializing in defense and military intelligence. I'd never occupied their radar and intended keeping it that way.

"Good to know."

It was. JJ had delivered an intel nugget. Whether it would help, unknown. But it tied back to Jules's contention about the Pentagon's interest in the missing scientists.

"Keep him safe," she said. "And out of my hair for a while."

JJ and I signed off, I called Bo, and we arranged a meetup in the Bay Area.

***

After we left the Halls' home and the Mossad spook and the FBI watcher down the street, we sat at a coffee shop near Stanford's campus along with another dozen patrons. Students, professors, and two beat-up ex-Delta operators. The professors chatted; the students eyeballed laptops and smart phones and each other.

"How's the tea?" I asked Bo.

"Sublime."

"I would hope so. A five-minute discussion with the barista on flavor profiles should have yielded something worthwhile."

"Don't get mad at me because I eschew more pedestrian beverages."

He referenced my choice—coffee, black, no sugar or sweetener.

"Who are you texting?"

He'd pulled his phone and begun a two-thumb dance on the small keypad.

"JJ."

"Leave her alone. She's fine. Let's talk clues, amigo."

He ignored me, finished his text message, and sipped tea. The end-of-day low light streamed through the coffee shop's large window and highlighted the lines on his face. Lines nonexistent months ago. The whole aging thing plus worry over JJ had left a trail. It hit hard—Jules was right. No longer spring chickens.

"They lead an eclectic lifestyle," he said, stretching with arms overhead. "Admirable."

"I suppose. A hefty tome on the collapse of Rome, da Vinci literature, and a thin book on Irish farm breeds. With black-and-white photos."

"Expansive minds, touch points across time, connectivity with the soil. I wonder if they share all those interests?"

"Solid question. Let's focus on that aspect."

"The *Joy of Cooking*. How dogeared was their edition?" Bo asked.

"Well used. Although you'd think they'd keep the thing in the kitchen."

"Let's chalk it up to limited space. They enjoy a meal together, prepared at their humble hearth. What might such an act give us?"

"Diddly-squat."

"Wrong, my goober. They shared, connected, and broke bread as one. A tight relationship."

"Could be a stretch."

"Or a foundational truth. Would you like a taste?" he asked, lifting the tea mug. "The hibiscus comes through admirably."

"No, thanks. What about the coffee table books? Impressionists and Hudson River artists?"

"Allow me conjecture, said the more expansive mind to the plodder."

"I'm not a plodder. I'm a grinder, just what's required right now."

"Fine, my miller. Grind this. Both artistic styles reflect outdoor settings."

He had a point, and it tied in with the outdoor photo of the two scientists.

"Okay. They cook together. Share meals. And like the outdoors."

"Don't forget the chocolate."

I shook my head, sipped coffee, stared out the window, and said, "I'm not getting any warm fuzzies off all this. We're pissing in the wind, bud."

"Two stalwart scientists. They may not appear the rugged type, but they forge ahead, towel-draped and undaunted, traipsing through the great outdoors while munching delectable chocolates."

"You finished?"

"Perhaps. But let us consider Rodin."

"Why?"

"Our next stop. A sashay through academic turf with a pause at a rare opportunity."

Fair enough. We sat and spun our wheels, while Ruth and Bart's offices on campus offered, at a minimum, activity. As opposed to tossing about clueless scenarios in a coffee shop.

As darkness fell, we stopped at Stanford's outdoor Rodin exhibit. Cast in bronze, the twenty sculpted creations included *The Thinker*. Bo, enthralled, tossed silent gestures into the cool evening air as he prowled the exhibit. Twilight provided sufficient illumination for a solid view of the Hoover Tower and red-tiled academic and administrative roofs at the center of the eight-thousand-acre campus. I'd visited years before, and the place remained an impressive monument to higher education and connectivity with Silicon Valley companies. Within fifteen miles from where we observed the Rodin sculptures sat the headquarters for Google, Cisco, Intel, Facebook, Apple, and more.

"Let's hit it, bud."

Bo drew away from the art, smiling, and said, "Rodin and skullduggery. The universe smiles on us, my Georgia peach."

We walked through the immaculate grounds, foot and bike traffic light on a weekday evening. The Halls' offices shared the same dimly lit building, hers on the third floor, his on the second. Several office lights burned, the rest dark, and no guards or campus cops protected the entrance.

I confirmed my jacket hid the Glock, and asked Bo, "You carrying?"

"I bear celestial love and universal harmony."

"How about things that go bang?"

A forefinger drew back his jacket hem and exposed the sheathed Bundeswehr knife. On him, it more than sufficed for any issues we might run into. Halfway up two flights of stairs, we ran into an older gentleman as he made his way down. He paused, stared hard, and shook his head.

"Much ado about nothing."

"Excuse me?" I asked.

Gray frizzy hair, reading glasses perched on his nose tip, corduroy jacket, and a bright red bowtie now askew as the day ended. He maintained a grip on the stair set banister.

"You two. The both of you. It's ridiculous."

"In what way? Sorry, I don't understand."

"More authoritarian agency snooping. At what point is enough, enough?"

"A bunch of us have snooped around, then?"

"Do not play the fool with me. You people have exhibited more than sufficient foolishness. I well know both the Halls. They are friends. And you people chase your tails. Foolishness."

He continued his downward descent.

"I'd be interested in hearing why you'd say that," I said as he passed.

But he wasn't interested in further discussion and waved a dismissive hand in the air, repeating, "Much ado about nothing."

When we heard the downstairs exit door open and shut, I asked Bo, "What do you think?"

"A Shakespeare fan. I well imagine others of your ilk have already conversed with him."

"My ilk? I shouldn't have to remind you I'm not connected with shadowland."

"Keep telling yourself that, goober. Shall we ascend?"

"How did he pick us out as sleuthing geniuses?"

"You lack a professorial air. I, on the other hand, blend right in."

"Wave your knife around on the next encounter and see how the blending works out for you."

As we stood outside Dr. Bartholomew Hall's locked office door with its white opaque glass panel, I pulled the slender old lock-picking tool set.

"How be ye skill-set-wise with this endeavor?" Bo asked.

"Rusty."

He extended his hand with a smile, and I passed the baton. It took him less than twenty seconds while I stood watch. The hallway remained quiet. Inside, I flicked on the light switch. They'd cleaned it out. Not a book in a bookshelf, steel file cabinets empty, a large whiteboard wiped clean.

As we rifled through Bart's modern wooden desk, I picked up a shadow appearing at the door's glazed panel. I tapped Bo's back as he bent behind a tall file cabinet and froze. He ducked farther alongside the cabinet, near the door. The silhouetted figure wore a hat, a fedora, and stood still for a full thirty seconds, then moved on.

"Perhaps another professor leaving for the day," I whispered as we resumed searching.

"No, my brother. The stranger carried an aura of ill intent."

Damn. While my aura detector remained inoperable, I'd learned over the years to heed Bo's warnings.

"We'll watch our ass here and upstairs. And when we leave campus. There isn't jack in this desk."

The drawers displayed a sum total of a breath mints container with three left, a paperclip pile, a pen and pencil assortment, and little else. Overhead, first arrivals had lifted ceiling tiles, and the space had been searched, with several tiles not settled back in their original position. They—whoever the hell they were—had fine-tooth-combed the office. A dry well, and I felt like an idiot for expecting anything else. And now someone tracked us. Someone with ill intent.

Chapter 5

I doused the office light, drew the Glock, and positioned at the door. Bo pressed between the doorframe and another tall and empty file cabinet. As the door opened inward, I kept the pistol's business end pointed at the widening opening. Nothing—an empty hallway, confirmed when Bo peeked his head out. We drifted toward the stairway, two casual dudes, my right hand inside a jacket pocket gripping the Glock.

"Adopt a scholarly demeanor," Bo said, voice low.

"Sorry, but I look like an over-the-hill former special operator gripping a hidden pistol. Which, at the moment and quoting Martha Stewart, is a good thing."

I couldn't foresee a gunfight in a Stanford research building's august hallways, but you never knew. We made our way up the stairs and down the hallway, passing an exiting elder dude who locked his office door, nodded our way with a pleasant smile, and made his way toward the stairs we'd just climbed.

"No ill intent auras there," I said.

"Righto. However, the character hidden around yon corner would fit the bill."

"You sure?"

We kept our voices at a near whisper.

"I could adopt your out-of-sight-out-of-mind attitude if you'd prefer."

"Just asking, Bo. Should we perform a meet and greet?"

"He would flee, hearing footsteps headed his way. Your footsteps, anyway."

"It's what us plodders do. Let's check Dr. Ruth's office and see what happens."

"Hand me the tools."

I did. Bo picked the lock inside fifteen seconds. We opened the door and flicked the light on, revealing another picked-clean office space. Door closed, we sniffed around. Empty bookshelves, empty cabinets, empty trash cans. Ruth's desk drawers displayed several pens and clean sticky notes and a granola bar wrapper. A large old-school calendar desk pad remained, displaying nothing but doodles violating individual day borderlines—tornadolike swirls, lightning zigzags, and several concentric circles. A small handwritten note along the right edge read "Stanley chocolate." Bo tapped the note with a proud smile.

"Chocolate."

"Yeah. I see it. Do these doodles mean anything?"

"Boredom at play. Although one might view the tornadoes as impressionistic."

"Good to know. This sucks, Bo. We've got nothing."

"We have an imminent incursion, goober."

Whoever had hidden around the hallway corner approached. I stepped toward the light switch as Bo climbed, silent, onto a file cabinet near the doorway and ascended until perched on the two-inch wooden sill above the door. Squatting, he appeared as a demented gargoyle, knife drawn and peering down with an angelic smile. They broke the mold when they made my best friend.

I doused the light and pulled the Glock. The gauzy silhouette appeared again outside the door, followed by a door handle turn and a gentle shove inward. As the door swung open, I ducked behind the desk and aimed at the entrance. The intruder had edged against the hallway-side doorframe, hidden.

"Come out. Slow."

The voice carried a distinct accent. Russian. The SVR, Russia's current version of the old KGB, had stepped onto the stage.

"No, thanks."

A brief pause until he whipped a free hand around the doorframe, flicked on the light, and resumed his protected position. Another silent pause, then he spoke.

"Are you armed?" he asked, his accented voice casual.

It wasn't this guy's first rodeo. Calm, questioning, assured—a pro.

"Yep."

"Ah. As am I. And your friend?"

"Nope."

"My apologies for not trusting you." His jacket rustled. He produced, I supposed, a handkerchief as he blew his nose. "Pardon me. Allergies, I am afraid."

"Sorry to hear it. Do you think a gunfight at this place is a good idea?"

"I do not. Are you familiar with the mutually assured destruction principle? A Cold War description?"

"Where's this going, Boris?"

"I will enter, weapon drawn. You and your friend will come from hiding, your weapons drawn. Then we talk. No shooting."

A classic spookville tactic—start a conversation, poke and prod, gather intel. This guy was good. But he didn't have an ace in the hole perched over the doorway.

"Fine. I'm standing up and aiming at where your head will appear. So is my friend."

"Even though he is unarmed?"

"I lied. My apologies."

His pistol appeared first, followed by a smooth slide into the doorway. We shared headshot aimpoints. He remained just outside the entrance, except for his pistol hand. Big mistake. The fedora's brim prevented overhead alerts and Bo, who'd sheathed his knife during our discussion, dropped as silent as a cat. Catching the spook's wrist and pistol, he continued his descent and rolled as he approached the hardwood floor. The audible snap of his wrist bone preceded the man's pained cry. Bo popped up, the Russian's pistol in hand as the spook cussed up a storm. At least I think he cussed—it damn sure wasn't a verbal recipe review.

He glared killer's eyes at us both but followed instructions when I signaled him to enter the office. Two weapons pointed at his head facilitated the activity. Door closed, I ripped the electrical cord off a desk lamp and tied his arms behind his back at the elbows. No point torturing the guy with a wrist tie. During my ministrations he switched back into a conversational mode. As much as I disliked dealing with spooks, the good ones could impress.

"I must ask. Are you two gentlemen with the CIA? The DIA?"

He spoke through gritted teeth—the wrist must have hurt like hell—but adopted a casual tone.

"Nope. Find something for his feet, bud."

Bo produced his knife and shaved off a length of the Russian's jacket.

"Sit," I said, guiding our captive toward an office chair. "And relax. And tell us what you're doing here."

"The same as you. If not the CIA or DIA, then who? FBI?"

Bo applied a solid ankle wrap and knot while I checked his pockets. Two items—a wallet and an extra magazine for his semiautomatic pistol.

"Perhaps you work for an agency I am not familiar with. If you will not kill me, it would be most helpful knowing."

His wallet held a couple hundred bucks and a Michigan driver's license. Samuel Kravchenko from Grand Rapids. Right.

"Or are you both freelancers? If so, perhaps you could share your paying client."

"Here's the deal, Samuel from Grand Rapids. Answer a few simple questions, and we leave your ass here without further harm. Did you follow us here, or hang out here on lookout?"

We locked eyes, and with a small tight smile he said, "Both."

"So the SVR assigned you to lurk and see who else dropped in, right?"

He returned a small, restricted shoulder shrug.

"How's campus life?" Bo asked. "Did you check out the Rodin Garden?"

"Freelancers then," he said. "Most interesting."

A dilemma. He'd confirmed we arrived late for the search party. Spooks galore visited the Halls' offices, and spooks galore still sought them. Good to know, I supposed, but why did my contract ask for Ruth

Hall and not Bart? Weird. In return, he'd ascertained our status as unaffiliated. A solid guess, and he'd also captured a visual of us both as well as our speech patterns, identifying us as Americans. Not quite tit-for-tat intel, but about as good as it gets with a professional spy.

Now what? Whack the guy? No, wouldn't happen. Neither Bo nor I desired his blood on our hands. Hold more conversation? I might own a dumbass streak, but I had to acknowledge he held all the cards in the conversational intel realm. Which left leaving his Russkie butt hog-tied while we slipped away.

I head-pointed toward the door. Bo nodded back, removed the guy's fedora, rubbed his head, and said, "Happy trails, comrade." We left after turning off the light and locking the door, the spook stating as the door closed, "Perhaps we will meet again when I can return the favor." He'd attempt to kill us if there was a next time.

We hustled downstairs and out the building's door. A few students with backpacks meandered about, visible from pathway lighting and a half-moon. I felt both empty and mighty inquisitive. Our house and office searches had yielded little, if anything. A lousy intel-collection exercise. But this gig immersed us neck-deep into a large clandestine swirl, with Mossad and the SVR making an appearance. Others, no doubt, also took part. Which opened a wide barn door of possibilities for what these two scientists worked on. Without doubt, spookville perceived a possible game changer for geopolitical advantage. A new whiz-bang weapon or a breakthrough in psych ops or a warfare application beyond current knowledge. Plus, the Ruth-only situation stuck in my craw, big time.

"He possessed a nice hat."

We strolled back toward the Rodin Garden and our vehicle.

"One among many, Bo."

"Not a jaunty or stylish look. But a fitting display, matching the countenance of a stalwart fellow."

"He'll try and whack us if we meet again."

"A fatalistic people, the Rus."

Two young students approached and passed, with smiles and several pleasant "hi's" exchanged. What a great slice of life for a young person—a student at a renowned university, the future bright.

"We have before us," Bo said, once the kids passed, "a tale with many facets. Perhaps others will sing songs of our exploits. I appreciate you asking for my assistance."

"Always a pleasure, bud. Now, about the tale. You realize the other players hold an advantage? They know, or suspect, what this is all about."

"An advantage mitigated with our universal ebb and flow embrace. An elevated mindset, providing higher level nourishment."

"I've gotten little nourishment from our house and office searches. I'd argue we're still clueless, in oh so many ways."

"Speak for yourself. Let the pot simmer, my worry-filled brother. And don't forget the chocolate. Stanley chocolate. Which, I will admit, lacks a Belgian ring."

"You take the chocolate. I'll dig elsewhere."

"Righto. For the immediate, let us consider a fresh addition for our shadowed family."

Damn. We were being followed. On a freakin' California campus, having already encountered a Russkie spy, another player had arrived in the night. Jeez Louise. Grand Central Station for espionage players.

THE SAWTOOTH JOB

Chapter 6

We strolled toward the Rodin Garden and paused for a false stare at the sculptures and a real back trail search. A tall thin man's silhouette progressed along a parallel path and halted, still at our backs. He pulled a cell phone, the device's illumination evident, and acted as if he answered a text message.

"That our boy?" I asked.

"One and the same. Once JJ heals, I may hang with you more often. You do not occupy a mundane spot within the cosmos."

"Enough with this BS. Let's find a quiet spot and bushwhack the SOB."

"Will this fall under the rubric of information gathering? If so, I might point out dead men tell no tales."

I pulled my phone and performed a quick Google Maps search.

"Don't intend to kill him. Do intend to get answers."

"Perhaps he's an ally, a wandering associate."

"Here's the deal on that, Bo." I found a spot on the map, pocketed my device, and edged alongside my best friend. "There are no field allies in my world. None. There's you, me, Marcus, and Catch. And Jules. A tight circle. Everyone else, and I mean everyone, is suspect. Period."

"You present a jaundiced view, Mr. Bond."

"A life-saving view. A short distance away is the Arizona Cactus Garden. Let's go."

We ambled north. Our tail pocketed his phone and followed.

"Do you have a sudden yen for arid environments?"

"I have a yen for no artificial illumination and tight gravel trails. Me and the tail will crunch while walking. You won't."

Bo would move with silent stealth. A given. The dumb bastard following us wouldn't stand a chance. Ten minutes later we left grass and concrete and entered a nighttime world filled with century plants, barrel cactus, cholla cactus, and yucca—all with spikes and needles jutting outward. Our mystery dude remained on our tail. Ten paces in, I turned for a quick whispered tactical ops review. Bo had already disappeared. Not a trace, not a sound. I paused, then continued at a slow pace. Thirty seconds later, a second set of gravelly footfalls joined mine.

I kept a lazy pace and moved deeper into the garden, stopping alongside a massive yucca plant. The half-moon provided sufficient illumination for a solid view, the evening cool, no other students or faculty anywhere nearby. The trailing footsteps hesitated at my silence, then proceeded with caution. I pulled the Glock.

He rounded a turn in the gravel path, sighted me, and halted. The cat stood four or five inches north of six feet, thin, wearing a dark windbreaker. Standing ten paces away, his hand rested on his holstered pistol's butt, his legs spread and knees bent in a firing stance. Five seconds of mutual silent assessment, then he spoke with a flat West Coast accent.

"You've drawn a weapon."

"Yeah, I'm not a big believer in Quick Draw McGraw bullshit."

Several silent seconds passed. Tire and engine noise from several passing vehicles drifted in from a hundred yards away. Then nighttime silence resumed.

"Where's your partner?"

"Tiptoeing through succulents," Bo said at the guy's back.

I still couldn't see my partner, but the tall guy whipped his head toward Bo's voice, evaluated the situation, and dropped his ready-for-action stance as his hand lifted away from the pistol.

Straightening up, he said, "The name's William Barrett, DIA. And you two?"

"Roving cactus lovers."

"Let me rephrase the question. Who signs your paycheck, asshole?"

This guy worked for the Defense Intelligence Agency, one of eighteen outfits under the US Intelligence Community umbrella. Because, I supposed, you just can't have enough spooks. He'd assumed our employer was one of the eighteen. His lone question, which one?

"That's need to know, Barrett," I said. "And you don't need to know. But since we've all gathered, let's have a chat."

"CIA? FBI? HS?" he asked.

"NOYFB."

His head cocked, quizzical.

"What the hell is NOYFB?"

"None of your business. You can fill in the *F*. Now, scooter, let's talk about why you're tailing us."

He glanced over his shoulder at the unseen third party then back toward me.

"Tailing you? I'm another cactus aficionado."

"Common interests. A good start. What's the DIA doing here?"

Stupid question, but this was a stupid situation. This guy wouldn't reveal anything, nor would I. Not that I had a helluva lot to reveal. Soon enough, we'd part separate ways with no additional gathered intel.

Everything at this point constituted a dry hole, a duster. Bo and I could futz around tomorrow, tossing wild ideas at each other, but I had no action plan, no next steps. And Barrett, standing silent, wouldn't add anything. So I threw a Hail Mary pass.

"Well, whatever you're doing, I'm sure it's going fantastic," I said. "With one minor hiccup. We left you an SVR agent tied up in Dr. Ruth's office. Courtesy of the Company. You're welcome."

His body jerked straight, and he took a step toward me.

"Wrong direction, cactus devotee," Bo said, his voice cold and flat. "Do more than consider a step backward."

Barrett stopped, all too aware his back remained exposed to the hidden voice, and reversed his step. Then he lit into my Hail Mary.

"The Company has no business here. None. This isn't your turf."

True enough. But I'd identified us as Company assets, and doing so would ring bells. Including a large bell at the top.

"He has a broken wrist, but I'd give it fifty-fifty he's found a way to untie himself. You'd best haul it over to the good doctor's office."

"People will hear about this, Company man. And you'll be in deep shit."

Bo sang a few woe-is-me lines from an old blues song, stopping as Barrett approached and passed him, headed for Dr. Ruth's office at a brisk pace.

I'd made a long shot claim, with hard reality and desperation prompting it. Barrett would holler up his food chain, head knockers at the DIA would complain to their counterparts at the CIA, and word would filter up Company command. Marilyn Townsend, the CIA's clandestine operations director and therefore the world's most powerful spook, would get word. And she'd contact me. It might take several days, but it would happen.

We went way back. During Delta days, Townsend was our Company field ops liaison. She'd develop mission objectives, work with us on tactics, and our Delta team would execute. Marcus, Bo, Catch, and I retired from Delta Force and moved on. Marilyn Townsend climbed the Company ladder. She was tough, focused, smart as hell, and cut from the perfect cloth for managing geopolitical three-dimensional chess BS. We stood as borderline friends who cast a jaundiced eye both ways, and we'd worked together on a few of my jobs. And on other jobs, she'd played me like a conga drum. Spookville's queen bee.

She would soon glom onto my Hail Mary pass. Barrett would attempt to describe us to his bosses, coming up short on me. And coming up blank on Bo, except for the silent movement, voice intonation, and unique phrasing. Then the DIA would bitch at the CIA. Townsend, having spent several years with us in the field, would snap instantly on the two mystery men in the cactus garden. At Bo's description, she'd smile. At mine, less so, wondering what I was doing sniffing around the Halls' disappearance. Then she'd contact me.

All good. If I'd approached her, the odds she'd reveal anything about the Halls fell in the same bucket as me winning the World Tango Championship. But when she reached out to me, I had a half-assed shot at garnering intel. Because right now I had nothing. And nothing sucked.

THE SAWTOOTH JOB

Chapter 7

"You got a fake identity with you?" I asked Bo. "Because from now on, we're deep cover. Too many armed players mucking around in this sandbox."

We sat outdoors on the Palo Alto bar's patio. No seedy dive bars here—the other patrons appeared as venture capitalists, high tech grand poo-bahs, hustlers and hangers-on. Fifteen buck drinks, twenty-five for a plate of shared nachos. Nachos with crabmeat and seaweed slivers.

"I carry an obfuscation grab bag. Same as you," Bo said, firing up a small weed-packed pipe.

False passport and driver's license, with a fake-named credit card tied to a Cayman or Cyprus bank account. Good knowing he remained prepped for certain eventualities. We'd stay below the us-seeking radars from this point forward.

"How'd you get through all the cactus without becoming a pin cushion?"

"It's not a matter of through. It's a matter of flow."

"Well, I appreciate you flowing behind our new DIA friend."

"The gentleman exhibited a too-tight winding. Perhaps he should practice meditation. By the by, pulling the trigger on our old associate makes for an interesting gambit."

"Desperate times, desperate measures."

"We sit with drink and smoke and comradeship and peculiar nachos on a lovely evening. Desperate doesn't define our path."

"Wanna bet? From Israel to Moscow, London to DC, other seekers know backstory and context. We've got Monet and hot springs and cooking recipes."

"Our way presents a less cluttered road, a potent advantage."

"Wish I had your optimism. Would you chase down Stanley chocolate? I'd guess a high-priced candy store around here."

Bo pulled his phone and searched. I considered calling Jess for help with our next steps. She might know an angle I'd missed and toss a life ring my way. I was floundering. As I pulled the phone, it rang. Marcus.

"Is the snow ass-deep yet?" I asked as a greeting.

Marcus Johnson, our former Delta team lead and current rare black rancher in the Montana wilds, near the town of Fishtail. Older than us and a blood brother, I often used him as a sounding board and advisor. The man defined rock solid.

"Why do you start off conversations highlighting America's wussification?" he asked. "Perhaps your delicate constitution requires climate-controlled settings."

He knew, all too well, I fared poorly in cold weather.

"A constitution less robust than your bovines, I'll admit. Help me remember what breed those are—Icelandic Browns?"

"You're a funny guy."

"Let's switch to not funny. How's the leg?"

Marcus had taken a bullet to the leg during a Texas job firefight. Like JJ, I'd checked in with him every few days during his recovery.

"I've still got a slight limp. The physical therapist in Billings, schooled at the Torquemada academy, insists I'm not working hard enough. I have explained, in no uncertain terms, that seasoned citizens take longer to heal."

"Words falling on deaf ears?"

"She ignores biological fact—due, I'd bet, to her looking like high school graduation is imminent."

"I won't comment on someone's personal struggle with wussification."

"I've got to get you a stand-up comedy gig here in Fishtail. You're a riot. Where is your butt right now?"

"Palo Alto. Sharing crabmeat and seaweed nachos with Bo. Living large, bud. Living large."

"Let me talk with our cosmic cowboy. I want an update on JJ's condition. Then have him hand the phone back. I want to hear what's going on."

A first. While Marcus respected Bo as the finest warrior we'd ever seen, their worldviews remained at polar opposites. Only JJ's medical situation could have driven his request.

"Felicitations, cow whisperer," Bo said after taking the phone. "Did you receive my healing salve?"

The server wandered over, I ordered another drink, and told her she could remove the quarter-eaten plate of nachos. With a wide smile, I listened in on the one-sided conversation.

"Yes, it contains a high THC content. An ingredient particularly effective for aged bipeds."

"…"

"That would be wormwood's aroma. Think turkey on a Thanksgiving morn."

"..."

"Have you considered yoga? It would please my heart gifting you yoga pants."

"..."

"Your words speak no, but I sense an underlying desire. Do you have a color preference? If not, I can foresee mauve as appropriate. Let's not deny mauve's royal aspect, a fitting accompaniment for your elevated deportment."

"..."

"She resides on an ephemeral path, smooth and supporting. I'll pass on your loving concerns. As for your situation, how often do you address it?"

"..."

"The injury, bwana Johnson. The healing wound. It will listen if you allow it. Flow and connectivity, my brother. Flow and connectivity."

I chuckled as, without doubt, Marcus's blood pressure skyrocketed. The Montana rancher tugged the tiller hard enough to refocus on JJ, and Bo assured him again all was well with her. Then he returned my phone.

"I require another bourbon," Marcus said, groaning as he lifted from his leather chair. No problem visualizing his movements in a place I'd often stayed. His bird dog sleeping on the couch, a cigar in the ashtray, a bourbon with cold water cocktail at his elbow, his large socked feet resting on the ottoman. "I should have grabbed the bottle before speaking with him. Now, tell me what's going on."

I did. We both spoke with 256-bit encrypted phones, our conversation semisecure. Semi because the NSA and China both had geosynchronous big birds far overhead, and you just never knew about their decryption technologies.

"Why does your contract seek just the one scientist?" he asked once I'd finished. "A red flag, son."

"Yeah. As someone warned from the get-go."

"The Chesapeake witch?"

Marcus held little truck with Jules of the Clubhouse. He viewed her as a rogue player, immersed in a subterranean sewer among killers, turncoats, and the anything-for-a-buck crowd. Not wrong, but the Clubhouse tendrils extended far beyond that collection, which he would begrudgingly acknowledge when pushed. But Marcus stood straight and true and viewed Jules as an apparition, floating in the deep shadows. Not his type, at all.

"She knows things, Marcus. Boy howdy, does she know things. And this gig has shitshow written all over it."

"Right up your alley. It must thrill the Swiss having someone who relishes wading in these messes."

"Any more inspirational comments on tap? Because so far, you're really helping out."

"Alright. Don't get your skivvies in a knot. Let's accept global interest in those two scientists. Hell, you might take a gander around your eatery and see if MI6 and MSS have made an appearance."

MI6 and MSS—the British and Chinese spy agencies. They'd both passed through Palo Alto, no doubt. And Marcus presented a legit point—they could both be sitting within thirty feet of us. Plus, given our location at the world's tech hub, corporate technology spies and financial ferrets and hedge fund intel collectors lurked among the crowd, adding their own spice to the clandestine gumbo. A freakin' rat's nest.

"I know. I'm discounting the spook participation because there're no answers coming from them, just distractions."

"A solid approach. Focus on the mission. Let's run through again what you've found so far. Then let me chew on it overnight."

We ground through details, with Bo interrupting us once. He'd searched for Stanley chocolates and come up dry. After a twenty-minute back-and-forth with Marcus, he signed off.

"My optimism meter rests on empty, bud."

"The professorial crowd might be talkative," Bo said. "We could visit Ruth and Bart's compadres tomorrow. We've already met Mr. Shakespeare."

"Pretty certain other players have run through them several times, starting with the DIA."

"So?"

I sighed, killed my drink, and said, "So you're right. It's better than nothing."

At our hotel we locked our room doors, and—without mentioning it to each other—both slept with a chair under the room door handle, blankets and pillows piled into the tub, a pistol on the tub's edge, locked and loaded. Helluva way to live.

The next morning, I knocked on Bo's door. He answered with a smile, a steaming cup of tea in hand.

"Enter, Sherlock Holmes. Tell me a tale."

"We've got a call with Marcus in ten minutes. He pinged me earlier this morning, and we worked through some possibilities."

"The universe has presented a fresh scent, a twisted trail?"

"Roger that. We might head for Idaho."

"Ah. The game is afoot. Most excellent."

THE SAWTOOTH JOB

Chapter 8

Marcus had sent a text at six in the morning.

Get your sorry ass up. You do not require beauty sleep—lipstick on a pig. Check out Stanley, Idaho. Expect a call in one hour.

And a jolly good morning to you, too, Marcus. I'd already hit the hotel's lobby for my day's first coffee when the message came in. Stanley, Idaho. Stanley chocolates, as per Dr. Ruth's desk pad. A thread, a whiff of a trail. Nothing that flashed bright, no pot of gold at the rainbow's end, but better than anything Bo and I had come up with. Back in the room, laptop open, I checked the possibilities.

In the middle of nowhere, Idaho. Nestled against the Sawtooth Range, close by the White Cloud and Salmon River and Boulder Mountain ranges. Population sixty-three. Man, geography tossed cold water on the likelihood Ruth and Bart hung out there. Cell phone service? Internet connectivity? I mean, sixty-three people. But I dove in and sussed the area, if for no other reason than to ensure Marcus wouldn't crawl my butt when he called.

Stanley sat sixty miles north of Sun Valley, accessed over the Galena Summit pass. As I researched, I realized those sixty miles represented much more than distance. On one side of the mountain pass— millionaires and billionaires, an airport handling private jets, high end designer stores, expensive restaurants, ski lodges. The entire jet set motif. Over the pass, a town with gravel roads in the minuscule downtown, several bars, one general store. Sixty miles, a mountain pass, two worlds.

Stanley had a short outdoorsy tourist season for hikers, rafters, fly anglers, mountain bikers. Short because Stanley was in a geographic bowl between those mountain ranges, where cold air collected. It could snow the Fourth of July. The high season ran about four months. Man, I just didn't see it as our focus. The weather caught my eye, and a quick scan displayed a current weather in the twenties at night, high thirties during the day. It had already snowed, and another storm headed Stanley's way. The winter months added nothing but more isolation to the tiny burg.

But giving it a solid effort, I accessed Custer County records and searched for property ownership. No Halls. A passel of corporate ownerships, several based in Nevada, which wasn't unusual. Nevada didn't require you to reveal corporate ownership, with a Nevada law firm of your choice acting as directors and officers. I checked cell phone coverage. It existed, but with limited range because of river canyons and soaring mountains. As for internet, one carrier had run a trunk line up the two-lane lonely highway, along the Salmon River and through Stanley. So those sixty-three folks had internet connections.

Marcus called on the dot.

"What'd you find?" he asked. "Besides the name Stanley?"

"No chocolate shops."

"Get off the damn chocolate. View the scribbled note she left as a reminder to shop in Palo Alto. I doubt the Stanley general store has a great sweets selection."

"It's in the middle of nowhere, Marcus. How did you know about it?"

"Allow me to remind you where I live. Fishtail, Montana. Near the Wyoming and Idaho borders."

"Great intel, Obi-Wan."

"Shut up and listen. I've hung out in Powell and Cody and Gardiner and Ennis and Lemhi and Leadore. It's called the West. My turf, you moron. After you mentioned Stanley, that nowhere town came to me late last night."

"Which is great. I mean it. But you've gotta admit it's a stretch."

"I'm not admitting jack or contending a eureka moment. Let's look at probabilities. Your two scientists have gone missing, which also raises the question why your contract focuses on Ruth Hall. Let's shove the Ruth-only aspect into the ancillary column for the moment."

"Okay."

"Don't do that."

Marcus's hackles rose when I tossed noncommittal "okays" into conversations. Which didn't stop me from doing it.

"Alright. Two missing scientists."

"Which leaves three prime probabilities. One, they had a horrific accident, and both lie dead somewhere. Put that one on the bottom of the stack."

"Agreed."

"Two, whatever they worked on together brought heat. Espionage heat. So they skedaddled away for their private hidey-hole. Stanley fits the bill."

"Wouldn't others know about it? Colleagues, friends, tax records?"

"We're dealing with two scientific geniuses, son. Those types may sit somewhere on the Asperger scale, which could include a desire for isolation and all the trappings to ensure as much."

He had a point. Brilliant folks often had peculiar ways. And they could exhibit incredible focus. If one of their focal points embodied anonymity, deep cover was a possibility. But still. Stanley?

"Let's look at the third possibility," I said. I'd spent time in the bathtub before sleep came thinking about this gig's landscape. "They've been kidnapped. Which puts Stanley in the moot point bucket. Unless they kidnapped Bart and missed Ruth. Hence my contract."

"And puts Stanley back in play."

"Thin gruel, Marcus."

"Did you investigate the hot springs?"

Wheels spun, clues rifled through. A dog-eared book on western hot springs, shelved near an old *Joy of Cooking*, remained at the Halls' house, perused and discarded by multiple spook outfits. I still didn't see a connection.

"Where, pray tell, are these hot springs?"

"Your enthusiasm moves me, son. They're sprinkled all over the Salmon River drainage, including Stanley. It's a massive geothermal area."

"Aren't we reaching a bit here, bud?"

"Not in my book."

The lone fact buttressing Marcus's contention—a big fat fact—was not one spook who'd combed through the Halls' possessions knew about Powell or Ennis or Lemhi. Or Stanley. Not the DIA, Mossad, SVR, or whoever else. Nossir. It took a man of the West to make the connection, and Marcus was every bit that. Besides, I had nothing better on the burner.

"Alright. I'll call back in ten. Let's get Bo involved."

"Why?"

"He's on the job with me, and don't start. Grit your teeth, and, well, allow the cosmic winds to blow."

"Not funny. If you're hell-bent on bringing him into this conversation, I'll need those ten minutes for the aspirin to kick in."

In Bo's room, with the phone on speaker, Marcus and I reviewed our best guess findings. Bo, a mug with steaming tea in hand, rocked slowly, eyes closed, a pleasant smile plastered on his face.

Then he asked, "What about the Belgian chocolate?"

"Listen. Both of you," Marcus said. "You can buy chocolate from Belgium in damn near any grocery store in America. So no more talk about either Belgium or chocolates."

"Our cow whisperer overlooks the more spatial picture," Bo said to me. "A focused man. An attribute not easily dismissed."

"Mission oriented," I said. "A man with a keen eye on the operational theater."

"A man with steam coming out his ass," Marcus said. "Will you two pay attention?"

I searched hot springs near Stanley. They abounded, most along riverways, quite a few along the Salmon River nearby the small town. Marcus may have cracked the nut, and I said so.

"I'm leaning toward an Idaho trip. Well done, Marcus. Iffy dots and iffy connections, but it beats everything else we've got. And there won't be any other bloodhounds on the Stanley trail."

"Anonymity and seclusion. Geothermal waters," Bo said. "Yet you two dismiss the third trace, a third indicator. The fourth if one includes confection from a mysterious northern European country."

"What, Bo?" I asked before Marcus could unload.

"Consider Minnie Mouse."

"Oh Lord," Marcus mumbled.

But Bo had struck gold. The Ruth and Bart photo, with Ruth wrapped in a Minnie Mouse towel. While water wasn't visible, they stood along a riverbank, the stones and slope evident. No doubt. And those weren't dirty lenses on their glasses. No way, Jose. Lenses fogged over because of steaming water. Hot springs. Oh, man. Marcus's long shot became more viable in an instant. I explained the photo to my Montana brother.

"There it is," he said. "Pieced together, it presents solid intel. I'll meet you two there this afternoon. It's a little under five hundred miles. Give me seven or eight hours."

And so it arrived—an action plan, albeit one leaning on the farfetched side. Still, a plan, movement, a fresh scent. And no more rubbing elbows with spooks circling Palo Alto. But while Bo and I would cross the Rubicon, I couldn't ask Marcus to join us.

"I don't think so, Marcus. You might remember getting shot in the thigh not long ago."

"He refused my healing unguents," Bo added.

"Since you two can take a charter jet, why not land near Sun Valley with the other sports," Marcus said, ignoring our comments. "Then rent a vehicle and hop over the pass."

"Let's return to you joining us. From both a strategic and tactical perspective, it's a bad idea."

"From a mission perspective, it's the one thing that makes sense considering you two couldn't pour piss out of a boot if they wrote the instructions on the heel."

"He's a trooper," I said to Bo. "A trooper with a limp and graying hair."

"He presents a certain je ne sais quoi," Bo replied. "As a workaround, we could avoid stairs, or curbs, so as not to exhaust him."

"You two clowns exhaust me. Why not land in Sun Valley?"

"We're landing in Boise. It's arctic conditions in the Sawtooths and we require outfitting."

"It's above freezing, you wusses. Get outfitted in Sun Valley."

"We require real deal clothing. Elk or caribou or musk ox or wooly mammoth hunting attire."

"Alright. Point taken. How are you two set for tools?"

He meant weaponry. Marcus never arrived in an operational area without more than sufficient armament. A habit that had saved our butts more than once.

"I've got the Glock. Bo took possession of an SVR asset's 9mm. And he's toting his knife."

"You forgot to pack feather dusters?"

"There's clearly a curmudgeonly virus floating around Fishtail. But we'd appreciate a solid tool-set collection. At least I would. I won't speak for Bo."

"A tallyho element bobs in the currents. The quarry scented, the hounds loosed."

"I'll bring tools for you, too, Bo. Case, don't let him purchase jodhpurs in Boise. We should make some attempt at blending in among Stanley residents."

My excitement level amped up, forward movement assured. Yeah, we grasped at a few straws—and we each knew it—but action, motion, drew me away from espionage turf and into an arena more aligned with my comfort level. But try as I might, spookville never fully disappeared in the rearview mirror.

"Marcus, stay deep on this one. The clandestine swirl remains active, big time. Cash only, bud. No credit card transactions while you travel. I'll handle accommodations."

"Roger that. Let's saddle up, men. I'll stay in touch."

Chapter 9

A charter flight landed us in Boise near noon. Once we exited the airport I pulled over, crawled under the rental SUV's left front fender, and disconnected the vehicle's GPS. Just to be sure.

Boise appeared as a clean, attractive small city. The state capitol building anchored a vibrant downtown area as folks in sweaters and light jackets walked the sidewalks under bright sunshine. Pleasant defined the look and feel. A pleasant town and friendly folks with well-kept neighborhoods. An atmosphere driven, I supposed, through self-reliance and isolation. The nearest large cities were far away—Salt Lake City a five-hour drive to the southeast, Portland over six hours to the northwest. Idaho had one phone area code, two time zones, and fewer than two million people.

We stopped at a grocery store for a few items—I lost Bo inside and waited ten minutes at the vehicle—then off to a sporting goods store where we outfitted with warm boots, winter jackets and pants, gloves and hats. In the fifties at Boise's lower elevation, we'd soon enough climb into the Sawtooth basin where it dipped well below freezing at night. Plus, the weather forecast for Stanley predicted a storm late the next day. Not my cup of tea—although I logged a mental note about not whining too much about the cold. Or harp on the salubrious weather along the Ditch in the South Carolina and Georgia sections. Or poke Marcus about life in a place with a few barbed wire strands between his neck of the woods and the Arctic. But no denying I was a warm weather dude.

As we left town, I contacted Marcus. He'd just passed through Butte, making good time. A few guilt pangs struck—the guy hadn't recovered from his wound but hauled it, solo, five hundred miles. Not a lot I could do about it, other than thank him. Twenty minutes north of Boise, we began sighting National Forest signage. The lion's share of our travel from then on passed through public land. National Forest, Wilderness Areas, Bureau of Land Management turf. I asked Bo for a quick intel search on Idaho's public lands.

"Thirty-two million acres."

"Gotta love it."

"A wonderous aspect. Barriers few, movement unbridled."

It was wondrous. Every American owned that land, along with the six-hundred-million acres spread across the other states. A vast ocean of deserts, prairie, sagebrush plains, forests, mountain ranges, rivers, and canyons. An American blessing.

We soon turned and headed into high country along the Payette River's east fork, running crystal clear. It wasn't long before we began passing hot springs.

"Shall we linger?" Bo asked. "The good doctors may while away a few hours immersed at these."

"Let's make Stanley, bud. If the Halls have a place there, the locals will know it. Or at least know them."

The small two-lane wove along the Payette, at times a thousand feet below us, with glimpses of elk herds as we passed. Snowfall remained on north slopes and in patches under pine and fir trees. Summer and early fall outdoor activities long past, the asphalt lay empty with occasional big game hunters in pickups sharing the road. The miles eased past as I traveled through gorgeous country with my best friend, an objective filled with hope not far ahead.

A little over two hours into the trip, we left the Payette River drainage and dropped into the Sawtooth basin. Ahead, Stanley and the Sawtooth Range. I'd seen mountains aplenty—many if not most pretty doggone stunning—but the Sawtooths fell into the jaw-drop bucket. Jagged peaks and spires, well above timberline, loomed over a valley filled with forests and meadows and creeks. As we approached the tiny town, the White Cloud Mountain Range became visible toward the east. Along the town's edge, the Salmon River flowed low and cold, its source the creeks and rivulets from surrounding mountains.

Stanley was shutting down. The hikers and rafters and other visitors had dwindled to a trickle, and the Sawtooth valley prepped for winter when the population reflected the sixty-three souls as stated on the road sign as we entered. The small cabin I'd rented in downtown would close for the season in another week, a seven-month hiatus on the horizon. A few bars and eateries abutted the downtown gravel roads. No traffic lights and the few stop signs more a suggestion than a hard and fast rule. A handmade sign announced a street dance that night, a last hurrah. Winter on the way, hunker-down time.

We pulled into the town's general store with adjoined gas station. They'd know the Halls. Or not. Anticipation and angst ratcheted up, success or failure soon to be determined.

"End of the line, bud."

"There is no line, my Georgia peach. And it never ends."

"That doesn't help."

"Do we seek help or direction?"

"Before we traipse down your rabbit hole, let's review. Charter flight, rental vehicle, outfitted with winterwear, long drive. So maybe it's not the end of the line. Let's call it a cul-de-sac. A cul-de-sac named failure."

"Loose hand on the tiller, goober. Allow the universe free rein."

A muddy pickup pulled alongside and parked. Two hunters in camo exited and entered the general store. I'd have bet good money on the store's interior. A grocery section, liquor aisle, sundries, and fishing gear. Propane tanks, ammunition, T-shirts, hoodies. And a large coffeepot the locals would take advantage of all winter. A place to hang, at least until dark, when the several bars would fill the bill as a gathering spot. Sixty-three folks. Someone who worked the general store would ID Ruth and Bart. If they had a place here.

"And if they've never seen nor heard of the Halls?"

"We wait for bwana Johnson, dance in the streets tonight, and soak in hot springs tomorrow. You can carry the gloomy weight. Regardless of the discoveries within this unique example of isolated mercantilism, I see all upside."

"I could hit Stanford again and become the seventeenth questioner of the Halls' associates. Right behind the DIA, FBI, Mossad, SVR, and every spook outfit you could shake a stick at."

Bo patted my shoulder.

"Rejoice in hope, be patient in tribulation, be constant in prayer."

"You can bet I'll rejoice if Ruth and Bart are known here."

"What are your thoughts on man buns?"

We locked eyes, smiling.

"I appreciate you delivering a potent signal the time has come to venture inside. You take the gas station, I'll take the store. You still have their photo?" I asked.

I'd made several photocopies for both Bo and Marcus so they'd be armed with something viable on this wispy trail.

"Do indeed. Let's sally forth, you and I, on this quest."

We did. The store displayed as expected. Wooden plank floor, scuffed, with a snow shovel by the doorway. The few shoppers moved slow with smiles and nods toward each other as they passed. At the empty checkout line, a local waited for customers. He wore a wool shirt, jeans, down vest, and sported long hair and a bushy beard.

I smiled, nodded a greeting, and said, "I'm friends with the Halls from the Bay Area and thought I'd drop in while here in Idaho. They don't answer their phone, and I have no clue where they live."

"Don't know any Halls."

My gut sank as a long shot became even longer. With a dose of desperation, I pulled the beach towel photo.

"I figured they might lay low out here. This is my favorite photo of them."

He eyeballed it, smiled wide, and said, "You mean Ruth and Bart. I've never known their last name. Hall?"

Oh, man. Christmas morning for a beat-up and frustrated ex-Delta operator. Relief flooded, a quick silent prayer cast, my grin toward the young man authentic. I could have crawled across the checkout counter and hugged the cat. I kept up the chitchat and hoped to glean more intel.

"No, Halt, with a *t*. They're great folks, sweet people, but a challenge from time to time. Known 'em for years."

They'd kept their last name hidden from the local scuttlebutt, and planting misdirection with "Halt" was a weak attempt at not upsetting the dynamic.

"Like you say, nice people but a bit off-center. We go months without seeing them, then they appear, pay cash for everything, and keep to themselves. But nice. Bart calls me Young Mountain Man. I'm Tom, and told him so a half-dozen times, but maybe he forgets. He, and Ruth, are getting up there."

"Happens with the best of us."

"Ruth came in here yesterday, so they're in town. But I don't know where they live. Somewhere north along the highway. I can't tell you exactly where."

Not an issue. We'd find them. Their presence here overrode any disappointment about their cabin's location.

"They're good folks. Oh, well. Any suggestions on next steps for us?"

"Go to the dance tonight. They could show up. Otherwise, sorry. Grab a cup of coffee, and hang out if you want. Although I would bet it'll be another day or three before they show up here again."

I thanked him, then thanked him again as I checked out after a liquor aisle perusal and brandy purchase. A wee dram in celebration and to ward off the cold seemed appropriate. While spies circled Palo Alto and Stanford and who knows where else, we'd found the Halls. Somewhere along the Salmon River in the Sawtooths. Yessir. I tossed one of Bo's cosmic messages into the ether for all the spooks who also sought the Halls—bite me, dumbasses.

Bo waited, leaning against the SUV, arms crossed, a knowing smile on full display.

"Bingo, bud," I said, a mile-wide grin displayed. "Bingo and eureka and hallelujah chorus, baby."

"A solid affirmation fills the soul, does it not?"

"It does, it does. What'd you find at the gas station?"

"Dr. Ruth filled up yesterday. They always pay cash. Dr. Bart calls the woman who runs the place Gas Lady, even though she's introduced herself several times. I would surmise our two scientists fill a local niche. The peculiar but benign older couple. Every burg needs one, you know."

Man, it felt good. Beyond good. I called Marcus, speaker on, his satellite phone available as he hauled it through empty no-cell-phone-service country.

"You two make Stanley?" he asked.

"Made it and planted a flag. They're here."

"No shit?"

A potent indicator even Marcus had cast a jaundiced eye at the odds of our success.

"No shit. Where are you?"

"North. Just passed through Clayton, so I'll make it in thirty. This hardtop is one winding road along the river."

I told him our rented cabin location in downtown Stanley, not a difficult find.

"Next steps?" he asked.

"Pause and reflection and tempered rejoicing."

"Sure. Besides reflection, Bo, let's talk next steps."

"The guy at the general store said they might show up at a street party tonight," I said. "Let's start there. It'll get dark soon, so soon after you arrive, we can check it out."

We signed off, Bo and I checked in at the cabin, and we passed the brandy bottle for a few small slugs. Then a first—a strange message from the gnomes of Zurich. My Swiss client, Global Resolutions.

Contract canceled. Submit invoice.

THE SAWTOOTH JOB

Chapter 10

"Weird."

I stared at the message on my phone. Bo and I stood on the cabin's front porch as the Sawtooths loomed nearby, snow-white in north face crevices and bowls. Hammers sounded around the corner and down the gravel street, likely construction on a makeshift band stage. The temperature dropped as the mountains became awash in alpenglow.

"Share the weirdness, goober. I may have a different perspective."

"They canceled the contract. It's over. Finis."

"Ah," Bo said, filling a small pipe with weed. "You stand within this glorious dusk burdened with contractual concerns. Allow me to quote a famous baseball player."

"Yeah, I know. It ain't over till it's over. But still. It's weird."

Bo didn't reply, enjoying the postcard view.

"Maybe the DIA was the Global Resolutions client," I continued. "The DIA cat in the cactus garden, who was none too happy, could have pulled strings and canceled the contract."

Bo took a hit off his pipe, exhaled, and said, "And now the inevitable. My Georgia peach struts and frets in his tedious manner across this vignette's small stage." He smiled my way. "We are joined on a quest, one true and keen. Let not your heart be troubled."

Marcus rolled into the parking lot as his SUV kicked up cold dust. He eased from behind the wheel, stepped gingerly on terra firma, and delivered a tight-lipped smile and nod. His leg clearly bothered him, and it bothered me he'd made the gritted-teeth drive. Not that I could have stopped it.

"Imagine my surprise," he said, limping our way. "To arrive and view two such fine gentlemen sucking down liquor and smoking weed. Operational prep, I suppose."

"To each their own, Marcus," I said as I stepped off the small porch with a heartfelt smile and shook hands.

Always a pleasure seeing him, and the gray hair that peeked out below his Stetson added a certain gravitas to the man. A meticulous dresser, he wore a clean canvas ranch coat over a pearl-button western shirt, pressed jeans, and western boots. A strange and unsolicited poignant mood washed over me, and I couldn't release his hand, using my left to pat his side. He returned the gesture. Don't know what brought it on or why that moment, but years-past Delta scenarios gripped me as we stood in twilight. Asia, the Middle East, Africa, South America—we'd been through hell and back, and now, older and maybe wiser, it struck me hard that an expiration date was woven into our connection. Time would pass, the mountains and meadows and rivers would continue, oblivious, while we mortals wove and dodged and, for a few lucky spells, glided through the here and now. Strange. So damn strange.

"You're not getting any prettier," he said, then glanced toward Bo. "Neither of you."

"Speak for yourself, cow whisperer," Bo said, stepping off the porch. "Clearly your aged eyesight is failing. I'll approach so you might take in this grand visage."

Marcus, with a headshake and snort and Bo-induced smile, stuck out his hand and then accepted the inevitable as Bo drifted past the handshake offer and wrapped him in a hug. Marcus, not a hugging fan, patted Bo's back.

"You can let go now, Bo."

"A difficult maneuver. I take great solace holding the physical you and knowing linear thinkers can attain an elderly, albeit crusty, status."

"It's liable to get a lot crustier if you don't let go."

"I've spent the day with another straight and narrow mind, another plodder, another intractable mind. So I'll release you, bwana Johnson. But know I'm here to help you both."

"Be still, my heart. Now, if you two hunyaks would help me unload the vehicle, we can get down to business."

Bo and I insisted he just negotiate the porch steps, sit on a porch chair, and sip brandy while he provided unloading oversight. He didn't argue and took the three porch steps with cautious leg lifts, hurtin' for certain. Bo grabbed his rucksack and a grocery sack while I hefted a massive duffel bag. Our armory. Inside, towel-wrapped, nested a weaponry collection. Soon enough we settled back on the porch. Marcus asked for a thick Pendleton blanket still in his vehicle, I donned a heavy coat and thick watch cap, and Bo appeared with a thick, bright alpaca shawl and vivid Peruvian cap, the earflaps tied across the top of his head.

"You got batteries for your getup, bud?" I asked. "I may require nighttime sunglasses just to look at you."

He grinned back, extended his arm, and requested the brandy bottle.

"What's the current status?" Marcus asked as his Zippo clacked open, a cigar lit.

"They canceled my contract."

"Did they give a reason?"

"Nope."

Marcus mulled over the new intel, and said, "Let's start with the knowns."

I ignored Bo's eye rolls the next few minutes as Marcus plowed a straight and narrow furrow. I appreciated it—the man excelled at operational landscape assessment and planning.

"Right," I said. "A simple contract. Find a missing scientist."

"But not her husband, even though he's missing too."

"Roger that."

"And now we've found her, or near enough, and the client on the other side of your Swiss outfit cancels the job."

"Yep."

Marcus puffed the cigar, background nail-pounding ceased, and tires crunched on gravel a hundred yards behind our cabin as the early street party arrivals assembled.

"I've pieced together a few things during the drive. Tell me what you think. Our two scientists collaborated on something that's got spy world's skivvies in a knot."

"Agreed."

"With the Defense Intelligence Agency appearance in the mix—and I'm sure you and Bo were absolute gentlemen when you met their guy—it points toward a military application for whatever our talented doctors worked on."

"Mossad's interest also points toward military use," I added.

"Alright. Does anything you've discovered about the Halls suggest they'd dabble in weapon systems?"

"Not at all. Marcus, my impression is they want to be left alone. They may have collaborated on some whiz-bang theoretical discovery, but I don't see them reaching for a high-paying job with a defense contractor. Not at all."

A snare drum, a few bass licks, and a pedal steel guitar's lonesome whine said the band had arrived and now warmed up. No highway noises sounded but more tire-on-gravel crunches indicated more arrivals as a crowd's low hum filled silent voids. Sparks of bright laughter interspersed with the crowd noise. Marcus's Zippo clacked again as he relit the cigar. I took a sip from the brandy bottle, waggled it toward Bo who declined the offer, and set it down on the porch alongside our wounded compadre.

"If the DIA contacted the Swiss and set up your job, they wouldn't pull the plug unless they had a handle on the Halls. I don't see it."

"Here's the deal, folks. Something changed. Someone met a trigger point, fresh intel shifted chess pieces. Who the hell knows what happened? But something changed today."

"Roger that," Marcus said. "As for the known unknowns—who hired you, what were the Halls researching, did the two go missing together, are they both here now, and why terminate the contract today? There're plenty others, but let's stick with the big ones."

"I'd argue the biggest one is do we pull the plug?" I asked. "This gig is officially over."

"So what? You hurting for money?" Marcus asked.

"No issues there."

"Then the mission isn't over. We move forward on our own dime. This entire deal holds prime interest for me. And it's a pleasant break from the ranch, although I'm doing much work there. Thank God I've got some remarkable neighbors."

"It's the Georgia peach's call," Bo said. "He mans the tiller, unsure, but as always undaunted."

"Alright," Marcus said, groaning as he pushed up from the chair. "Call it, Case. Just don't expect me to stomp up any gravel dust if we head for the street party."

"Stomped Dust," Bo said. "Not a bad name for a country band."

It was my call. The Russkie and Mossad agents aside, the job hadn't displayed bright warning signs, no life-threatening danger. At least none we couldn't handle with minimal effort if I kept Marcus away from the fray. His groan lifting from the chair was the real deal. But we were all alone here, the spook scramble in the Bay Area a long way away.

"We're on a hot trail," I said. "Let's tree these two critters, or at least the one we know is here, and see how they or her are doing. Maybe they could use some help."

"Then we start with the fandango," Bo said as he stood and stretched. "Ruth and Bart might surprise us as older rockers, cutting a rug under a half-full moon."

As if on cue, the band broke into "Jumpin' Jack Flash," the pedal steel guitar blending with the lead guitar, the drums and bass pounding.

"We know who to look for," I said, "so let's wander over there."

I'd texted Marcus the photo, so he had a grip on their appearance. At least when they stood hand in hand and dripping wet, wrapped in beach towels. The cloudless sky and bright moon provided more than sufficient light for navigating our way. Three ex-Delta operators. One in a heavy ranch coat and Stetson, one covered with bright Andean colors, and the third bundled up with everything I'd purchased in Boise. And I was still cold.

The scene we approached was Americana personified. The Sawtooths reflected bright moonlight as electric illumination from several bar and eatery front windows shone onto the gravel main drag. Folks—end-of-season tourists and locals numbering maybe a buck fifty—wandered in and out of the bars with plastic cups as they laughed and waved at friends and acquaintances, attired in well-used warm clothing with more than a few Carhartt labels on display.

The dancing had started with the band's first song as hiking boots, western boots, Sorrels, and sneakers helped create an ankle-level dust cloud. Couples, singles, moms with young sons, dads with young daughters, shook and stomped and twirled with the kids giggling as they observed their parental dancing partners cut loose. Smiles and joy aplenty as older folks shuffled and moved with the music as well, one arm static, ensuring they didn't spill any liquid from their cups. At least a dozen dogs, unleashed, wandered through and among the moving mob, tails wagging as they wondered what these crazy humans were up to.

Sixty miles away over a mountain pass sat Sun Valley where people drove expensive vehicles and congregated in pre-ski season finery at pricey restaurants and bars, the music muted, conversations held with an eye out for someone they might know, including celebrities. Give me Stanley, anytime.

Marcus found his spot on a bar's porch and leaned against a roof post, taking weight off his bad leg. I bought him a top shelf bourbon and water and stood with him for a few minutes as he lit another cigar. We both acknowledged, unspoken, that the master sniffer worked the crowd in his alpaca outerwear.

"I'm thinking about what if we find them?" Marcus asked, his voice raised, overriding the band's CCR song. "You mentioned help. I agree. But I'm wondering what help looks like."

"No clue, bud. At a minimum, we can tack a 'The End' on this strange tale."

"The weapon system facet bothers me. On several levels."

"Me, too. But we're still dealing with conjecture. You okay standing here?"

"Good as gold, and quit acting like I'm incapacitated. I could still whip both your asses and not spill a drop of this fine drink."

I smiled, patted his back, and moved through the crowd, stopping at regular intervals and performing a slow one-eighty. No sign of the Halls. And no sign of Bo. I circled the area three times—asking Marcus if he required more medicine on the second pass—and resigned myself to a fresh chase the next day.

Standing at the crowd's far end, opposite the band, Bo spoke into my ear and spooked me.

"Hi-ho, Fred Astaire."

"Dammit, Bo. I've asked you a thousand times not to do that."

His cloak of invisibility routine—an incredible tool against the enemy—disconcerted within benign environments. Every doggone time.

"If you would ease open, with acceptance and love, your cerebral cortex you would sense my approach."

"I'm deficient in cortex-opening endeavors. Any sign of our two scientists?"

"Several."

"They're here?"

"No."

I locked eyes with him and waited. He shifted close, a knowing grin and eyes twinkling under the goofy knitted cap, and bumped foreheads with me. His breath smelled of ginger and brandy.

"We are not alone. Several associates lurk. They lie in wait, as do we."

I shot hard stares across the crowd and along the periphery and couldn't pick up anyone who would set off alarms.

"What about Mossad and the DIA?"

"A difficult assessment. They each had winter wear, parka hoods covering their heads. One, however, is tall and could represent a fellow cactus lover."

"Where?"

"They skulk in the shadows, my goober. Deep shadows."

Spooks. Here in Stanley. Great. Just freakin' great.

THE SAWTOOTH JOB

Chapter 11

We stayed until the band quit and the crowd dispersed. I kept seeking Levy, the Mossad agent, and Barrett, the DIA guy. No luck. Which didn't mean they weren't there, skulking as Bo said, far back in the shadows among the main street buildings and parked vehicles. Both Marcus and I considered siccing Bo on one or two but nixed the thought knowing such an altercation would alert them to our presence. Which they may or may not have already figured out.

Two items stood clear—the Halls were a no-show, and the game had changed. It threw me into an indecisive mindset, with walk away on the table. Back inside the cabin, Marcus insisted we sit on the porch and distribute weaponry. Not a big deal from a public perspective—in Idaho, Wyoming, Montana, and other western stretches, the general populace wouldn't blink an eye at three guys passing around firearms, an activity not worth a second glance. But Marcus insisted it was a big deal if unfriendly eyeballs took a gander our way. Nothing subtle about the message, and a Marcus Johnson trademark.

"How about we do it inside?" I asked. "It's colder than a well digger's ass out there."

"Such wussification negates the entire point of the exercise."

"Well, at least give me time to stoke the fireplace so we can come back into warmth."

"We should send a pleasant note, handwritten in cursive on fine linen paper, requesting our favorite goober be exempt from any cold weather adventures. The Swiss, I believe, would view such a gesture with approval," Bo said as he tossed chunks of firewood at the room's hearth.

We assembled on the porch and extracted weapons from Marcus's duffel bag. Three Colt 901 .308 caliber assault rifles, each with an Elcan Specter scope wired for night vision. Two MK18 Mod 0 assault rifles. A CQB weapon. Close-quarters battle. A tight-situation rifle and Bo's favorite. Marcus had added something new—the two MK18s displayed green dot laser sights. Put the green dot on your target, squeeze the trigger. He'd also brought two M870 pump shotguns, a box of double-aught buckshot shells, and an extra H&K pistol for himself. He'd given up on me switching from the Glock. As a package, the weaponry represented Marcus Johnson's prime battle philosophy, one exhibited often during our Delta forays. If it's a knife fight, bring a gun. If it's a gun fight, bring more and better firepower. Hard arguing against his standard approach to conflict.

Bo snatched up an MK18, engaged the laser sight, and a pencil-thin green light displayed across the parking lot, settling on a tree stump. The green dot wavered a bit on the stump, then held steady as he settled in with the weapon.

"You've added a new feature," I said.

"A needed addition," Marcus said. "There's environmental variety here where we might engage."

"I'm hoping no engagement at all."

"This is way cool, fearless leader," Bo said, still aiming the laser-equipped weapon.

"No engagement would suit me just fine as well, and this little exercise fosters a hands-off reaction from bogeys. If they're around, right now, they'll view our armed-to-the-teeth status as mess with at your own risk. Rack a shotgun several times, would you?"

I did, as the pump shotgun's clack—a universal sound—carried a fair distance in the frosty night. An audible statement, not subject to misinterpretation.

"Let's talk bogeys," I said, "We can't whack a bunch of spooks here. And we don't know if we'd want to. Several might be, ostensibly, on our side."

Neither Marcus nor I questioned their appearance. If Bo said they lurked, they did.

"First, how did they know to congregate here?" Marcus asked.

"Bo and I both checked our rucksacks for tracking bugs when we left California. We're clean. And no one tailed us from Boise."

"And I kept my phone's GPS off and credit cards in my wallet. I made a clean entry from Montana."

"Which circles back to something changed. And it changed today. Contract cancelation, spook arrivals. And how did they get here so fast?"

"Sun Valley," Marcus said. "The airport there handles private jets daily. The high-net-worth crowd. And now, it looks like, the unmarked jet crowd as well."

It made sense. Even so, something had triggered their arrival. An element or action had changed behind the curtains, and we didn't have a clue what it might be.

"Alright," I said. "We assume the Halls are good folks, solid and sound. What if they're weirdos, and have a hankering for developing some new game-changing weapon system? If, in fact, it's a weapon system they worked on."

"They seek shelter from the storm," Bo said. "A slip-away, and a potent totem placed in the cosmic swirl showing their desire for anonymity and seclusion."

He'd curled up on a chair, wrapped in alpaca wool, his goofy hat's earmuffs pulled down.

"I must have had too much bourbon," Marcus said, "because I both understand what Bo just said and agree with him. Check the night sky for flying pigs."

We each knew we'd reached a pull-out point. Exit, scoot away, wash our hands clean of the entire affair. A solid option, except for a major collective mindset among us. To haul it away translated—given our history together—as ceding defeat, a white flag waved. Fat chance.

"Then let's play out what happens if our side, the DIA or Company or FBI, finds them here. Then what, and do we interfere with it?" I asked.

"Kenneled with regular feedings."

Bo was right, and we each knew it. They'd snatch up the Halls and hide them at a safe house somewhere in Maryland or Virginia, under constant surveillance. No ventures into the hills and woods, no hot springs, no freedom. They'd inform the two their research should continue and omit weaponizing their findings. Meanwhile, the data points, discoveries, formulas, or whatever they produced would slip out the back door and off to a weapons lab. And if the results were positive or poor or inconclusive, the end game remained the same. At some point both Ruth and Bart Hall would find themselves disappeared. Permanently.

"Which clarifies the game plan," I said. "We find them first. Then figure it out."

"While we dodge bogeys," Marcus added.

"Yeah. Dodging bogeys. That's not a rock band's name, Bo. It's a mandatory approach. If we whack a foreign spy on US turf, it won't ring any alarm bells if carcass disposal remains up to snuff. Taking out a US asset, well, that's another story. Discernment is the key."

"Rules and strictures placed into the universal current as if they held reign. The best-laid plans of mice and men, my brothers."

"It's an operational framework," Marcus said. "A framework without input from Scottish poets."

"Poets provide the muse for operational frameworks, fearless leader. Acceptance is the key."

The Zippo clacked as Marcus muttered, "Shithouse mouse, Bo."

"The person at the general store said they lived somewhere north, along the river," I said. "It's where we focus in the morning. Keep an eye out for power company wires headed off the main line, and signs of buried internet cable. There'll be a cabin or three along the river. We'll find them. So will the bogeys."

"Yet we carry an advantage over the assembled amorphous parties, fellow seekers."

"Which is?" I asked.

"We alone shall check on fissures, releases, from deep in the bowels of Mother Earth."

"You mean hot springs," Marcus said.

"He means deep bowel releases," I said. "Get with the program, Marcus."

"Here's the program, you mullets. Three-hour watches. I'll take the first one. This leg is protesting and would prevent shut-eye, so I'll take some ibuprofen and wait for it to kick in."

"I'll take the second," Bo said. "Our goober requires rest from the fretting."

I required clarity, and only Dr. Ruth and Dr. Bart would provide it.

Chapter 12

Daylight arrived late while we ate at an excellent breakfast diner. The establishment would shut down in a few more days, then reopen in May. A chilly morning, and the sky indicated a weather pattern change as gray clouds moved in. A weather forecast called for snow later in the morning. We'd loaded up our vehicles as the day's events, often the case, might have required a hasty action-provoked exit. A late start for us, accommodating Marcus's slow movements without a word said.

Stanley's small diner held a dozen other folks. The ones who looked up from their coffee or meal as we squeezed past didn't bother me. Those who feigned indifference did. One cat replied, "No, thank you," when the server asked if he'd like more coffee. He spoke with a British accent. An MI6 spook? Maybe. Maybe not. When we removed our heavy coats—Bo now wore regular outdoor clothing—our pistols remained hidden under fleece vests or thick untucked shirts. Strong odds we weren't the only ones who ate bacon and eggs while armed. The British accent guy left without a glance in our direction before we received our breakfast.

It struck hard we had no skin in this game other than personal interest. Much larger interests, powerful and deadly interests, held sway over finding the Halls. We were bit players, plain and simple. Bit players engaged because of curiosity and a desire for closure. Weak tea for placing ourselves in danger. But our involvement also spoke to an unstated desire nested deep within us—do the right thing. Maybe not full throttle and not with gleeful anticipation we could engage the bad guys. No caped crusaders among us, but the situation offered a feeding opportunity for tamped-down skill sets honed through years of training. Skill sets employed when doing the right thing stood clear and present.

The Salmon River ran alongside the town and flowed tight against a two-lane headed north. Our two vehicles rolled slow, Bo and I in the lead SUV. The river showed shallow, close to its source, a foot or two deep in most stretches with darker pools at irregular intervals. Also known as "The River of No Return," it flowed for over four hundred miles through central Idaho's wilderness. Outside Stanley, Redfish Lake sat at the base of the Sawtooths where salmon formed nests, laid eggs, and died. Their journey began in the Pacific Ocean, up the mighty Columbia River, then the Snake River, and finally the Salmon. Awesome stuff.

Less awesome—any clue what we planned if we found the Halls. While we shared the winding highway with few others, powerful forces circled and sought, with unknown intent. High odds it involved capture, kidnap, and a rapid whisk off to Virginia or Tel Aviv or Moscow or a country village in England or China. Some may have intended to kill them on the spot. Hard to say.

Uphill entrances with creosote power poles and overhead electrical lines showed on our left. We stopped at the first three. At each one, less than fifty yards up their dirt entrance roads, days-old snow, shaded with forest trees, showed no tire tracks or footprints. Not a definitive sign, but a decent indicator the cabins hadn't seen an owner for several weeks—a reality confirmed as we drove farther up the access roads and viewed empty, quiet structures. At the third cabin's entrance road, we made a disturbing discovery. Three sets of fresh footprints, men's boots, had tromped through shaded snow, and returned. They'd parked their vehicle at the driveway's bottom, and after sussing out the cabin situation, came back and moved on. We parked at the bottom as well and exited our vehicles, armed. Bo and I carried the green laser-equipped MKs, Marcus the Colt rifle.

"You hang, Marcus. Bo and I will check it out."

He could do without a walk on his bum leg.

"Stow that BS. Bo, you're on point."

Our former team spearhead veered off the road and disappeared into thick forest. Marcus and I eased our way up the road. No recent tire tracks, no woodsmoke, no indications of occupancy. As we approached the small cabin, Bo stood outside the front door and shook his head. Nothing, nada.

The found footprints, attributable to a variety of possibilities, remained unmentioned. We knew who'd created them. Other seekers, their intentions unclear—either capture or kill. Take your pick. Why the first two cabins showed no sign of other parties remained unspoken as well. The clandestine cavalcade had zeroed in on this specific area. We were closing in.

"We'll run out of these small entrance roads soon," Marcus said. "I passed this way headed for Stanley, and it's lonely turf between here and Clayton, thirty miles up the highway."

"How big a town is Clayton?" I asked.

"The sign said seven."

"As in seven people?"

"It's what the sign said. And it may have overstated things. Let's keep moving. We're burning daylight."

A half-mile north, the road well above the river, a small empty pull-out appeared on our right. Steam showed far below, down the steep river slope. I pulled in, Marcus followed, and we collected at the drop-off. A tiny footpath wound down the slope, ending where near-boiling water entered the Salmon. River rocks, arranged in semicircular designs, created small pools. Ice-cold river water, partially dammed, flowed and mingled with the hot outflow and produced, I supposed, decent soaking spots. The air carried a sulfur hint, and no brave souls occupied the makeshift hot tubs below us.

"Not a Ritz-Carlton setup," I said. "But pretty cool. Hidden from the road with a DIY soaking spot. I get the appeal."

"An exercise in hydraulic engineering," Bo said. "With an ever-changing environment as the river rises and falls. A chance for hands-on communion with ancient and potent forces."

A lone light snowflake fell before my face.

"An opportunity for freezing your ass off. It's snowing."

Marcus sighed and said, "It's not snow, son. It's a few snowflakes, although the sky says real snow comes our way."

"Would have been nice if they'd bought a place on the beach in Florida. Or the Caribbean."

"Let's roll," Marcus said, limping toward his vehicle. "Bo, your mission between here and our next stop is fixing his whining."

"I'm not whining. I'm just sayin'."

Within a half mile, another cabin road proved fruitless, the hidden vacation home boarded up. Prior to finding out it stood empty, we parked again near the blacktop and sent Bo ahead because six sets of booted footprints showed, three together, the others separate as solo players. The playing field had become crowded. Bo squatted beside the displayed indentations in the shaded snow.

"The same group of three as the last place. Plus two unknowns. And the Brit from the diner."

Marcus and I didn't question his statement's veracity, but curiosity mandated I ask.

"You know it's the Brit how?"

"He stretched his legs under the table at the diner. I had a clear view of the pattern on his boot soles."

He took off into the woods. Marcus's limp, pronounced, pained me as we made our way upward until we found the cabin with the boarded-up windows and, again, Bo.

"Someone picked the lock and checked out the interior," he said upon our arrival. "It's still unlocked."

"Not surprising. Anything?" I asked.

"Midthirties couple own the place. They're from Boise. You gents want a gander?"

"I won't ask if the heater is on because it will only rile the elderly among us. So, no."

"Then I shall lock the front door as an act of consideration. Photos show a pleasant loving couple, with two golden retrievers."

Surrounding fir and pine treetops swayed as wind noise increased, joined with sporadic tire sounds as vehicles passed on the highway below us. The snowflakes increased and midmorning daylight decreased as the clouds became darker. At least five bogeys worked the terrain nearby: one the Brit, the others unknown, everyone hot on the trail. The moment had all the earmarks of turning into a bloody circus.

"Extreme caution from here on out," Marcus said. "We don't need some trigger-happy spook taking a potshot in our direction."

"Roger that."

We made it back to our vehicles and again headed north. My anticipation and excitement redlined—couldn't help it. The quarry close, others joined in the chase, unknowns out the wazoo.

A mile later, Bo made an announcement.

"We just passed Ruth."

"What?"

He returned an angelic smile filled with surety, eyes bright. I could have kissed him. Our opponents had the weight of entire nations behind them. We had, well, three over-the-hill ex-Delta operators, one of whom could track an ant across smooth granite. I found a pull-out that afforded a five-point turnaround. While I maneuvered, Marcus pulled alongside, lowered his window as cigar smoke exited, and waited for an explanation.

"Bo found Ruth."

He nodded back, raised the window, and joined me in the one-eighty maneuver on the empty blacktop. Several hundred yards later, Bo pointed toward a seldom-used two-track above the river, its entrance suggested with lightly bent bunchgrass. We turned, rolled downhill, and ran into an old parked Subaru on a flat spot where any trail indications ended. A hundred yards below us was the Salmon River, pressed hard against a cliffside. At the cliff's base, far below, steam and hot water rivulets. An older woman sat in a self-made hot pool, a clothes pile and beach towel collected on a nearby boulder. We assembled and watched. Marcus puffed his cigar, I patted Bo's back and pulled small field binoculars.

"It's her, bud. Retro cat-eye frames. Short gray hair. Skinny as a rail."

"Speaking of glasses," Marcus said, viewing through his binoculars, "hers are so fogged up she can't see five feet. And with the river noise she won't hear anything either, which makes her vulnerable as hell. Let's fix that."

He limped toward his SUV, pulled the Colt rifle, and returned, eyeballing the steep cliff's rim where the highway passed by. Dr. Ruth extended her legs, toes above water, and pulled them back, having run into either a too cold or too hot spot. She stood—more an unwinding—and rearranged fair-sized rocks to correct the flow.

"She's butt naked," Marcus said.

"Somehow I'm not surprised."

Bo left us and retrieved a small paper grocery bag from his rucksack, along with a towel. Ruth, satisfied with her river rock rearrangement, sat back down, the water at armpit level.

"Allow me the initial introduction," Bo said. "Join me in fifteen, my weather-challenged Georgia peach. You as well, fearless leader. A hot soak would do wonders for your leg."

He headed downhill on an indistinct path.

"He's the right man for addressing her," Marcus said. "And within ten minutes, head down there as well before he corrupts whatever linear thought processes she might have."

"Yeah. Solid point. Snow is collecting on the river rocks near her soaking spot. How cold do you think the river water is?"

"Damn cold."

"Maybe Bo can convince her to get out and come up here."

"I don't see it playing out like that. Get engaged, you moron. Get wet. I'll provide cover for everyone from up here. My leg hurts."

"Suddenly your leg bothers you."

"Go talk with her. I'm providing cover."

He was right. I would go talk with her after Bo introduced us and the situation. I'd tote a satisfied smile and relief and satisfaction we'd outdone the spook circus. A circus with multiple ringmasters and dangerous acts. Although no vehicles passing above could view us or the hot springs or the rising steam, which dissipated as it lifted, I collected my borrowed MK rifle and fished a towel from my rucksack, then rejoined Marcus.

"You don't require the rifle," he said. "Although the towel will come in handy."

"Are you sure you won't join me, Mr. Man of the Mountains?"

"I'm not the one who took a contract to find Ruth Hall."

"Thanks for the insight, Dr. Phil."

Bo approached the river, unnoticed at seven paces from Ruth's back, and began a silent river rock collection. Freezing cold aside, the moment was filled to the brim with right and tight. Dr. Ruth Hall, and answers, soaked in a hot spring below me. To hell with my contract. We had found her.

Chapter 13

Marcus and I watched through binoculars as Bo started his introductory ministrations. The river flowed alongside what appeared as ancient archeological formations, underwater circular rock structures, as an immersed nude older woman lifted her toes again above the waterline. The light snow now arrived in flurries, not heavy, but a precursor for a larger weather pattern. Bo, still unnoticed, assembled a rock cairn until the small stone pile reached two feet in height. Then he pulled a small box from the paper bag, set it on the cairn's top, and supported the item with smaller rocks, facing Dr. Ruth.

"What the hell?" Marcus asked as we viewed events through our binoculars.

"Belgian chocolates. He must have bought them in Boise."

Satisfied with the presentation, Bo stripped naked and must have spoken with soft tones. Ruth first lifted her head at the sound, not alarmed, then removed her fogged-over glasses, dipped them in the water for temporary clarity, and sighted Bo. Wearing nothing but a wide smile, he used both hands as presenters and pointed toward his gift as a visiting nobleman paying tribute to royalty. Ruth smiled. They talked. Then Bo joined her in the small hot pool she'd created.

"I'll admit he's got a way," Marcus said, lowering his binoculars.

"Yes, he does. Wish me luck."

I headed downhill.

"Avoid firing the rifle. It might spook her."

"Thanks for more world-class advice. You oughta get a syndicated radio program," I said over my shoulder.

I picked my way downhill at a slow pace, which allowed Bo more time for setting Ruth at ease with an armed man's approach. Halfway down, she again dipped her glasses, looked in my direction, and continued chatting with her soaking buddy. Several minutes later, I stood by Bo's clothes pile and laid the rifle down.

"Hi, Dr. Hall. I'm Case Lee."

Another eyeglasses dip, a close inspection of what I hoped came across as a friendly player, and a simple statement.

"Bo says you will not harm me."

Her voice, with each word enunciated in full, came across as soft, gentle.

"Yes, ma'am. Bo's right."

She continued staring, assessing, as steam-induced fog reclaimed her eyewear. Satisfied, she stood and began rearranging rocks at the pool's interface with the Salmon River. Bo joined her. I looked overhead as the clouds darkened, tiny snowflakes more numerous. Then stripped naked. Before the plunge, I shot an uphill glance toward Marcus, who wore a wide grin under the binoculars and delivered a thumbs-up.

My first tender steps proved a rookie mistake, placing my bare feet into three-inch-deep water pouring from the cliffside. Water that could have cooked eggs. I danced backward. Then cautious steps on smooth rock tops just above the steaming rivulets, and finally the chosen pool where I joined the two as we rearranged more rocks and expanded our makeshift hot tub while I froze my ass off. Satisfied with the stone-age construction, we sat.

"Are you good, Ruth?" Bo asked.

She scooted a few inches over, an underwater sand and mud cloud raised then washed away with the pool's light current.

"Yes. Yes, this is good."

I soon enough grasped the reason for her small maneuver. An ice-cold current from the river pushed against my right side, I scooted too far left, and brushed against a teapot-hot inflow. So I scooted back a few inches and found the sweet spot. We sat three feet apart, shoulder tops above the waterline, as the river pressed against us with its riffles and icy flow just below eye level.

"Dr. Hall, can you tell me where your husband is?"

"No, I cannot." She adjusted position again, sighed, and said, "You can call me Ruth."

Then she wrapped her arms around lifted knees, lowered her chin, and stared into the pool's depths. Her voice inflection indicated a tender soul.

"What do you think happened with him?"

She pinched her nose and sank below the waterline for a few seconds, then reemerged, hair dripping.

"They took Bart." She locked eyes with me. "Bo said you are three, and you will help. I do not know how you can."

I didn't either. With clarity, with purpose, maybe. But no guarantees.

"Do you know who they are, Ruth? The ones who took your husband?"

"Americans?" Bo asked.

Great follow-up. Bo's question implied US government assets.

"People from the US government?" I asked.

She shook her head with small, tight movements.

"I do not think so. It is a possibility. But I do not think so."

"Why not?"

"A man and a woman arrived at our house. They wished to move us, they said. They wished to move us away from our home in Palo Alto."

"US government people?"

"Yes. It does not seem fair."

"It's not fair. But we can't do anything about them, and I'm sorry. When did the US government people appear at your house?"

She hesitated and stuck a forefinger in an ear, rubbing. A raven cawed from across the river as light snow fell and the river gurgled past.

"Why would you three help me?" She removed the finger from her ear and used both hands, creating surface swirls, lost in the water's movement. "It is wonderful not feeling all alone. Wonderful. But why?"

Bo and I locked eyes. Personal reasons galore, left unspoken among us three. But Ruth deserved an answer. I wouldn't plunge into Swiss contracts or clandestine maneuvering. No, she sought human rationale, internal motivators. Reasons that neither I nor Bo nor Marcus would fully dissect.

"A sense of duty," I said, an answer lacking full disclosure or great clarity, but the best I could do given my head ping-ponged on reasons and rationales.

"Universal obligation," Bo said. "Fulfilled with commitment and affection."

Duty, obligation, right and wrong. A package deal, a mindset we three seldom dwelled on. She lifted her head, smiled at us both, and returned her gaze toward the hand-induced swirls.

"Ten days ago."

"When the government people appeared at your house?"

"Yes. They appeared ten days ago."

"When did Bart go missing?"

"You use such a strange expression. Go missing. Forgive me, but I do not believe this is accurate. They took him."

With gentle prying, we gained a few answers. During our conversation she proved frail, off-kilter, but endearing as hell. Bart Hall disappeared five days ago. We never found out why she thought with certainty it wasn't the US Defense Intelligence Agency or the FBI or the Company. I gave it fifty-fifty odds as Mossad, and the Russians and the Brits sniffed around as well, so the kidnapper's affiliation remained wide open.

One thing for certain—whatever the Halls worked on required them both. An incomplete weapons system design was worthless when new discoveries from both Ruth and Bart made up integral components for a working system.

As the clock ticked, I made an operational decision and shifted toward the immediate. We could excavate for both bigger picture and Bart's trail later. Meanwhile, we required an exit plan to move Ruth to a safer spot. I had no clue how or where, but my team would, come hell or high water, act. In which direction and with how much force a TBD, but action created opportunity.

"Ruth, other men have arrived in Stanley who want to take you, too. I believe it's best if we move you somewhere safe."

"Somewhere safe. I do not believe Bart is somewhere safe."

"First things first. Let's find refuge for you, then work on finding Bart. Okay?"

"Refuge. Is this a temporary condition?"

Temporary. For sure the two US spooks who'd approached her and Bart in Palo Alto hadn't used the term. Their solution had permanent stamped all over it. Whether she, and Bart, could ever feel safe again in Stanley, an unknown. No point sugarcoating the reality.

"Maybe. But I don't know. Sorry. I just don't know."

She nodded toward the water's surface. Seconds ticked off.

"Bo. Bo and Case," she said, then looked up. "Who is the third person?"

"Marcus. He's alongside your Subaru."

She nodded and hugged her knees again.

"I am afraid I made a mistake yesterday."

"Mistakes and stumbles and wrong turns create our life's fabric. It's true for us all," Bo said. "And often we surface on the other side more enlightened."

She smiled in his direction and scooted an inch or two, adjusting her water temperature.

"Thank you for the chocolate."

"You are most welcome."

She sighed and returned to her mistake.

"I used the GPS function on my phone yesterday. There is a new bookstore in Twin Falls. I checked for directions and drive time, something I should not have done. Bart and I have a pact never to use GPS while here in our hidden getaway. It is a function not integrated within our phone's encrypted framework." She shifted her gaze toward me. "I did not have it on long."

There it was. Everyone and their brother had waited for a crack in the Hall wall. Clandestine services in the US, Israel, Russia, Britain, and likely several more backdoored systems with software programs designed to flag and alert when a Hall credit card transaction appeared, or an airline manifest listed a Hall. Or when a Ruth or Bart Hall encrypted phone switched on the GPS function. An unencrypted function tied to their phone account. Ruth's action yesterday had kicked off a spookville scramble. Contract cancelation—no need for ol' Case anymore—and private jet flights into Sun Valley, with a spook brigade crossing the mountain pass and descending on Stanley.

"Where did this happen?" I asked.

"I started a drive into Stanley when the thought struck me how nice it would be to wander around a good bookstore."

"So, somewhere near this spot?"

"Yes, near this spot. Perhaps a mile away."

Which explained why we found footprints at several cabins. They'd captured a location on the highway. Not the Halls' cabin, but close enough for horseshoes and hand grenades. The pursuing entourage had by now discovered the Halls' cabin. No doubt. And they'd wait for Ruth's return.

A few more questions for clarity and then dry-off time and action taken. As Marcus would say, we burned daylight.

"How did you arrive in Idaho?"

Her old Subaru had Idaho plates, so she didn't drive here. And a commercial flight would list her as a passenger, guaranteed to create a bevy of spooks at the Boise airport.

"I flew. We always fly."

"On an airline?"

"No, not on an airline. We have a friend with a large propeller plane. He loves flying, so he takes us. Bart and I buy the fuel. We store the Subaru in Boise."

"Is this friend associated in any way with Stanford or your research?"

"Oh my, no. We met him at a coffee shop in Palo Alto on trivia night. Bart and I love playing trivia games. Our friend is also very good at trivia within the entertainment and sports categories. Bart and I remain deficient within those classifications. Our friend joined us, creating a three-person team."

She'd become animated while speaking about home and small pleasures. She began her hand swirls again, halting once and dipping her glasses.

"We often win. The prize is our choice of pastries," she said, her voice now wistful. "The pastries are a day old but still quite delicious. Bart enjoys croissant variations. I prefer scones." Then her body language collapsed when she added, "I do not wish for refuge. I wish for Bart, and for us to be left alone."

"I know, and I'm sorry. May I ask you a few more questions before we get going? It will help us paint a bigger picture and formulate an action plan."

She nodded back.

"Do you only use cash while you two are in Idaho?" I asked.

"Yes. And cryptocurrency for larger transactions. Are you familiar with blockchain technology?"

"Yeah, a little bit. Did you and Bart purchase your cabin through a corporation? A Nevada corporation?"

"Why, yes. How on earth did you know that?"

"An educated guess."

Alrighty, then. The Halls had created a decent hidden trail between California and Idaho. All for naught at this point—when she switched on her GPS, even for thirty seconds, system alarms sounded across the globe. Man, technology could bite you in the ass.

"We should get moving, Ruth," I continued.

I glanced at Bo, and he returned a tight-lipped nod.

"I must tell you, I do not relish leaving this spot. It is very peaceful." She took a deep breath, exhaled, and dipped her glasses again. "We were married in graduate school forty years ago. Almost every night we work on a jigsaw puzzle and discuss the day. Sometimes we listen to classical music while we talk. Bart often drinks a glass of wine." She stared, once again, into the pool's slow current. "Since they took him, I have become quite lonely."

A powerful wave of anger and disgust and screw-all-of-you-SOBs flooded me. I possessed little bright knight or avenging angel within my makeup, but this situation irritated the fire out of me. A gentle soul soaked across from me, and all indications pointed toward a like-minded individual as her partner. Sure, they'd collaborated on some out-there technology or theory that had held their interest from a researcher's perspective. Leave it to spookville and geopolitical chess players to take their research and roll it up into a bright and shiny and new leverage point for use against others. Screw 'em.

"We should get moving, Ruth. I'm not sure how this will all play out, but I can tell you this. The two guys soaking with you now, and the third one up the hill, are your best bet for living the life you and Bart want."

She and I locked eyes.

"Will you find him and bring him to me?"

"No promises, except for one. I'll give it my best shot."

Chapter 14

We gathered inside Marcus's vehicle, filled him in on what we'd learned, and planned. The snow continued, collecting on the SUV's windshield. Marcus started the engine and heater and wipers. Ruth expressed wide-eyed concern over all the weaponry in our midst.

"Ma'am," Marcus said, "in our experience, it's better to have it and not need it than need it and not have it."

"Do you believe such devices are required?"

"Unknown. What we do know is quite a few players want you, none of whom I'd classify as benign. We can go over why later, but right now I'd suggest we head north and leave this area. Bo, you drive Doctor Hall."

Ruth stared out the back seat window, lost.

"We should never have collaborated on our research," she whispered toward no one in particular. "Bart always asks me about my location. They make him do it."

This was new, and as hardened operators we'd have to accept her intel would arrive in dribs and drabs.

"You communicate with Bart?" I asked.

"Oh, yes. Every day, and it is a heartening experience. He is alive. I do not believe he is well."

"But you are certain the unknown 'they' have him?"

I'd twisted around in the front seat, one arm over the backrest. She explained her husband's voice and word choice conveyed a desire for her to remain hidden, even as his captors pushed for the geographic revelation.

"Did he contact you on the day they kidnapped him?"

"Oh, my, yes. A most disconcerting call."

"Where was he when they nabbed him?"

"He walked home. Bart enjoys his walks."

"In daylight? Near Stanford?"

"It would seem so."

The kidnappers displayed no subtlety, which winnowed the field a bit. Russians, maybe. They could have parked a van along his walking path and nabbed him within seconds, observers be damned.

"Where were you, ma'am, when he called?" Marcus asked.

"Shopping. We had planned on a Stanley trip this week."

"Chocolates?" Bo asked. "Belgian?"

"Why, yes. And Dutch and Swiss as well. Thank you again for your gift. Would you like a piece now?"

"Perhaps later, although Marcus may desire one. When Bart contacted you the first time, why didn't you reveal where you were?"

"My husband is quite clever. He explained they had taken him and stated his captors wished to know my location and then asked if I was at Mr. Stanley's house. We do not know a Mr. Stanley."

Good for Bart. The guy kept his cool, protected his wife.

"How did you reply?" I asked.

"I said no. He said he understood if I did not wish to reveal my location. The Mr. Stanley reference implied I should flee. Flee here. Then they struck him."

"Struck him?"

"Oh, yes. What terrible people. He cried out, and his phone clattered to the ground. Terrible people."

112

"Ma'am," Marcus said, "he won't call today. They've found you."

"Oh."

She absorbed the hard truth, sighed, and stared out the window again. Bo slid his hand into hers and she gripped, tight, as he whispered, "It's alright." I twisted back forward and watched snow collect on the windshield between wiper swipes.

Hauling ass constituted a solid near-term plan if we employed specific tactics. Marcus and Bo didn't live in my world and lacked the convoluted mindset required when engaged with spookville.

"We have to separate on the drive. All three vehicles. If you find a semi headed north, stay on its tail."

"Explain," Marcus said.

"One of our intel agencies may have a drone over this area, although this snowstorm could ground that approach. But they'll have a big bird overhead. So will the Chinese and maybe the Israelis. I've never had a good read on Mossad's capabilities in the overhead surveillance area."

"Heat signatures?" Marcus asked as he glommed onto the dangers.

"Roger that."

The snowstorm would prevent look-down visual capabilities for a drone or big bird geostationary satellite, but thermal imaging—a vehicle's engine heat, for instance—would still work. And a two or three vehicle tight group exiting our area would draw unwanted attention.

"We spread out. Hook up with a semitruck if you can. Its heat signature will be much larger, and a lone vehicle trailing a semi in this weather won't raise an eyebrow in DC or Beijing. Or Tel Aviv."

"You surf interesting waves, goober. Don't worry, Ruth, I'll drive us. Where shall we reconvene?"

113

"If this weather pattern keeps up, they might shut down the highway in the next hour or three," Marcus said. "At a minimum, we make Challis. The town of Salmon is preferable."

"Because it's farther away?" I asked.

"That, plus it offers another small highway south, between the Lost River Range and the Lemhi Range. It intersects with a smaller road, which can take us into Montana."

Man, it was excellent traveling with someone who knew this vast turf.

"Alright," I said. "Everyone on board with travel plans? We make Challis. If the weather allows, on to Salmon."

"Roger that."

"Hi-ho."

"What about Bart?" Ruth asked.

"We'll deal with finding him once we've gotten you to safety. Okay?" I asked.

"We must stop at our cabin."

A hard stop as three operators remained silent and wondered how best to steer Ruth toward the situation's danger. Her cabin was out of the question. There be dragons there. Bo took the lead and gently pressed, citing at least five bad guys on the prowl in, at, or near her cabin.

She listened, nodded, and said, "My laptop computer remains there."

Shit, oh dear. One thing for certain—her laptop now sat in some spook's hands.

"Does this computer contain your research?" I asked.

"It does."

Marcus removed his felt Stetson and rubbed his head. I let out a puffed-cheek exhale. Snow continued falling.

"We could leave it," Marcus said. "Although it might trigger a series of damn unfortunate events."

"I do not understand," Ruth said.

And we wouldn't elaborate on the implications. If her laptop fell into hands associated with Bart's kidnappers, Ruth's life became less valued. They had Bart, and her research. She might become a loose end that required snipping. Assassinations were easier than kidnapping.

If her research fell into someone's ownership not associated with Bart's captors, it could set off executions under the rubric of zero outcome—if I can't have both halves of this knowledge, the safest play is no one gets it.

Under the first scenario, adios Ruth. Under the second, call it a draw, let's go have a beer, and adios both Bart and Ruth. Welcome to the shadow world's morality play. Oh, man.

Then there was the dead mule on the table. If we engaged with those at her cabin, we crossed the Rubicon. At least I would. Marcus and Bo weren't on anyone's radars and could engage, scoot, and remain anonymous. Not me.

No doubt the Mossad spook, or one of his brethren, was in the area and knew my identity. High odds the DIA guy, William Barrett, had arrived. And the world's most powerful spook, Townsend at the Company, would find out I'd engaged in a Stanley area fandango and at Stanford. Thank God I lived on a boat with constant movement along the Ditch with no known address. But tangling with the gang at the Halls' cabin guaranteed the Company would be on my ass. What a freakin' hair ball.

Taken together, the dangers and perilous outcomes did nothing but bolster my commitment. Call it hardheadedness or dumbass on display, but I wouldn't back down. Marcus swiveled his head in my direction and locked eyes. No words required—the mutual message clear. Do the right thing. I turned toward Bo in the rear seat.

"Let's dance," he said, smiling.

Decision made, Rubicon crossed, we peppered Ruth with tactical questions.

"What is the distance, as close as you can estimate, between your driveway entrance and your cabin?" I asked.

Through back-and-forth, we gathered the lay of the land. The entrance road for the Halls' cabin was a half mile farther down the highway. Their driveway road ran uphill a couple hundred yards and ended at the cabin. Forest surrounded both the road and the cabin. No other cabins after theirs until many miles up the highway in Clayton. Their cabin marked the end of Stanley's suburbs.

"Bo, why don't you take Ruth and fire up her vehicle," Marcus said. "Get the heater going."

They slid from the back seat as three retired operators understood we'd hold the next conversation away from her earshot. Marcus and I exited as well, lifting the SUV's back hatch as Bo fired up the Subaru, left Ruth inside it, and returned. Marcus handed Bo an MK with laser sight and an ear mic for communications. I slid an extra magazine into a coat pocket and inserted my ear mic as Marcus lifted the shotgun and chambered a round. The scattergun would join his Colt rifle in his front seat.

"Tight discernment, gentlemen," Marcus said. "We're liable to find semifriendlies there."

He referenced DIA or FBI or Company assets.

"Pretty much guaranteed," I said. "And they're semifriendly at best. Let's not forget likely outcomes if they nab Ruth."

"That's not a green light to start whacking Feds."

"No, it's not, Marcus. I wouldn't squeeze the trigger on a US asset. But they're not taking her. Period."

"Understood. So tight discernment and upper hand frames the ROE."

ROE. Rules of engagement. Bo, Marcus, and I acknowledged that conflict lay ahead. Of what variety, and to what level of ferocity, unknown. I climbed into my SUV and fired the engine, turned on the wipers, and cranked up the heat. The next conversation, overheard via ear mics between Bo and Ruth, took place as we each made multiple-point turnarounds so we'd hit the highway moving forward.

"Bart and I have done nothing wrong. Nothing. What if we arrive at the cabin and talk with these people? They must know where he is."

"I believe we sit immersed in a warm flow, accepting currents and eddies that will keep you safe and offer answers about Bart," Bo said, his voice pleasant, calm.

"So you will talk with them?"

"Soft whispers, perhaps, leaving the door open for communications of a more argumentative nature."

She sighed and said, "Good. I believe reasonable communications might provide answers."

Ruth Hall was unaware she spoke with—if communications became "argumentative"—the last person on this good earth you'd want to tangle with. I led, the SUV in four-wheel drive, which didn't prevent the tires spinning as I crested the two-track path and turned onto the highway. Snow blew horizontal with the occasional gusts but otherwise fell steady, thick. Bo goosed Ruth's Subaru and hit the highway, followed by Marcus. A quarter mile north, a parked SUV appeared on a tiny turnout over the river. It had sat there awhile with no tire tracks in the snow indicating its arrival.

"Bo," I said, "ask Ruth if there's a hot springs down there."

He did. Her reply, discernible over his ear mic, was negative. She added the tight turnouts we'd encounter were for anglers, who'd scramble down the riverbank. No one fly-fished during a snowstorm.

I slowed at the Halls' entrance road. Although snow covered the driveway, earlier tire tracks from a single vehicle remained discernible. No stealth approach through the woods for those cats. They'd barreled up the entrance road, which set off mild alarms. Russians, maybe, although my gut said even they would take a more circular, a more subtle approach. As would the DIA or FBI or Mossad or MSS or MI6. Strange stuff. I continued rolling forward.

"Peculiar," Bo said as he and Ruth passed the entrance.

A few seconds later, Marcus added, "Damn peculiar," as he rolled past.

A quarter mile later, another angler turnout with a parked vehicle and several hundred yards past that, another. Both lacked recent signs of arrival, the surrounding snow fresh and unmarked.

"We're late for this soirée, gentlemen," Bo said. "We can only hope a few hors d'oeuvres remain."

I continued for another mile until a wide pullout appeared, sufficient for the three vehicles to pull over and make a turnaround. A pickup truck rolled past, followed by a semitruck, both headed north.

"Let's park it at the entrance road," Marcus said as we waited until the two passing trucks had disappeared around a curve. "Then approach on foot."

"Roger that," I said and made the one-eighty, headed south.

I pulled into the Halls' entrance road just far enough so our three vehicles parked in a line off the highway. Adrenaline meters rose as bogeys and semifriendlies and who-knows-what waited up the snow-covered road.

Marcus, carrying both the shotgun and Colt rifle, cracked open Ruth's passenger door and said, "Ma'am, would you please crawl into the back seat and lie down?"

She did, without comment or questions. For all her strange mannerisms, she understood she'd entered an alien and unknown realm. A place where three strangers recently met projected surety and professionalism, undaunted by whatever lay ahead. Not a comfortable situation for her, but protestations about having done nothing wrong aside, she had to know she sat smack dab in the middle of a shitstorm.

Bo and I both wore camo winter coats and dull brown watch caps. Marcus kept his Stetson on—not a bad play as it kept the snow off his face—with a muted dark scarf wrapped around his neck underneath a heavy ranch coat. Left unsaid—his bum leg prevented him joining the uphill dance. He'd stay behind and protect Ruth.

"Discernment, gentlemen," he said. "And keep me informed. I'll make it up the hill pronto if necessary."

"Roger that," I said and edged toward the forest on our left.

Bo didn't respond, and my glance toward the forest on our right displayed his snow prints disappearing into a thick cluster of fir trees. I moved ahead slow, weaving through timber with caution and all senses cranked up. Ahead, competing forces, unaware the big dogs had arrived. And for what? A laptop containing research on something we had no clue about. We—three ex-Delta operators—moved against US and international forces within the Idaho wilderness during a snowstorm. Freakin' ridiculous. But we'd committed, the deal sealed, and I reminded myself it boiled down to those competing forces messing with two nice old scientists who wanted nothing more than to be left alone.

Then gunfire exploded ahead. Two automatic weapons, ripping bullets and sharp cracks into the snow-muffled setting.

Chapter 15

I sank to a knee, rifle against shoulder, when silence returned… the brief firefight over, outcome unclear. With one exception. High odds someone just died. The setting had now changed, shifted. I used my teeth and pulled off the tight, thin glove on my right hand, pocketing it. For a reconnoitering, the glove had utility. For battle, I required full-feel forefinger against trigger. Fat snowflakes poured down, shifting and swirling with the occasional wind gust. Ravens called, hoarse and grating; unconcerned forest watchers, their cries lost in the snowfall.

I eased left and uphill and used pine tree trunks and thick fir tree foliage to cover my advance. The automatic fire had taken place at or near the cabin, another hundred-fifty yards straight uphill. I didn't relish engagement with whoever still stood using a single-fire MK, at least not up close. Distance was my friend, so I continued veering left and uphill, movement slow, calculated, with regular knee-drops to scan the area. Our team's positioning, solid. I circled left, Bo the same on the right, as Marcus anchored the downhill exit.

A slow fifty yards later, a massive spruce tree, lowest limb-tips brushing the ground, offered shelter from the storm and an excellent observation point. I crawled into a bone-dry environment, four paces wide, as the air changed from crisp snow to dusty duff. All the snowfall collected on the fir's limbs above me, and a belly crawl across the space put me at the sanctuary's opposite edge. I waited, scoped, all senses jacked. Five minutes passed, then ten.

A blasting automatic gunfire rip sounded uphill and to my right. Three quick, sharp cracks from a pistol responded. I couldn't see squat from my position, so I crawled forward, back into the snow, for twenty yards and took a position behind a thick fir tree trunk. Another five-shot burst from the full-auto rifle, and a single pistol shot returned. The pistol's sharp crack ID'd the shooter's position, and I scooted sideways to obtain a target.

The Brit, the MI6 cat at the Stanley breakfast diner. He, too, hugged an enormous tree trunk, on one knee, pistol at the ready. A side-spot on his tree displayed chewed-up bark and wood where bullets had pounded, his assailant still unseen. What wasn't unseen—this spook had brought a pistol to a machine gun fight. He could have hauled it downhill as he slalomed among trees and dodged chasing bullets, but he hadn't yielded, even with the armament odds in the other guy's favor. The Brit was a fighter.

I altered focus farther uphill, and movement caught my eye. Heavy coat, a fur cap, and steady weaving progress downhill toward the MI6 spook. A full-on assault, an almost desultory use of cover, willing to take his chances against a single pistol. I sighted on his face, and internal alarms sounded. His facial structure pronounced one thing—Korean. A North Korean. A Nork. For a myriad of reasons, starting with our location inside the US, I was certain he wasn't South Korean. Oh, man. This entire mess now took on even uglier potential.

Rumination on the larger implications shoved aside, I focused on the immediate. An armed Nork operator with ill intent on US turf headed my way. Simple decision. I sighted the green laser dot on his chest and squeezed the trigger. The sharp blast dropped him like a rock as the Brit spun in my direction, pistol aimed. Pressed against the tree trunk, I altered aim. The MI6 agent and I sighted on each other, a *High Noon* moment. My laser sight held steady underneath his extended two-hand grip, centered on his chest. It didn't take him long to acknowledge the dime-sized dot on his vitals and internalize its finality if he engaged. He lowered his weapon, placed it on an exposed tree root at his feet away from the collecting snow, and strode several paces away. He stood still, palms facing me. I approached within three paces, the green dot still painted on his chest. Because you never knew.

Pocketing his pistol, a Walther, and voice low, I asked, "How many Norks?"

"Four, I believe. Three, it would appear, still on the prowl. You could use my help. We are on the same side, you know."

A statement designed to elicit a clarifying response from me—who I was, what organization I associated with, and any other tidbits he could pocket. Freakin' spooks. They never stopped.

"Who else?" I asked.

"One of yours, I'm afraid, was killed near the cabin. As for other players, it's rather difficult to state with any certainty."

One dead US asset plus three Norks and possibly others still on the hunt.

"Take off your coat and turn around."

Something in my voice or 'tude or both prompted his compliance. I was checking for Ruth's laptop. I'd do the same with the Nork I'd just popped once the dust settled on this weird-ass vignette.

"Alright. You can put it back on."

He did.

123

"Here's the deal," I continued. "I've always gotten along with you MI6 people. Not as bosom buddies. That'll never happen. But I don't want to pop you, and I'm uncomfortable with you on my six."

At my back. Everyone but my team fell in the bogey bucket, this guy included.

"There's the off chance I've heard about you," he said. "Name?"

"Stop it."

"Fine. Then, without a weapon, I believe I'll sit this one out, sport. If it helps, I will stroll downhill toward the highway."

And toward his parked SUV where communications and more weaponry waited.

"Nope. Try an uphill stroll. Away from the dead Nork. I'll watch."

He shrugged, turned, and headed farther uphill, angled away from both the dead man and the cabin. He'd circle back at some point—the cat was a pro—but his future actions fell far down the immediate worry list. Yeah, I'd run into and worked with MI6 assets in the past and halfway liked them. Which was still a far cry from trusting them.

My single shot, its sound signature far different from the Walther pistol, signaled to other bogeys in the area the game had changed, a new player introduced. They'd adjust accordingly, accept the change, and commit to killing the new intruder. At least the Norks would. The North Korean secret services were renowned for a few distinct characteristics—seldom seen, seldom encountered, and an ops mode best described as brutal. With their country's mindset, failure wasn't an option. Do it or die trying. Period.

I checked the Brit's progress—he wasn't busting ass on his climb—and side hilled toward the cabin. The snow eased off, no longer dumping, although the air remained filled with flakes.

"You have practiced catch and release, my goober. Quite a change."

Bo's voice came through the ear mic. He, and Marcus, had listened to my one-sided conversation with the MI6 guy. I dropped to a knee, nestled against a fir tree.

"An MI6 asset," I said, shedding light on the situation.

"Give me a Nork count," Marcus said, joining the conversation. "I didn't hear his response to your question."

Classic Marcus. No questions or comments on the North Korean introduction into this spun-out-of-control gig. Instead, a simple request for bogey numbers and the operational implications.

"Three remain. Other players unknown."

"As we reflect on head count," Bo said, "allow me a minor correction for the north of the thirty-eighth parallel contingent. Two, not three."

Marcus and I both responded, "Roger that." Bo had taken a North Korean out with his knife, silent and sure. The dumb bastard on the receiving end never stood a chance.

"There's a US asset dead at the cabin. Two Norks remain, positions unknown," I said. "And my gut says there're other players, somewhere. Too many parked vehicles on the highway."

"You tight?"

Marcus asked for confirmation I had a handle on the situation.

"Tight. Headed toward the cabin."

"Watch your six," he said. "The Brit won't leave the theater."

"Roger that."

I slumped to a belly crawl and snaked through fresh snow, focused on forward progress in a zigzag manner, working fir tree to fir tree. After ten minutes, the cabin came into view. Log construction, decent size, with an SUV parked near it. And twenty paces from the entrance, a sprawled body with dark-red snow collected around the torso. William Barrett, the DIA agent from the Stanford cactus garden. His automatic weapon lay nearby, half-covered with snow. Shit. I didn't have any great affinity for the guy—I hardly knew him—but SOBs had arrived from overseas and taken out a fellow countryman. Whacked him on my turf, here in the middle of Idaho. Bastards.

Chapter 16

I parked it, stretched out and well-hidden, and waited. The Norks would show soon enough. No cat-and-mouse for them. Succeed or accept death, an ops plan tailor-made for ruthless dictatorships. Decent odds at least one remained in the cabin.

Five minutes passed, a raven called as it passed overhead, and I flexed my right hand in a vain attempt to keep my fingers warm. Then a shotgun's distinct boom shattered the forest silence, followed by the metallic clack of another chambered round. Marcus, downhill at the parked vehicles.

"One Nork left."

His voice came across matter-of-fact, a focus forward at the one remaining bogey. I tapped the ear mic twice as recognition. The shotgun's blast prompted cabin movement. A side door alongside a stacked woodpile cracked open. No target showed, my view hindered by the woodpile. The man opened the door as an assessment process, figuring next moves. I remained still, waiting, and blinked away snowflakes landing on my eyes.

Several minutes passed when a sudden burst of automatic fire sounded from far on the cabin's other side. I recognized the weapon's sound. An Israeli submachine gun. An Uzi. The noise prompted an instant reaction from the cabin Nork, who flew out the side door and headed toward the cabin's back side, a clean shot still unavailable for me. The Uzi had sounded from Bo's hunting ground, and mental claxons rang loud. My position removed me from the action. Screw that noise.

I scrambled upright and hauled it toward the cabin. Take the Nork out, then cover my best friend's back. The snow silenced my footfalls as I dashed past the cabin's front, slowed, and edged along the stacked woodpile, weapon at my shoulder, pressure on the trigger. No time to fart around, I made the cabin's back corner and spotted the Nork standing, weapon at his shoulder, scoping the woods where the Uzi had fired its burst. He stood five paces away, unaware. I whipped the scope's green dot toward his head, settled, and pulled the trigger—all within a split second.

"Status?" Marcus asked, barking into my ear mic. He'd heard the Uzi and my shot, the situation confused, our status unknown.

"Last Nork down," I said, heart pounding. Ahead, deep in thick snow-covered forest, a Mossad agent and my best friend danced a deadly waltz. I prayed Bo had put away the knife and now stalked with the MK. "Sounds like Mossad cut loose at Bo."

"Bo?" Marcus asked.

Three taps on his ear mic signaled status okay, unable to talk. Translation: the Mossad spook had blasted fire at a ghost and now faced a terminal situation as Bo approached him, unseen. Relief flooded, as did urgency.

"Headed your way," I said.

Two taps returned as confirmation. I'd brought Bo into this mess and wouldn't stand aside as the death-dealing vignette ahead played out. Best bet—plow forward and draw the Israeli's attention and, maybe, fire. No worries. If he aimed my way, Bo—knowing I'd entered the fray— would cut him down.

Quick dashes, tree to tree, adrenaline meter pegged. A couple inches of fresh snow muffled my footsteps as pine trunks offered brief scanning opportunities. After fifty rushed paces with intermittent stops I spotted him, or at least his position. He'd parked behind a massive fir tree trunk. Scattered about were 9mm shell casings, the brass bright against the stark white ground. His earlier full-automatic blasts toward Bo's position had left firefight debris, and while I could make out footprints in the snow approaching his ambush spot, no evidence showed his departure. I had his ass.

"That you, Levy?"

High odds the Mossad asset was the same guy we'd run into at the Halls' Palo Alto home. But it didn't matter. Whatever his identity, he was screwed. He just didn't know it yet.

"Sorry about the earlier fire, Lee. I didn't realize it was you."

"It wasn't."

A low chuckle from the tree trunk's other side.

"Right. Now tell me I'm surrounded."

"Not going to tell you jack shit except put down your weapon."

Thick bark scraped as he shifted position, pressed hard against the tree. Separated by twenty-five paces, he figured the Uzi would provide more than enough leverage for an advantageous discussion. No doubt he could use the weapon with great effectiveness. And no doubt he'd use it on me given the chance.

"Allow me to use American vernacular. What we have here is a Mexican standoff."

Bo whispered in my ear mic.

"Green near his head."

Bo's laser sight now placed a small green dot on the tree trunk, unnoticed, near Levy's head.

"No, Levy. What we have here is a dreaded green-dot bark beetle issue."

"I have business to attend to, Lee. Let's work this out."

"The little critter appears on tree trunks around here. It's unmistakable. You might want to have a look at your tree trunk. About eye level."

Within two seconds, Hebrew curses flowed. High odds Bo had allowed him a close perusal of the laser dot as it shifted from tree bark to his head.

"Now, toss the Uzi."

Levy weighed odds, then tossed the weapon onto snow, accompanied with more cursing.

"And your pistol."

It soon followed.

"Now walk backward ten paces."

He did and became exposed. My laser dot joined Bo's. Levy had dressed for combat. Whatever the Halls had cooked up was perceived as game-changing stuff. But I tempered spookville's perception with knowledge they always saw things as game-changers. It kept them in business.

I advanced, retrieved his weapons, and said, "Stand there. A bark beetle will keep you company for a while. On your back."

He glared and remained silent. I worked my way back toward the cabin, the Mossad agent's pistol in a coat pocket, the Uzi slung across my chest, the MK pressed against my shoulder. No telling who the hell still lurked. Exiting the woods at a different spot—my footprints in the snow leading into the woods told a tale—I captured a just-in-time image. The Brit spook had returned, and now leaned over the DIA agent, retrieving the dead man's assault rifle. Jeez Louise. These clowns never gave it a rest.

"You don't want to do that."

His body froze and his head twisted to see a guy with an Uzi draped across his chest aiming an MK at him. With discretion as the better part of valor, he straightened up.

"Given the recent gunfire," he said, cool as a cucumber, "I assumed you might require some assistance."

"Sure. Come toward me. We're taking a little walk."

As we headed back toward the Mossad spook's pissed-off and bark-beetle-awareness stance, I asked the MI6 agent for a legit favor.

"You know people in the US intelligence services."

"I do."

"The dead man is a guy named William Barrett. Do me a solid and contact the appropriate people for a cleanup. I don't want him lying out here for the ravens and coyotes and cougars."

He halted, turned, and addressed me.

"I will, of course, see it done. And this, right now, is an appropriate time for joining forces. We both want the same thing. Keeping critical information from the wrong hands."

They never stopped. Never.

"Just do me a favor and contact the right people. You good with that?"

With an expression conveying both affirmation and resignation, he nodded back. When we approached Levy, I explained the situation.

"Stand six feet apart, both with your backs toward the north." I head nodded toward Bo's hiding spot. "My companion will rotate his laser sight from one man's back to the next at irregular intervals. He has an itchy trigger finger and would love to put a bullet in either of you. Turning your body and checking if the laser is still sighted on you brings an instant bullet. Are we clear?"

"How long?" Levy asked, tight-jawed, face red, still pissed.

"An hour. You can risk cutting it short, of course. The coyotes would appreciate it. They like carrion."

I headed back for the cabin, approached with caution, halted at the forest's edge, and waited several minutes. Just to be sure. While waiting, and with a near-whisper, I asked Bo how the two under his guard performed their stand-still duties.

"They are not idle with their craft, engaged in a fascinating conversation. Each endeavors to out-spook the other. Through the looking glass, my Georgia peach."

"In more ways than one, bud. In more ways than one."

Chapter 17

Fifteen minutes ticked off, the killing floor still, quiet. Post-battle scenes always struck me as eerie. Death dominant, bodies splayed, life snuffed out as peaceful surroundings framed the place and time. Nature, potent and standoffish, absorbed the scene. And shrugged.

Marcus had listened to all the conversations, albeit one-sided between me and the spooks, but he remained silent, situational awareness satisfied. A raven flew overhead, landed on a tall pine tree, and croaked its call. Other clandestine players—at a minimum, the Russians—would join soon enough, and find the party over. Time for artifact collection and haul it north.

I fished in the backpack of the Nork I'd killed at the cabin and found a laptop. No doubt Ruth's. A quick perusal of the cabin proved reminiscent of the Halls' Palo Alto home—ransacked, picked over.

"I've got the laptop," I said, providing Marcus and Bo my status. "Let's exit, stage right."

"She wants more items from the cabin," Marcus said.

I didn't fault Ruth. She'd internalized the situation, no doubt triggered when Marcus blew away a Nork approaching our vehicles. The act highlighted a hard reality—no temporary evac for Ruth and Bart. The cabin would no longer do as a Hall hideaway, destined to be a government focus for at least a year, if not longer. What a mess. Find Ruth had morphed into help Ruth escape, hide her, and find Bart. Then what? No freakin' clue as I stood among the scattered Hall possessions, the surrounding terrain polluted with four dead Norks and a DIA agent.

Then toss in a Brit and Israeli spook frozen nearby, exchanging lies. This job had spun out of control, and gratitude filled me, knowing my friends would help navigate our next-step decision processes. Because the immediate shouted, "Now what?"

"Roger that," I said, replying to Marcus. "It's clear here, so you might as well drive up."

He, and Ruth, did. Marcus's large SUV could carry quite a load, her Subaru station wagon less so. Before they pulled up, I took two sheets from a clean laundry pile spread on the floor near the washing machine and dryer. I covered the DIA agent at the cabin's front and the Nork at the rear. The act didn't hide their condition, but at least Ruth wouldn't have a bird's-eye view of a dead body.

Marcus exited his vehicle with the Colt rifle. Still within a battle area, he remained prepared. Ruth hesitated inside her Subaru, stared wide-eyed at the sheet-covered body, then slid out and glanced my way.

"I'm sorry, Ruth. It's a mess. Everything is a mess."

She nodded and hesitated at the cabin's open door, surveyed the ransacking's aftermath, and with a heavy sigh, entered.

"Just point out what you want. I'll tote it."

She didn't respond, stood stock-still, and captured in her mind's eye a last look at their personal Shangri-La. Their cozy reprieve from the world, their hidden hideaway. Poignant and painful moments as she remained frozen.

"We should get going."

I kept my tone as gentle as possible, with a hint of urgency. The Russians and who-knows-who-else hadn't yet appeared, late on the stage. But sooner or later they'd show.

"All the pictures," she whispered. "And quilts."

I gathered items and carried them first into her vehicle, then Marcus's. He remained still, alert, and smoked a cigar. We locked eyes once and shared a mutual acknowledgment that we might have bitten off more than we could chew.

Dresser drawer contents, some items scattered on the floor, collected and dumped into her vehicle. Closet clothes, a CD player, speakers, CDs. Books upon books. An old rocking chair shoved into Marcus's SUV. A fireplace poker, she explained, Bart had bought her in Stanley. We dang near cleaned the place out and filled both vehicles to the gunwales. As I hustled back and forth, Bo sidled up.

"They should remain on unsure ground for another twenty minutes," he said. "The Brit appears as an accepting soul. The Israeli remains burdened with anger issues."

He edged beside Ruth.

"An adventure, Ruth. One with bumps and twists and pain, but the path holds promise."

"I want Bart."

"A key item on our amorphous agenda. First, let's escape the storm."

She sighed again and placed a light hand on Bo's chest.

"Why are you three doing this?"

A repeat question, but one with more significance given the clear death and destruction. Events had slipped off the rails, and more rational people would have waved a white flag and exited the entire endeavor. I still lacked a solid answer, other than Delta didn't wave white flags.

"We are simpatico wayfarers," Bo said with a gentle smile. "Delivered through cosmic currents that have swept us together."

For a brilliant, rational scientist, it surprised me when she returned an accepting tight-lipped smile. Explanation enough, I supposed.

"We're burning daylight," Marcus said from his guard-duty position.

We were and completed the loading, then rolled downhill as Bo drove Ruth, stopping at my vehicle where we reiterated travel plans.

"Marcus and I will flatten tires on all the parked vehicles," I said as we gathered at the Subaru. "Bo, you and Ruth take off. One of us will catch up and pass you. Remember, the more varied our separation and movement, the better. Big birds hover overhead. We try and make Salmon. If they shut down the road, we stop in Challis."

The Subaru took off, and Marcus followed them with plans to stop at each parked vehicle and drive a knife blade into at least two tire sidewalls per vehicle. I turned right, toward Stanley, to perform the same and then play tail-end Charlie on the way north. The two spooks left behind, finding their vehicles incapacitated, could walk the several miles back toward Stanley. The tight highway had collected several inches of snow, and flakes continued falling. As I completed knifing spookmobiles, a snowplow ground past, its blade shoveling surface snow off the highway. Perfect. I fell in behind it until Clayton, where the snowplow performed a one-eighty and headed back toward Stanley. Communicating via satellite phones, we parked it in Challis, sixty miles from the cabin. The storm's intensity increased, and the highway would shut down until it passed.

Challis, with fewer than a thousand hardy souls and the county seat for Custer County, displayed a wintry main drag with five bars and two motels. We checked into the one farthest from the highway, paid cash for two upstairs adjacent rooms, and piled in. Bo would stay with Ruth,

Marcus and I together, although the rooms had an adjoining. We gathered in the room where Marcus and I would bunk as the open curtain displayed a blizzard, with blowing snow collecting on our covered second-floor walkway. We seated Ruth against the curtain, out of sight. The shotgun and two MKs rested on the small table and elicited another wide-eyed look from Ruth. Our Alamo felt safe, secure. Given the outside conditions with its limited visibility, bogeys would have a hard time taking us on. Marcus produced the brandy bottle and poured healthy snorts into four motel glasses. Even Ruth took a sip.

"Ma'am, we have a lot to discuss," Marcus said. "Are you up for a discussion?"

She nodded back.

"First, tell us what you and your husband worked on that created so much interest."

She shoved her cat-eye frames up her nose and said, "I have a doctorate in biomedical science."

"Yes, ma'am."

"Bart has a doctorate in engineering physics."

"So we understand."

"We both have a keen interest in the human brain."

She leaned sideways for a look out the window, interested in the snowstorm.

"Ruth, please don't peek out," I said. "Bad people still seek you. Let's not provide them any opportunities."

She sat back and said, "I wonder if a nice cup of tea is possible? Bo has been kind enough to explain the unfortunate events that have just transpired. I must tell you, it is all most disturbing. The events also make me fear, more than ever, for Bart."

"I'll tell you what," I said, "we'll see if we can rustle up some tea after we go over what you two worked on. Then we'll address Bart's situation. But first, we'd all appreciate it if you provided information on your research as a CliffsNotes version. We're not scientists."

She blinked, twice, and took another tiny sip of brandy.

"The human brain is staggeringly complex."

"Okay."

"It contains a hundred billion neurons. A hundred billion. Standard dogma assigned a single type of neurotransmitter for any given neuron."

"What's a neuron? In terms us three will understand."

"They use electrical impulses and chemical signals for transmitting information between different areas of the brain, and between the brain and the nervous system."

"So they're information messengers."

She chewed on my statement for a moment.

"Yes. Information messengers." She gave a slow nod at the tabletop. "I have discovered many neuron classes contain multiple neurotransmitters."

"A big deal?"

She smiled, pushed her glasses up, and said, "I am afraid it is too big a deal."

Genius scientist humor. I didn't have a freakin' clue regarding her punch line but smiled and nodded as if I did.

"You see, the brain has eight hundred trillion constantly changing connections. Eight hundred trillion."

138

"Big number."

"A daunting number. Individual neurons, some with multiple neurotransmitters, use very precise rhythms and work with other neuron groups, oscillating together with very specific frequencies."

"So pretty doggone complex."

"Yes. Complex. But Bart developed some fascinating frequency mapping constructs. Absolutely fascinating."

Marcus finished his brandy and asked, "Ma'am, what was the end game? The ultimate purpose?"

"We had a dream of repairing specific pathways in individuals." She glanced at us. "Those whose neurotransmissions do not function properly."

"Rewiring and repairing those connections?" I asked.

A poignant endeavor—my younger sister CC was mentally challenged.

"Yes. But I am afraid the issues proved too complex from a knowledge-base and computational and engineering perspective. Bart and I moved on to other research when the government people showed up."

The three of us understood where this headed—reverse engineering, weapons development, a new manner of warfare.

"Department of Defense?" I asked.

"Yes. Them. They sent two scientists who asked us to continue with our research but reverse our methodology. They claimed that the intentional altering of random neurotransmissions held great interest for them. Then they offered a large financial grant for continuing our work, redirected toward outcomes the opposite of which we had intended."

I glanced at Marcus and Bo. We all got it.

"Bart and I started the redirected research. Until."

She shook her head, absorbed in thought, and stared unblinking at the cheap tabletop.

"Until what, Ruth?" I asked, voice low, gentle.

She looked up.

"Until they asked Bart about actual delivery, from a physics and biomedical perspective, of neurotransmitter alterations across a large area. A large geographic area, affecting thousands."

Delivered via drone or chopper or plane over a battlefield. Directed brain-scrambling technologies. In totalitarian regimes, they could also use it on their own people for crowd control. Or genocide. Whatever the application, the world didn't need such a weapon.

"Ma'am, if it worked, would the people affected ever recover?"

"We do not know. Perhaps it would create a temporary manifestation, although the residual time frame for the affected people could vary wildly. An hour? A month? We do not know. There is the possibility the damage would be permanent."

"When they asked about the efficacy over a large area, what happened next?" I asked, redirecting her back toward the "until" statement.

"Bart and I told them no. And we asked they take their grant back."

"Their reaction?"

"They were not pleased. Later, they talked about moving us away. Moving us to someplace near Washington, DC."

Which didn't explain leakage. Marcus glommed on to the same issue.

140

"Ma'am, what happened between the time you and your husband refused further research and when they talked with you two about moving someplace else?"

"Nothing happened. Our lives continued as usual."

"So you stayed in Palo Alto?" I asked. "And at Stanford?"

"Yes, we did. Except for one trip."

"Where?"

"An international biomedical conference in DC. Bart and I attend every year. We enjoy long walks among the monuments. We always visit the Lincoln Memorial at night. The caterers at the conference provide wonderful sweets."

Fertile turf for scientific skullduggery. I could envision the event—brilliant scientists from across the globe as spooks worked the crowd.

"Did you or Bart engage in conversations about the Defense Department request with any friends or colleagues?" Marcus asked.

"Over the years, so many of our colleagues have become friends."

"I'm sure, ma'am. Did either of you talk with them about the Defense request?"

"I am quite certain we did. Why would we not?"

Because, Ruth, you weren't at a scientific conference. You and Bart were smack dab in the middle of spookville.

THE SAWTOOTH JOB

Chapter 18

Bo, a tea aficionado, made a selection for Ruth, and—using the small drip coffeemaker in the room—prepared her a cup of Earl Grey. Marcus and I tossed on our heavy coats, toted weapons, and stepped outside onto the second-floor walkway. His Zippo clacked, cigar lit, we pressed against the room's exterior wall, and avoided the whirling snow. Down the main drag and barely discernible, a pickup's headlights shined as it pulled in and parked at one of the multiple bars.

"You realize North Korea might have been your client on this job, right?" he asked. "Which highlights one of many holes in your business model, Mr. Case Lee Inc."

"I've considered it. Smart money would bet on MI6 or Mossad as the client. Or a US entity."

"Kim Jong-un attended school in Switzerland."

North Korea's Supreme Leader—a brutal dictator who followed in his father's and grandfather's footsteps—had attended a private school in Switzerland as a young man. Still, Norks wouldn't venture outside their own tight circle to nab Ruth Hall. Too much risk.

"Yeah, but they're not called the Hermit Kingdom for nothing. They'd keep their actions tight and among themselves. Which leaves another spy organization as the client," I said. "Once Ruth fired up her GPS, they located her and didn't require my services anymore. My money's still on the Brits or Israelis or us. Maybe not the DIA, but another US intel service. Plenty to pick from."

Bo slid outside with his cup of tea. I angled a look through the window. Ruth read a book, her steaming mug on the table.

"Norks," Bo said. "In Australia, they use the term for a woman's breasts."

He'd lived in Australia a short while, zipping around in the outback on a motorcycle with sidecar.

"Thank you, Bo," Marcus said. "You've added great clarity to our situation."

My gut, already knotted, pushed hard reality onto the table.

"The North Koreans lack sophistication and resources, so they pooled those limited resources and glommed on to Ruth's GPS signal like the others. But unlike the others, who did it as a get-in-the-game move, smart money points toward the Norks having a damn compelling reason."

"I agree," Marcus said. "They've got Bart ratholed somewhere."

"Yep."

"Shitty situation."

I sighed. "Yeah. Shitty situation."

We remained silent as snow blew halfway across the second-floor landing. An occasional set of headlights pulled in and parked along main street. Late afternoon, and Challis stalwarts braved the snowstorm for beer and cocktail hour. If nothing else, they could gather and talk about the weather.

"Darkest before the dawn," Bo said, "so take cheer, gentlemen. Ride the maelstrom, and know we have a face card itching to be played."

"I don't see it, Bo," I said, staring into the big lost, now covered with a white blanket.

"And therein lies your problem. Feel, sense, my favorite goober. See is not the lone option."

"What about the face card?" Marcus asked. "In terms normal people can understand?"

"I wouldn't concur that you two fall into such a limited categorization, cow whisperer."

"Dammit, Bo."

"Let's assume you two sleuths are correct. The north of the thirty-eighth parallel gang has our good Doctor Bart. By now, they will have expected a report from their field team. A team resting in perpetuity among forest denizens."

I smiled as I realized where Bo was headed.

"They'll start the Ruth calls again," I said.

"Posthaste, I would imagine."

"You both overlook a showstopper issue," Marcus said. "If the Norks have him, he's in North Korea. Even our intrepid shadowland contractor can't pull off a rescue there."

Marcus had a point. North Korea's incessant national obsession with secrecy defined locked down and sealed shut. South Korea might have assets there, but even they couldn't rescue a hidden and high-value asset like Bart Hall. And any westerner wouldn't have a snowball's chance in hell. But my gut said he wasn't there, a feeling fed through too many interactions with the espionage mindset.

"I don't think so, Marcus. The Norks are halfway batshit crazy, for sure. But not crazy enough to risk it."

"I don't follow."

"Everyone and their brother knows about the North Koreans' involvement now. Or if not now, by tonight. The Brit will heads-up MI6, and he'll contact US assets about the killed DIA agent. US assets will recover the four Nork bodies. Mossad damn sure knows about them. The Russians won't be far behind."

"You make it sound like clandestine services around the world leak like a sieve."

"Dribs and drabs. And even those have ulterior motives. But not regarding the North Koreans. Nossir. If the Norks got battlefield brain-scrambling capability, as Ruth described, it would create a global hair-on-fire moment. It'll be all-hands-on-deck."

"What about the Chicoms?" Marcus asked.

Helluva question. The Chinese remained North Korea's closest ally. Followed by Russia and Cuba. The Russkies would want this brain-scrambling technology for themselves, and the Cubans weren't a player. China's role in this hair ball—unknown. The North Koreans may have gone rogue and captured Bart Hall on their own. Or worked under China's guidance. Hard to say. Easy to say—this whole deal sucked, and the deal's fulcrum point rested on three beat-up ex-Delta operators who stood on a motel porch in Challis, Idaho, in the middle of a blizzard. Great. Just freakin' great.

"Hard knowing with the Chinese. They like pulling strings from the shadows, so this could fit their standard operating procedure. Or, the Norks took this on themselves."

"Do you just dial up shitstorms, or is there planning involved?"

"Yeah, this thing has spun out of control. Plus the cherry on top— Townsend will be on my ass before long."

"Pass on greetings and salutations," Bo said. "And gritty reminiscences. Old times not forgotten."

"I don't think her call starts with hail-fellow-well-met."

The Zippo clacked, cigar relit. Darkness peeked through the blinding whiteness. Ruth continued reading and Bo, after firing his weed pipe, hummed an Andean chant—he'd put his alpaca attire back on.

"Back to why Bart's not in North Korea," Marcus said. "I still don't get it."

"A global three-alarm focus on North Korea starts now. Satellites, drones, South Korean spies, beaucoup pressure on China, you name it. The Company, MI6, Russia's SVR, Mossad—everyone who's anyone in spookville. The North Koreans, or the Chinese, would have planned for this if word got out. And word is damn sure out."

"So?"

"So they picked a spot early in the game where clandestine services wouldn't look. Or the Chicoms picked a spot for them. Either way, they wouldn't risk the entire world coming down on them if someone discovered Doctor Bart on their turf. The Chinese, being their closest ally, wouldn't want spookville's collective eye on their bosom buddies because everyone would follow the connection upstream, all the way to Beijing."

"There's hope for you," Bo said. "Truly. Even as a plodder you show aptitude for dwelling in an alternative reality."

"Solid point," Marcus said. "We've allowed him entry into the twilight zone. Nothing is as it seems, fog and lies, logic so convoluted we should patent and market a board game."

"You both realize I don't ask for this stuff, right?"

"So you tell yourself," Bo said. "Yet you receive these cosmic thunderbolts with open arms, undaunted. Admirable, my goober. Admirable."

"Let's get with Ruth and go over phone call strategy," I said. "I'm thinking she'll get a call tonight."

With coffee and more tea, we huddled again around the small table, Marcus and I with laptops open.

"First, Ruth, will you let me disable your phone's GPS?" I asked. "Just to be sure?"

She nodded, handed it over, and I disabled the app. Then she closed her book—Anthony Doerr's *All the Light We Cannot See*—and sipped tea and waited. She'd shifted focus toward me because of my statements about finding Bart. I may have represented her lifeboat, which bothered me. A lot. Bart Hall was so far beyond my reach it wasn't funny, while global powers jockeyed for the golden fleece. On the flip side, I had Ruth.

"How often does he call you?" I asked.

"Almost every day. When he does not, I become worried."

"That's on purpose. Tell us about the conversations, please."

She did. He always asked how she was doing and where she was. Nothing subtle there, a Nork hallmark.

"I reply I am in a safe place. Then there is a pause, and he asks, again, where?"

His captors stood around him and prompted the repeated question. No doubt.

"Do you ever ask him where he is?"

"I do ask him."

She blinked behind those retro glasses. It would take gentle hands for a Ruth Hall intel extraction.

"What does he say?"

"Bart says he is doing fine. They do not let him divulge his location."

"It sounds like a somewhat disjointed chat."

"It helps me. There are nonsensical things he says, but knowing he is well lifts my spirits."

I glanced at Marcus and Bo. Marcus nodded; Bo smiled. Bart Hall sent signals using nonsensical words or expressions. He'd already shown the ability when he'd mentioned Mr. Stanley.

Captives did what they could to convey intel—metaphors and allegories and absurdities. They had time aplenty on their hands for conjuring up hidden messages. Military prisoners, if on visual comms, had even communicated with Morse code, using eye blinks. Delta Force operators specialized in hostage rescue, and the three of us hadn't forgotten our training and real-life missions.

"Ma'am, let's focus on those nonsensical words and statements," Marcus said.

"At least they do not strike him when he says those things."

"What has he said when they struck him?" I asked.

"I enquired about his diet. He responded the seafood was excellent. Then they struck him. I cannot describe my worry when he yelled in pain. After that, I no longer asked about his nutritional intake."

"Smart move, Ruth." I patted her hand. "Does he repeat any nonsensical words or phrases?"

"Yes, he does."

"What might those be?"

She sipped tea and stared at her book before answering.

"Bart asks if I have found a solution for the EQ equation. There is no EQ equation."

Marcus's boot tapped my leg under the table. I returned a brief, tight nod.

"What do you reply when he asks?"

"I reply no, I have not."

"Good, good. What else does he say that might come across as strange or different?"

"He says he feels like a guinea pig. Bart says this often. I cannot imagine what physical or mental methodologies they subject him to."

"Ah," Bo said.

He clasped his hands and cast a peaceful smile toward Ruth. Marcus began an internet search.

"Anything else?" I asked.

She mulled over the question, and said, "Time and tide wait for no man. He has expressed this twice, when he asked about my location."

"Bo?" I asked.

"Chaucer," he said.

Sometimes you roll the dice and come up with snake eyes. Sometimes seven or eleven. We'd hit the jackpot. Within one brief conversation and one fell swoop, we knew Dr. Bart Hall's location.

Not an exact location, but which country the Norks held him. And narrowed his location to that country's coast. Alrighty, then.

Chapter 19

The Spanish word for equator is *ecuador*. In US military intelligence parlance and within CIA field ops and in slices of the scientific community, EQ is shorthand for the equator. Bart Hall, thank God, knew about the abbreviation.

Toss *guinea pig* into the mix as confirmation. During Delta days, a Maoist revolutionary group in Ecuador had gone on a rampage, entering villages in the Andean foothills and slaughtering everyone. The Ecuadorian government, unable to cope with the situation, asked for help. We arrived—along with Marilyn Townsend who was then our Company field liaison—and went to work. The Maoist group wanted a revolution. We handed them their asses instead. Within any operational realm, local customs and mores became part and parcel of our experiences. Food included. A popular dish in Ecuador—maybe the national dish—is cuy. Guinea pig.

Bart's seafood comment that had bought him a head blow—large old telephone books are popular around the world for such treatment as they don't inflict permanent damage but hurt like hell—spelled out coastal town or village. His reference to time and tides reiterated it. Bart had moxie, not knowing what clue he could spill without a head blow.

The Norks had him in Ecuador, somewhere along the coast. Why Ecuador? A singular reason shouted from the rooftops.

"What's the Chicom status down there?" I asked Marcus.

He'd been on the same wavelength. Closing his laptop, he said, "I need a cigar."

The three of us trooped back onto the motel walkway, telling Ruth we had some potential good news, but it required further analysis. She smiled and her eyes lit up—her first expression with hope and expectation. A good thing, with an asterisk. Man, I didn't want her hopes too high with odds still stacked on the side of abject failure.

Full-on darkness had arrived, a surreal backdrop for thick, swirling snow. Marcus fired a cigar, Bo a small bowl of weed. Down the main drag, the windowed neon signs of Challis's drinking establishments shined, faded, and shined again as snow flurries dominated the scene.

"The universe has looped us back on an old trail, my brothers."

"True enough. What's China's play in Ecuador?" I asked Marcus.

"They almost own the place now. People hold Ecuador up as an example of China's influence in South America. They have a near monopoly on Ecuador's crude oil exports, buying over ninety percent. Some politicians down there say it threatens their national sovereignty."

A perfect play. Use North Koreans as kidnapper proxies and a South American country under heavy Chinese influence as an operational base. Gain a new weapon system, a brain scrambling technology, while they kept their hands clean. Classic Chicom ops.

A tap on the room's picture window brought us all back inside. Ruth held up her phone, eyes wide and questioning as her other hand pointed toward the phone. We hustled back inside.

"Answer it, and don't change anything you've been saying," I said. "Same answers to the same questions, the same conversational tone and expressions. Please, Ruth. It's very important."

"Should I put the call on speaker?"

"No. Change nothing. Okay?"

She nodded and received the call. I stood alongside her, my ear close to the phone. Bart's voice reflected stress and maybe a touch of depression. His sentence structure included drawn out, repeated words. "I'm fine" came out as "I'm fine. Fine." The conversation followed the previous scripts as Ruth had described, with one exception.

"I must know. Where are you, Ruthie? This has become a very pressing issue. Very pressing."

"I am safe and comfortable, love."

Bart tried again and received the same answer. Later, he mentioned he felt like a guinea pig. And he asked her about the EQ equation, with Ruth's standard response. Then he was clearly pressured to end the call, with "I must go, dearest," repeated twice. They exchanged loving signoffs.

"Well done," I said, patting her back.

Tears welled; one ran down her cheek, wiped away with the back of her hand.

"Do you have any idea where he is?" she asked. "He sounds very depressed. And he has never pushed so hard for my location."

"We have an idea about his location, but I won't give you more than that. For a reason. You were excellent on the call. I don't want you changing a thing when he calls you. Knowing our thoughts on his location might alter your speech pattern. Which could be bad, Ruth. Very bad."

She blinked, and several more tears cascaded.

"But I want you to change one item next time you talk with him. Just one thing. Okay?"

She nodded back, sniffled, and pushed her glasses back up. Man, excitement aside, my heart ached for her. And Bart.

"When he asks about the EQ equation, tell him you've made progress."

"Why?"

"It will give him hope. He could use some right about now. But don't expand on EQ. If he asks for details, tell him you don't want to talk about it until you've made further breakthroughs. Okay?"

"It will give him hope?"

"Yes."

Her back straightened, glasses removed, face wiped with her sleeve. I hadn't lit a fire, but her fingers had found a crack large enough for a grip in a terrible wall. Something to hang on to. Hope.

"Bo, would you mind staying with Ruth while Case and I rustle up some chow?"

"No worries."

"Would a burger work for you?" I asked Ruth. "It may be all we can find."

"A hamburger would be good. I also have the chocolate Bo brought me. I will share those."

We bundled up and headed down the street. I was reasonably confident we'd lost any big bird tracking. At the second bar, a small kitchen worked food orders. We received drinks while waiting for the burgers and fries, and Marcus, as always, dived straight into key mission points.

"I'll take Doctor Hall," he said. "Bo can drive her."

"To Fishtail?"

"I'm the one not on anyone's radar. Multiple outfits know about you and Bo. They haven't seen or heard from me. What will you tell Townsend when she calls?"

"First, where's the nearest airport? One not in Montana."

The Townsend call would start with a finger snap, a summons, and the nearest airport's location. She'd demand a sit down over this mess… a meeting I required as well.

"Boise. Go through Arco. They will shut down the way you drove to Stanley due to snow. Now answer my question."

"I'll proclaim Ruth's location a mystery. An accurate statement as long as you don't tell me whether there's a place in Fishtail you're thinking about for her or if your ranch house is the hideout."

"You mean you'll lie."

"I'll obfuscate the truth, although it won't matter. Townsend won't buy my BS, which brings leverage. I know Ruth's location. And Bart's. Sorta. Bottom line, I'll do what I can and put the two near-retirement scientists back together. You got hot springs in Montana?"

"Are you still buying in bulk?"

"The dumbass pills?"

"Roger that."

"Look, Marcus, everything has just worked out this way, not through design."

"Why are you headed down this one-man-show path?"

Helluva question.

"I told Ruth I'd find her husband."

The best I could come up with without performing a deep psychological dive in a Challis, Idaho, bar with a blood brother. Yeah, the

Ecuadorian scent triggered my pursuit instinct, the trail hot. But tactical considerations aside, something far deeper drove my actions. Do the right thing, I supposed. Perhaps prove I still had it. Pull out the oiled rag and shine the Case Lee Gets It Done plaque. But all else aside, the mule pulling the wagon was commitment. I'd committed. Backing down would reveal a large and bitter and regretful pill to swallow. A regret I'd live with forever.

"We have found him," Marcus said. "Or near enough."

"Not the same."

He scanned the crowd, shook his head, and delivered a low, throaty exhale.

"Shithouse mouse, Case."

"Look," I said, "I'll tell Townsend I have a decent idea about Bart's location. And I could use the Company's help."

"Which, with a normal person, would lead down a common-sense trail and recognizing your limitations. It wouldn't hurt you, for once, to let them handle things. Yes, they will pull both the Halls in and hide them. But Townsend could give you her word their disposal stayed off the menu."

"You trust her that far?"

"We did in the field."

"She doesn't occupy that space anymore. Not by a long shot. Are you willing to give Ruth up?"

He sighed, took a sip, and said, "No. No, I'm not. But I sure wouldn't hold it against you if you did."

Rock, meet hard place. He'd tossed Ruth's federal handover onto the table as a feeler, an outlier concept. My reaction—and we both acknowledged this was my show—pulled it back off the table. And I appreciated he'd done it for my sake, an option for a blood brother. And an act of love. Marcus saw where I was headed with this whole mess.

"Don't forget, I'll have leverage," I said.

We locked eyes.

"So, you think you'll leverage her and her husband's locations for Company help. The world's largest clandestine outfit at your beck and call."

"Reciprocity, baby. A finger snap back at 'em. Listen, I really appreciate you taking Ruth. A big freakin' deal."

"She requires safe haven while you, a man with more wild hairs than the law allows, figures out next steps." He broke eye contact and muttered, "Reciprocity. Shithouse mouse."

A decent crowd surrounded our position at the bar's end corner, backs against the wall. We both packed semiautomatic pistols, which no doubt put us in good stead with multiple patrons. Pool table balls clacked, the jukebox played a George Strait tune, smoke and fried food smells and friendly chatter filled the air. Carhartt ranch coats, many with mends, hung on hooks. Marcus asked the lady behind the bar if he could light a cigar.

"Don't care if you fire up a cow turd. Just don't leave without paying your tab."

We both ordered another drink.

"You'll ask her for a contract through the Swiss."

Statement, not question.

"Yep. They can afford the expenses."

"And ask her for help in Quito."

"Yep."

Quito, Ecuador's capitol and home for US, Chinese, and Russian spooks. Same for any South American capital.

"Then use the Company's assets, both human and technical, to pinpoint Bart Hall."

"Great minds think alike."

"At which point you'll dump the Company asset and smuggle Hall back into the States."

"Good knowing you haven't lost your touch for operational plans."

He took a long draw on the scotch and puffed the cigar. Our food arrived in brown paper bags, the grease already staining the bag's bottom. I settled the tab.

"Before we leave, let me clarify a few things," Marcus said. "Otherwise, I'll look back on this and consider you slipped a hallucinogen into my drink."

"Fire away, Montana Slim."

"You intend whacking a collection of Nork abductors and fleeing with the good doctor. On your tail, a pissed off Company who, at this point, would whack you in a heartbeat. Plus, Chicoms who would also whack you in a heartbeat, likely more Norks, and additional take-your-pick spooks from around the world. How might you intend to pull this off?"

"I'll work on it. I admit your precious known unknowns are sprinkled throughout the recipe."

"Then you'll sneak the good doctor back into the States, reunite him with his wife, and the two live out their lives among rainbows and unicorns and hot springs while a heavenly chorus serenades them."

"Something like that."

"I swear, Case," he said with a hard stare at the bar top. "I swear."

THE SAWTOOTH JOB

Chapter 20

Townsend called as we finished our burgers. I donned a heavy coat, stepped outside and, as always, spoke first.

"Director."

"Mr. Lee. It has been less than joyful tracking your exploits through secondhand accounts. I should also add I occupy the dubious position of the least surprised person on the planet. Where shall I send the plane?"

"Boise. That's in Idaho."

"As I am well aware, thank you. Noon tomorrow."

She hung up.

Later, we collected, sans Ruth, on the walkway.

"I appreciate it, Bo," I said. "Getting her to safety. Then you gotta cut out."

"We'll stop and rent you a vehicle in Bozeman," Marcus said. "Use your illegal as hell false ID. Doctor Hall can drive and follow me from there. Then fly out of Spokane. It keeps Montana off their map. Cut across northern Idaho. Interstate highway the whole way, six hours travel."

"Can do easy," Bo said, "although our intrepid goober's path forward includes an uncomfortable decoupling."

"You can't join me, bud. JJ expects you back. I'll have Company assistance in Ecuador. At least I think I will. There's always the possibility Townsend blows a gasket and refuses to help."

"As uncomfortable, and irritating, this situation is for her, you're her best bet," Marcus said. "You might place a bundle of descriptive labels on her, but *stupid* wouldn't stick."

"My heart pushes me toward accompanying you far south. Knowing you engage without enlightened accompaniment, footloose and fancy-free, disturbs me."

"I have a long list of disturbing aspects about this mission," Marcus said.

"Not a mission, bwana Johnson. No. A grand quest, motives pure, tightrope encounters with a litany of brigands assured. Jealousy pangs pierce me."

"Better pangs than bullets, my brother. I can't thank you both enough. This has been one convoluted trail, and I wouldn't be standing here, right now, without huge help from you both."

Truer words were never spoken. I didn't deserve such friends, such blood brothers. They'd entered this fray without question, and in return I'd exposed them both. Bo remained unknown to the players, except for Townsend. She'd connected dots and understood he'd been with me from the get-go, which added my best friend to her immediate shitlist. And true enough, Marcus had avoided engaging with spookville, aside from the North Korean he'd blown away at the cabin, but there were no guarantees he'd remain undercover. Neither blinked an eye at their current status. No problem, water off a duck's back, glad we could help. Man, I was blessed.

Upside motivations for moving forward rotated around a stone-cold fact. I brought special skills to the table: hostage rescuing skills. The Company didn't. Which was why they used Delta for those efforts, adding another twist I'd deal with. If the Company assets in Ecuador pinpointed Bart's location, they'd call in Delta Force and dump my butt. In a heartbeat. Then place Bart in an isolated location near DC and leverage his collection to gain Ruth as well.

Keeping things simple was my commitment to Ruth. I'd try. She'd hung her hat on my commitment. Which implied, in my book, no half-assed attempts, no white flags waved when things got hot. Find Bart, haul him away from Ecuador, smuggle him back into the States, rejoin him and Ruth. Maybe not a piece of cake, but not beyond my abilities. No brag, just fact.

Dawn broke bright and clear without a cloud in the sky. Snow everywhere, cold as hell, but given overnight snowplow work, passable roads. We collected at the vehicles.

"Stay in touch," Marcus said, extending his hand. "Remember there's no shame in making a focused effort and coming up short."

"Will do, bud. I'm not intending to commit suicide by hostage rescue."

Bo and I hugged, his forehead bumping mine.

"Don't fight the flow, my goober. Loose hand on the tiller, acceptance and righteousness the constant commands."

"Tell JJ hi, and safe travels. And thank you. As always."

Ruth approached me with a strange shyness, explained when she endeavored a bundled-up hug, cautious and unsure. I pulled her toward me and squeezed, hard.

"I'll give it my best shot, Ruth. Just please understand there are no guarantees."

"I wish you had eaten some chocolates."

"Maybe next time."

"You have arrived from nowhere and provided a measure of relief. I understand there are no guarantees." She spoke into my heavy coat's front material. "But now I have something to believe in. Someone to believe in. And it is enough. For now, it is enough."

They pulled away from Challis, headed north. I headed south. Four hours later I strode into Boise's private air terminal, through the tarmac doors, and onto an unmarked black jet. After a five-hour flight we taxied into a DC hangar where other unmarked aircraft sat parked. Two Townsend fetchers stood alongside an all-black SUV, waiting in their black suits, white shirts, black ties. We drove into a Langley neighborhood without exchanging a word. Fine by me.

Chapter 21

Two additional large black SUVs sat parked outside a small bistro in a quiet neighborhood. My escorts joined them. Early evening, a glance through the establishment's window showed a handful of after-work folks with coffee, beer, wine, and cocktails sprinkled among them. Around the bar top's corner, removed from window sight, sat the queen bee.

A rocky road, Marilyn Townsend and me. During Delta field ops years earlier, we'd formed a tight bond—not through an instant liking or personal connectivity but through thoughtful planning and dangerous tactical execution and jobs well done. Our small Delta squad and Townsend had formed a team mentality. When created under pressure-cooker conditions, such a bond held permanence, if not bonhomie.

My current vocation guaranteed we'd cross paths multiple times. The world's top spook held a royal flush every time and used me either overtly or from behind the curtain. The latter, the string-pulling from deep shadows, resembled playing me like a freakin' puppet master. On other occasions, I'd asked for her help, a request outright denied several times. At other times, she'd lent a hand when it suited her grand three-dimensional chess game. And at least once, she'd damn near killed me. So yeah, a rocky road.

This time, my approach bordered on the absurd, an acknowledgment best internalized up front. Use the Company for my ends, then ditch them and haul ass with the prize. Man, she'd be pissed beyond measure if I pulled it off. Too bad, so sad. Small recompense for placing my scarred butt in harm's way on multiple occasions for her and the Company's benefit. And yeah, she held powerful cards with direct command and control of the world's largest and most potent spy outfit. But I held a big-ass hole card. One she needed. Bart's location.

I stopped at the bar and asked for a black coffee. On normal sit downs with her, either pre- or post-ops, I'd order a Grey Goose on the rocks. But I wanted all my wits about me on this one. Townsend tended toward getting straight to the matter at hand and was much better than me at intel excavation and uncovering lies. Such a reality didn't thrill me, but there it was.

As I approached her black-suited phalanx, each with a discernible bulge under their jackets where small submachine guns rested, they greeted me with angry stares. Among all the folks on this good earth, I stood as the sole individual allowed top-dog access while armed. The Glock nested in the waistband of my jeans, covered with a light jacket.

"Evening, boys. As some fellow named Moses said, let the sea part."

I sat my rucksack on the floor and waited. Silence and stillness for several beats, then four dour men stood and scooted their chairs farther apart, creating an alleyway. None too happy, their glares intensified.

"Thanks. Job well done. Is there a tip jar?" I asked, passing through.

I took a seat beside Townsend, both our backs against the wall.

"Your abusive approach toward my people remains both persistent and unwarranted."

"Evening, Director. It's a preemptive move. For some reason, they don't like me."

"Wonders never cease. How was Idaho?"

"Cold and snowy."

She sipped white wine. Light laughter carried from a table near the front door. The locals in this quiet Langley neighborhood appeared inured to viewing a spook collection gathered in the establishment's corner.

"You found Doctor Ruth Hall."

Statement, not a question.

"We found her cabin, the same as the Norks, the DIA, Mossad, and MI6. The Russians couldn't have been far behind."

"How is Mr. Dickerson?"

Oh, man. An early screwup. Tossing the other players onto the table as an act of candor—a solid play. But I used "we," exposing Bo. A dumbass move, instantly regretted.

"He's fine."

Townsend took another sip and locked eyes.

"Where is she, Mr. Lee?"

"I don't know. But I have a lead on Bart Hall's location."

"You don't know?"

"Nope."

"Allow me to reiterate something you *do* know. At critical junctures in our operations, we often squeeze information from individuals."

A first. She'd never played the intimidation card with me, and I chalked it up to both an obligatory reflex through top spook habit and, more importantly, a lack of control. Holding a permanent spot at the top of her expectations list—control. Good. I could leverage it. I surveyed the half-dozen black-suited members of her praetorian guard.

"You didn't bring enough suits to pull that off."

"A fact, Mr. Lee?"

"Yeah, Marilyn. A fact. You and I both know it."

She shifted gears.

"Who contracted you?"

"They've canceled the contract."

Hooded eyes stared unblinking in my direction.

"Do try and stay on task. Whatever your little dance might be, it is already tedious. Have you considered the North Koreans contracted you through the Swiss?"

"Yeah. But dismissed it. It's not their style. My contract arrived from more standard sources. MI6, Mossad, maybe the Chicoms. Or you."

"The Company, while engaged, did not take the lead on these endeavors. The DIA led operations, highlighted with an expired asset found in the snow."

"Something neither of us were happy about."

"As even you might understand, national security takes precedence over my happiness. Critical technologies are at play. Technologies which cannot fall into others' hands."

"From what I understand, it's all theoretical. Not even close to an experimental phase."

A statement exposing the lie about finding Ruth, but I was obliged to try and crank the heat down a notch or two regarding this whole mess. Every damn thing with spookville entailed code red, end-of-the-world, survivability at stake BS. Townsend understood this but also understood the grand game's framework. A framework she continued working within.

"Perhaps the expired North Koreans near Stanley shared this with you."

"Maybe. Are we going to talk about Bart Hall?"

She delivered a long inhale and exhale, weighing whether the Ruth Hall train had left the station, at least for the moment. She'd return there for a Company derailment once Bart's situation became clearer. The fun never stopped.

"Fine," she said. "Doctor Bart Hall. Tell me."

"I'll go find him."

"Safe travels."

She knew where I was headed with this and as response wafted a high and mighty hand in the air.

"I could use your help."

"Oh?"

"I'll ID the country. It provides a great start. Then work with your assets there and pinpoint his location."

She held up her wineglass until a dark-suited minion spotted the gesture. He headed for the bar to collect more wine.

"I'm listening," she said, once assured another glass would soon appear.

"I require a flight and a full complement of weaponry. Along with a vehicle. I'll join at the hip with your asset, and we'll find Bart."

"Do you expect payment for these gilded services?"

"A contract would help. The usual channel."

It would. The Company could well afford to foot the bill on this venture, and she'd used the Zurich gnomes for contracting me in the past. They wouldn't pay my invoice this time once I'd hauled ass with Doctor Bart. But asking for payment provided cover. At least I thought so.

"Do you have cash flow issues, Mr. Lee? I've never known you to focus on money."

Inevitable, and unwanted. She'd excavate for motivations, mine for golden intel. Not a lot I could do about it other than sprinkle a few truth nuggets on top of my ultimate ops plan.

"The cash wouldn't hurt. And there's a personal driver. I'm invested in this hair ball and want to see it through. The North Koreans have Bart. However this plays out, we can both agree them capturing him won't do."

We shared unblinking stares, broken when her wine arrived. She took a sip and said, "It will not do. We have agreement on one facet. What concerns me is your personal investment."

It concerned me too. The moment—sitting with the CIA's clandestine operations director in a Langley bistro while attempting to orchestrate an end run—cast internal doubts. Big time. A here and now reality absurd on its face, and the hand-it-over door cracked open again. Toss a plea bargain on the table asking that the Halls wouldn't face disposal once their usefulness played out. Couldn't help it. I'm human. But I'd given my word. I'd try. Come hell or high water, I'd try.

"Two brilliant American scientists, near retirement, and by all accounts friendly folks who want to be left alone. They deserve better than what's happening."

"So sayeth Saint Lee."

"Drop the sardonic bullshit, Marilyn. The human element still holds reign in my world, if not in yours."

Her shoulders sagged, and her face displayed an expression tinged with sadness, regret.

"It's a matter of affordability. I cannot afford your perspective." She raised her glass, hesitated, and placed it back down. "As for my personal investment, I'd be remiss not pointing out you are a small fish in vast and piranha-infested waters. A cold and deadly reality I am unsure you grasp."

Inner relief flooded—she drew on our past shared experiences back in the day, and still held a unique perspective toward me. Not one swathed in love, but perhaps affection. The same affection I held for her. Arm's length, a jaundiced eye, but a bond only attained through a shared hang-it-on-the-line history. The cat-and-mouse conversation up to this point ceased. She'd internalized acceptance, knowing I did, for a fact, bring special skills to the table. And knowing I held a potent hole card: Bart's location. Our discussion shifted toward details.

"I am unclear on the weaponry requirement. The contract would stipulate your duties as assisting our efforts. Hardly cause for heavy armament."

"You'll need to make it clear to your assets my role as an associate. Assisting, yes, but not an assistant, a spook lackey. I'll require independent movement. You and I both know things work better that way."

"Hmm."

"We're talking about a major sticking point."

She remained silent.

"C'mon, Marilyn. Let's go find him."

But Townsend had a burr under her saddle, no doubt related to subsequent actions once I'd pinpointed Bart. She knew me too damn well.

"If you identified our subject's exact location, you would deliver the intel and back off. A younger version of our old team would deploy. Understood?"

She'd pull the trigger on an active Delta Force team, which she'd preposition in Quito along with a fast black-painted chopper on standby.

"Understood. And I'm not your people's assistant."

"Understood."

She eyeballed me, one eyebrow raised, and waited for the golden prize.

"Ecuador."

I stood, let the reveal marinate as her three-dimensional chess pieces moved about, and fetched myself a Grey Goose on the rocks. Done deal, and I could relax a bit. When I returned, she'd shifted into a handler's role with her contracted asset. Me.

"Can you provide a more detailed location?"

"Not at the moment."

She was fishing. I wouldn't reveal Ecuador's coastline as the target. My one advantage within this ungodly mess, and I'd keep it in my pocket.

"Are you aware of the broader implications?"

"Yeah. Chicoms out the wazoo."

"Let us use the appropriate lexicon, Mr. Lee. MSS. I would also note, firefights on Quito's streets would constitute unacceptable action, in the extreme."

MSS—the Ministry of State Security. China's version of the CIA.

"I sure don't plan on OK Corral reenactments. But the weapons cache for me should reflect that things often go sideways."

In her convoluted, messed-up world, I now represented a new and optional role. Her personal muscle, someone who could take on and take out MSS interference while she kept her—and the Company's—hands clean and used the Delta team against the Norks for Bart's extraction. Her game plan. Not mine. Either way, game on.

THE SAWTOOTH JOB

Chapter 22

Townsend and her entourage departed while I nursed my vodka. She'd text me an encrypted message with the flight time and assembly point—no doubt before dawn. A six-hour flight and integration with her Ecuador team lay ahead. Time aplenty for kneading how it might play out, but two items required immediate action.

I texted Marcus.

Status?

He responded within minutes.

In place. Cosmic traveler exited. You?

I replied with broad terms, but he'd get it.

Big dog on board. Travel ahead.

All good. He and Ruth were situated in Fishtail or at his ranch house, with highest odds on the latter. Excellent. And Bo had departed for Spokane. We'd scattered like a covey of quail, our back trail nebulous, confused. I breathed an internal sigh of relief and felt buttressed on my upcoming mission. We'd pulled off Ruth's escape against high odds, and a repeat performance hung on the horizon—albeit a performance that included a long line of adversaries on my butt. Norks, Chicoms, you-name-it. And while not adversaries, Delta Force, the Company, and Townsend would chase me down if I managed my own Bart extraction.

Which highlighted action item number two. I required my own Ecuadorian team assemblage—rickety, unreliable, and with backstabbing potential. Welcome to my world. I texted Jules.

Quito fixer.

She'd respond soon enough. I didn't require this cat for weapons or a vehicle or Ecuadorian officials' access—the Company would handle those things. No, I required someone just in case. A backup asset, with fingers crossed the fixer didn't already have a pipeline into the Company's Ecuador contingent. You never knew.

I ordered a second drink and viewed the bistro's small crowd. Normal folks out for the evening. They chatted, laughed, and stared at iPhones. The disconnect with my life palpable, but with a peculiar satisfaction. A wry smile accompanied acknowledgment that I relished this stuff, the hang-it-on-the-line aspects. Perhaps not healthy from a mental standpoint, but there it was. My phone pinged. Expecting a Clubhouse response, I was semisurprised it came from Townsend.

0600 Private Aircraft Terminal

She didn't fart around when engaged with enemies. She'd have someone tote me across the airport for the CIA hangar where my plane waited.

Roger

My immediate response reiterated we sat on the same team, with the same objective. Case Lee, team player. She wouldn't buy it, but appearances mattered among lesser players, ones I'd meet upon landing.

Soon after, Jules pinged me with an Ecuadorian phone number and a terse message.

Full service.

Bless her. A back pocket face card and someone who could provide most anything required. Excellent. I didn't respond as Jules disliked needless electronic communications.

Jess called. A pleasant break—off into personal territory with fretting set aside for a while.

"How's New Hampshire?" I asked.

"I haven't left for the job yet. How's wherever you are?"

"DC, dancing a sidestep among shadows, enjoying a Grey Goose, and contemplating supper."

We talked for fifteen minutes, a great chat, grounding, and a feel-good experience. Man, I appreciated her bringing that to the table. After we signed off, I booked a room—a hotel in DC and an Airbnb in Quito, plus a rental vehicle. The Company would have a room for me when I arrived, with audio and visual bugs plastered all over the thing. And they'd insist I didn't require a vehicle, providing whatever ferry services I required. Not happening for either, and they'd be pissed. Not the first time.

I paid the tab, lifted the rucksack, and waited outside for an Uber. Nighttime, little traffic, a quiet neighborhood. And somewhere close, a Company spook eyeballed me. Another Ecuador team member, assigned to ensure the newest player, Case Lee, behaved. Yeah, well, part of the deal.

As I waited, rationalizations pinballed inside my head. I'd chosen a dangerous path, with leveraging the Company for my own means near the top of the list. But they'd used my scarred butt plenty—in New Guinea, the Caribbean, Orcas Island, and northwest Africa. Played me like a freakin' kettle drum. Such thoughts eased the angst over blindsiding the Company, and Townsend, but did little when other, higher risk elements loomed.

Failure raised its ugly head—implications, outcomes, leverage points. If the Norks, and by default the Chicoms, scooted away with Bart, pressures and threats became too complicated as Townsend made demands I'd, at some point, acquiesce to. Hated the thought.

If the Company rescued Bart, a new poker game started. One in which the house, the Company, held all the cards. Oh, man. I recalled Apollo 13's flight control when disaster struck the moon mission. It all boiled down to a simple fact when bad things happened: failure was not an option.

Before dawn a Company man met me at the commercial private aircraft terminal and drove me around the airport, arriving at the CIA's massive hangar. Inside, planes of all shapes and sizes. Small single-engine prop planes, twin-prop planes, small jets, and new large transcontinental jets. A few carried tail numbers, a few had fake company names painted on the fuselage. Most had neither. Two sleek Gulfstreams, black with no markings, were in the prep process with spooks and mechanics and pilots hustling about. Alongside one, a Delta Force team. Five operators. I would fly alone. Townsend hedged her bets keeping us separate—no time to create bonds, no intermingling under the rubric of brotherhood. They had a job to do. So did I. And she intended to ensure our jobs remained separate and distinct.

Delta Force doesn't officially exist—the worst-kept secret in the US military's arsenal. Seal teams were another story. Heralded, rightfully, and pointed toward as an example of what the bad guys could expect if the need arose. But the bad guys knew about Delta as well, and feared us as much if not more. Organizational gestalt and operational approach separated the two entities.

Seal teams came at you with full military battle regalia. State-of-the-art weapons and tools and assorted battle hardware. Delta, depending on the circumstances, would strike while led by the tourist who was last seen snapping photos of old cathedrals, or the guy who took long walks around a neighborhood in shorts and T-shirt, stopping to pet people's dogs. The same guys who you'd next meet in your bedroom sitting on your chest at three a.m. or unleashing a hail of bullets with a tourist brochure in the back pocket of their Levis.

The team before me fit the bill—jeans, sneakers, several ponytails, a few with bushy beards, two with ear studs, multiple tats. They had rucksacks and duffels filled with fatigues and weaponry and modern hardware—which they'd don if the situation called for it—but their plan upon their Quito arrival, one I well knew, would entail a briefing at the US embassy, transfer to a safe house, and then spread out in two- or three-man teams as casual tourists, blending in. The deadliest tourists on the planet.

One approached me—sporting stylish long hair and groomed three-day-old beard growth—and introduced himself. I returned the favor.

"I know the name," he said. "Former operator?"

"Yeah."

No surprise. Delta, past and present, was a tiny and exclusive community.

"You're the contractor they mentioned who sniffed out the trail?"

"Pretty much."

"Good for you. Point out the nail. We'll bring down the hammer."

There was an inferred "old-timer" in his statement, which grated because, well, I saw myself as a long way from a front porch rocking

179

chair. We chatted for a few, separated, and his team boarded the aircraft. By design, I'd show up in Quito after them—standard operating procedure. Embed the warriors first. Then trigger them. Ten minutes later, the engines fired and they rolled from the hangar.

A large hard-sided case waited for me on board my plane. While waiting to roll, I checked the goodies. An M4A1 Carbine with semi- and full-auto modes. Two scopes—a Leupold with a variable zoom that would adjust between 2x and 8x magnification, along with a battery-operated thermal scope. Sweet. Not so sweet, only two thirty-round magazines. But I now knew a guy in Quito who might supplement backup ammo. The pistol—an M9 Beretta 9mm with a threaded barrel for the included silencer. I appreciated the weapon with its rock-solid reliability but preferred a larger caliber. Too late now. No grenades or other explosives—a disappointment but not surprising. Townsend held a tight rein, worried about yours truly and Ecuador carnage. Fair enough. Even so, a big bang option would have made for a handy-dandy tool in Case Lee Inc.'s tool kit.

Six hours later we began our descent into Quito, Ecuador's capitol. It sat high in the Andes Mountains foothills at an elevation over nine-thousand feet and sixteen miles from the equator. Built on the foundations of an ancient Incan city and established in 1534, it has a colonial old town with European, Moorish, and Indigenous styles. When our former Delta team had spent time there, it impressed us as a cool city—both the look and feel and the weather. The old town immersed you into centuries past, with brick and cobblestone streets and narrow passageways. The weather seldom varied, with lows in the fifties and a daily high of seventy. Sweater weather year around. And a city filled with friendly folks.

Quito lies flanked with volcanoes, a few snowcapped, visible on clear days. Toward the east, and over the mighty Andes, the land descended into the Amazon basin. Toward the north, Colombia, and to the south, Peru. And westward, the Pacific Ocean. My search area and Bart Hall's current   residence.

THE SAWTOOTH JOB

Chapter 23

We taxied alongside the private air terminal where a jet-black SUV with tinted windows waited. A spookmobile. I wouldn't pass through customs or immigration—the Company had handled those formalities. Rucksack and hard-cased weapons cache in hand, I exited the plane and approached a young lady standing beside the vehicle. Man, they kept getting younger. Not a day over twenty-six or twenty-seven, shoulder-length dark hair, business suit. An overcast day in Quito, she had no need for the ubiquitous Ray-Ban aviators, so she'd folded and hung them from her blouse's V-neck.

"Case Lee," I said, setting the luggage down and extending a hand. "Call me Case."

"Officer Linda Rodriquez." We shook. "They have assigned me to help you with your stay in Quito."

She didn't offer herself on a first-name basis. A junior member of the Ecuador CIA staff, she spoke with an officious tone and deadpan expression. Overcompensation for her inexperience. High odds a nice young person, and years and mileage and life's speedbumps would soon enough lighten her presentation. For this job, and for a change, the Company didn't bother with Agricultural Liaison or Economic Development cover titles. Straight to Officer Rodriquez.

"Thanks. Let me step inside the terminal and get my vehicle. I'll follow you to the embassy."

I'd requested that the rental vehicle be dropped off at the private air terminal—after reserving and paying with a false ID and credit card linked with a Caymans bank. A midsized SUV, I'd ensured it had enough punch to scoot if necessary.

"You don't require a vehicle. I'm assigned for any required travel. For example, I'll take you to your hotel this evening."

"Thanks for the offer, Officer Rodriquez, but I've already booked a room."

I had used the same ID and credit card as for the vehicle. She blinked several times, wheels grinding the monkey wrench I'd tossed into her assignment.

"Not a big deal," I continued. "I'm a contractor. It's how I work. Be right back."

Avoiding any more back-and-forth, I strode into the small terminal, retrieved the vehicle, loaded it, and joined her again at her vehicle, still on the tarmac. No doubt she'd spent my absent time on the phone, talking with one of her multiple bosses.

"They have instructed me to inform you a vehicle isn't necessary, and we expect you to reside at the hotel we've selected during your stay in Ecuador."

"It's fine, Officer Rodriquez. Why don't you swing by the parking lot on the other side of this building? Look for a silver midsized SUV. I'll follow you."

I turned and headed back again into the small terminal, feeling a bit like a jerk. Not the actions themselves, but knowing she'd get an ass-chewing because of my insistence on going it alone. Oh, well—probably not her first and for sure not her last. Still, it bothered me.

The US embassy, eight miles north of my colonial old town Airbnb, sat on extensive groomed grounds, surrounded by a sturdy and tall steel fence. Projection of power and all that jazz. The embassy building—three-story blocklike, and quite large. I followed Rodriquez toward a private back gate and waited while she chatted with the marine on duty, explaining the cat behind her was allowed entrance. The parking lot held employee vehicles and now my SUV. Within an hour they'd plant a GPS tracking bug on it, a good thing.

She led me inside without a word and not a smile, up a small elevator, through a locked door—opened with a retina security scanner—and into the Company's inner sanctum. Where I waited in a small windowless holding room. Thirty minutes later I heard the Delta team troop past and exit. Someone had briefed them, a game plan set, mission rules of engagement reiterated. My turn.

A guy in his forties, average height and build, opened the door.

"Officer Carl Fischer," he said, standing in the doorway without extending a hand, his expression dour.

Alrighty, then.

"Case Lee."

"What's the deal with your own vehicle and hotel room?"

"Standard operating procedure."

We locked eyes while he considered responses. Word had come from on high that I was key for this operation, so he balanced such reality with a desire, as the Company lead on this mission, for control. He understood someone up the food chain had initiated my arrival. Someone so far up the food chain he'd need a fire ladder to meet them. Not Townsend—this guy wouldn't even know her name. But someone, in his mind, high enough to stomp on his career should things go sideways. Which, if events went as planned, damn sure would. Sorry, scooter.

With a head nod indicating I should follow, he turned on his heels and led me into a large briefing room with another retinal scan door lock. Inside, no windows and a large conference table. We sat at one end. I would have appreciated coffee, but niceties weren't on the menu. He pulled a satellite phone from a jacket pocket and slid it toward me.

"Sat phone," he said. "I assume you've used one. You're required to answer it twenty-four-seven."

"No worries."

"It has my number preprogrammed. It's the only one. Call me the instant you find something."

"Got it. Have you triggered any field assets?"

People on the Company's dole. Informants, underground dealers, government officials, businesspeople.

"Not your business."

"I'd strongly advise against it. Those same assets, and odds are high on this, could also work for the Chinese. And if MSS gets wind you've started a search, they'll get antsy, to say the least."

And make my job more difficult, with the added possibility they'd move Bart Hall, perhaps to another country.

"You may not know this, Lee, but we are tight with Ecuador. We share a long and positive history, including military endeavors."

Yeah, I know, Fischer. Not long ago, I took part in one of those "endeavors."

"Times change," I said.

"What the hell do you mean?"

"China is Ecuador's largest trading partner, by far. And here, just like everywhere else in the world, money talks. And bullshit walks."

He bristled at the statement. Couldn't blame him—while the US had lost influence to the Chinese all over the world, it remained a bitter pill to acknowledge, much less swallow.

"If you trigger field assets, MSS will hear about it," I continued. "Guaranteed."

My gut said it was too late for such admonitions, and high odds this was Fischer's first heavy-duty field ops. Having a Delta team at your disposal remained a heady experience but the best application with such potency, as Townsend had demonstrated with us years ago, focused on less exposure, not more.

Shaken, Fischer lashed out.

"What's your background?" he asked, voice raised. "I don't have a thing on you other than 'prime asset,' which doesn't tell me anything."

Thank you, Marilyn. She'd kept my Company dossier blank.

"What's important here, Fischer, is letting me do my thing. Starting with local intel and big bird access."

Local intel ranked lower on the priority list, but I wouldn't insinuate as much with Fischer. Satellite imagery, big bird, held the key. I'd scour Ecuador's coastline with care as they'd track every keyboard entry and mouse movement I made inside the building.

My statement, at least in part, synched with Fischer's plans and lowered the stovetop heat. His jaw muscles stopped working overtime, posture less defensive.

"I have a workstation prepped for you. You'll have limited database and dossier access, but full imagery access. Since I don't have information on your security clearance, you'll have to live with that."

"I can come to you with intel questions?"

A head nod acknowledging his role with a touch of misdirection and an act I'd likely never perform. It helped lower the heat even more. Left unsaid was a viable option, which I'd trigger as a last resort, regarding encrypted satellite communications from coastal areas. The Company couldn't hear the conversation, but they might have the capability for identifying locations. And release the Delta team.

"Of course. Anything which might lead to Doctor Bart Hall's extraction is fair game."

"Thermal capabilities on big bird?"

The satellite, and maybe a drone or two, would have incredible visual imagery available, both real time and stored. A remarkable tool, if the sun shone. Daytime cloud cover and nighttime rendered visual imagery problematic. Thermal or heat signatures—people, vehicles, generators, cattle and horses—worked through the issue. A poor second place in many ways—while you could make out individuals and their actions, confirmed personal identification wasn't possible. But thermal images created a better-than-nothing option. We'd entered Ecuador's rainy season, with cloud cover an ever-present issue.

"Yes," he said. "Right now, we're performing broad sweeps. For repositioning a bird for specific areas, see me."

Wouldn't happen. I'd take my chances that satellite imagery had captured large swaths of the coastline.

"Roger that. I'll likely perform field ops as well."

"No need."

"Nothing beats feet on the street. I'm an unknown, unlike your officers and your local assets. I can move around without suspicion. We want Bart Hall, right?"

I failed to add MSS had my facial image and name on file, plonking me outside the unknown bucket. At least with MSS. Nothing I could do about it. Fischer cogitated on my plans and tapped the conference table with an index finger.

"Use the satellite phone," he said with resignation. "If you see or hear anything, contact me. I'm kept in the loop on anything and everything. Understood?"

"Understood."

Field rules set, he led me into another room with a dozen workstations, no cubicle dividers, and five others—analysts, no doubt—working away. I dived in, playing a dangerous game, but with a less than needle-in-a-haystack lead. The Company analysts—three very young, two near retirement—nodded in my direction, said, "Hey," and "Hi," and exhibited friendly but aloof behaviors. High odds they also focused on finding Bart, using imagery and communications and whatever else they had at their disposal.

I pulled up imagery and focused first on Ecuador's eastern side. Rain forest turf. I piddled around and zoomed in on a few villages, knowing full well they recorded my search in-house. An ass pain, but no other options presented. An hour later, the Andes, and the same false trails laid and nurtured. I itched, big time, to focus on the coast, but spent the false flag time mulling over Ruth's clues. Chocolates. A Ruth thing, and I couldn't tie it in with Bart.

Seafood. Fair enough, but seafood was ubiquitous along Ecuador's coast. Guinea pig. I could get grilled cuy down the street, another everywhere nonstarter. Time and tide wait for no man. Yeah, no kidding. And tides affected every ocean coastline in the world.

I took a break when an analyst invited me down to the embassy canteen for coffee and a sandwich. A nice guy, we chatted about life in Quito. A mental break, needed. Thirty minutes later and back at it, I rifled through a few databases, brooming my trail, tossing gorilla dust in the air, and wasting time.

I considered other possibilities while bouncing between useless databases. A large local population or, on the flip side, extreme isolation also presented as key. A gaggle of North Koreans would draw attention within any small town. Too much attention. Which left a large coastal city where a half-dozen Asians would get noticed, along with other population anomalies, and not raise any eyebrows or alarms or questions. One Ecuadorian city fit the bill—Guayaquil. About the same size as Quito with over two million folks, it stood as a possibility. But my gut pointed toward isolation. North Korea, the most isolated country on the planet regarding access and openness, would rely on segregation and seclusion during field ops. The hard-bitten Nork operators had a mission and would perform it within their comfort zone. Their overlords, the Chinese, would have accommodated their desire for anonymity and pointed them toward an out-of-the-way coastal location. Maybe. And the maybe had me twisted around the axle.

Plus, the clock ticked. If Fischer had released his local assets, and I sat there convinced he had, MSS could contemplate an immediate move for Bart and direct the Norks to a location change. A location in another country.

Hours passed as I flipped from the coast to foothill towns to Guayaquil to the ancient town of Cuenca. Then back again to the coast, seeking anything, any sign, that would set off my personal alarms. The workday over, the analysts around me left the office. What they'd worked on all day would remain unknown. I plowed ahead, grinding, and played the silly-ass game of switching satellite views from one location to another.

Early evening, I found it. The starting point for the great escape. Heart in throat, mental fist bumps with the cosmos, relief and excitement meters redlined, I didn't linger over the images and moved on.

Time and tides, baby. Time and tides.

THE SAWTOOTH JOB

Chapter 24

Tire tracks across beach sand leading to a tiny village grabbed my attention. Their disappearance rang the bell. Hidden SUVs lit the fuse.

A fishing village, marked with a half dozen small wooden boats hauled onto the beach. Ten miles from a hard-top road, with the last five miles along a narrow beach, waves lapping. A temporary sand highway, smooth and unobstructed. I took mental note of the village's location and the image's time stamp, and jumped back to inland satellite imagery, another diversion. What an ass pain, and it was a major effort pulling away as my heart rate and expectations rose.

Twenty wasted minutes later, I focused again on the fishing village and used images from a different time of day. The tire tracks, and the beach passage, were gone. High tide had shut down the fishing village's access—an isolated spot, big time. And access dependent upon time of day, in rhythm with the tides. Time and tide wait for no man. Attaboy, Bart. Well done, you.

As close to confirmation as I'd get arrived from shapes under a scraggly coastal tree collection fifty yards inland from the village. Two vehicles sat discernible beneath the thin foliage. SUVs—their shapes a far cry from the several old rusted-out pickups parked in the village.

I spent another twenty minutes fake scouring other Ecuadorian locations, repeating previous searches so the fishing village wouldn't stand out as a two-time look-see anomaly. Antsy to get moving, I lacked a hundred percent certainty I'd stumbled onto the right place, but— desperation and a ticking clock aside—gut feel said, "Do it."

Hands over head, I stretched when Fischer strode into the room.

"Anything?" he asked.

"Nope. And I'm brain frazzled. I'll return early a.m. and get after it again."

He stood, arms crossed, showing signs of hesitancy over spilling personal beans.

"I noted your concerns about triggering field assets. But I've made a tactical decision and pulled the trigger a few hours ago. I couldn't abide you as the single point of failure."

I nodded back, expressionless, and said, "Understood."

In his boots, I might have done the same thing. Sands dribbled in the hourglass, and releasing the bloodhounds presented a viable option. In his boots. In mine, it would make for a shittier situation. Ears always to the ground, MSS would get wind of the Company enquiries and become concerned, nervous. And trigger-happy regarding someone like me.

"Are you headed for your hotel?" he asked.

"Yeah. I'll noodle over some options for tomorrow's search, then back at it."

"You realize if our field assets make a discovery, your services aren't required anymore."

"Yeah, I get it."

I exited the building, climbed into my SUV, and headed for a modern part of town in the opposite direction from my Airbnb with three action items on the immediate agenda. Lose the Company's physical and electronic tail, visit the fixer, and use Google Earth for a detailed a.m. plan. The job's undercurrent, palpable and lifting, buttressed my energy level. A hot trail, ugly resistance guaranteed, the aftermath a crapshoot. I performed an involuntary headshake with acknowledgment this was my type of gig. Couldn't help it—weird and at the table's far end from normal and a hardwired attribute. And no apologies.

While driving I called the fixer. He answered with the sounds of children and kitchen clangs in the background. Home, supper prep underway, engaged with the kids. I requested a visit at his place of business to purchase a few specialty items. My American-accented Spanish prompted clarification on his end.

"You are American, no?"

"Yes."

"May I ask how you acquired this phone number?"

Thin ice, but no point crawfishing away from reality. I required this guy's services. The dice would roll across the table more than a few times over the next day or two, so I went ahead, started with this guy, and tossed the bones.

"The Clubhouse."

"Ah, of course. Allow me two hours."

At some point in life, I'd cease amazement at Jules's reach. I hadn't reached that point. He provided an address. Good to go.

Hesitancy at revealing my source was based on connectivity. With Fischer setting off the alarm and cash waved about among the Ecuadorian underground network, someone like me could prompt a phone call or two. This fixer occupied a spot on the underground network, guaran-damn-teed, and the Clubhouse connection placed me in the professional bucket. Hell, he might make several phone calls—China's MSS had little problem wafting Benjamins in the air as well. MI6 less so, and Russia's SVR remained a wild card. Mossad, not so much. With more limited resources, they wouldn't have the infrastructure for tapping into a small South American country's shadowland. Then again, you never freakin' knew.

The evening was cool, cloud cover thick, and a light drizzle fell as I made a dozen sudden turns, checking for a physical tail. Clean. Twenty minutes later I pulled under a valet parking overhang at a large, modern, and busy hotel in Quito's business district. I kept to the left under the wide overhang, away from the hotel guests' vehicles lined up for valet service, and parked. In short order, a young man approached my rolled-down window.

"This is for you," I said, displaying a Benjamin. "I will park here for twenty or thirty minutes. I don't want you or the other valets approaching this vehicle. Understood?"

"Of course," he said, with fingertips on the bill.

I maintained my grip and added, "Should anyone ask, you never saw me."

"See who?" he asked with a smile.

I released the Benjamin, pulled the satellite phone Fischer provided, and disabled the GPS function. Exiting the vehicle, I crawled under the vehicle's front and disabled the car rental company's GPS. Then the big search. Somewhere, without doubt, another GPS tracker lay hidden, applied while I worked at the embassy. It took fifteen minutes. Small and attached with powerful adhesive, they placed it at the back bumper's inside edge. I dropped the device on the ground and several boot stomps eliminated the issue. All tracking devices now kaput, electronic feedback to the Company pointed toward my checking into the hotel, where the signals stopped. They'd scramble and search for my room among the many travelers and come up empty—a ruse without legs, but it would do for the immediate.

Back hatch opened, I crawled inside and closed it. Next, weaponry, still encased within the Company-provided weapons cache. The 9mm pistol, silencer, and extra magazine slid into my jacket pocket, constant companions from this point forward. I slapped a loaded magazine into the M4A1 carbine and chambered a round. An extra thirty-round magazine would join me and my new friends in the front seat.

I tossed the rucksack onto the back seat, pulled extra clothing from it, and then crawled forward. I kept the pistol in my jacket. The rifle and extra magazine rested on the front passenger seat, now draped with a towel, jeans, and shirts. My arming process signified both comfort and kickoff, bringing a hardened mindset. On my own, and let's do this.

I waited for the right vehicle, which took another ten minutes. A late-model sedan dropped off a friend at the hotel and, after goodbyes, eased away from under the large overhang. I followed. Satellite thermal imaging, if now focused on my last known position, would pick up two vehicles, one friend following another, departing together. I stayed close for ten minutes as the sedan wove its way home, then peeled off. Overkill, maybe. Paranoia, no doubt. But with a high degree of confidence, I now traveled untethered.

The fixer's address displayed a tiny real estate office in a gritty part of town. I pulled over and waited. When he arrived—a man in his midforties—I exited the SUV. He heard the vehicle door close, turned, and with a casual air waved a friendly hand as he unlocked the office door. I joined him. We exchanged no names as we shook hands.

"I understand you have a need for specialty items," he said, casual and matter-of-fact.

"I do. As well as information."

"I am certain I can provide both. Come, come. Would you like some coffee or something stronger?"

I declined and followed him past stacked For Sale signs. This cat's real estate business provided a great cover, with payments for special tools providing, I'd bet, a substantial chunk of his cash flow. He unlocked a thick padlocked door, flipped on the light, and we headed downstairs into the basement, with him bolting the stairway door shut behind us.

More well-used yard signs, file cabinets, shelves filled with papers and rolled-up blueprints and other assorted odds and ends. I stood silent as he slid open a large steel file cabinet's lower drawer and produced a half dozen steel rods, each two feet long.

Rods in hand, he approached the basement's back wall with its exposed two-by-four wooden studs and began sliding the rods through large predrilled holes in a set of closely spaced studs. He created a ladder, using the lower rungs to complete the process as he climbed. At the top, he shoved open a trapdoor and climbed up, switching on another light. I followed.

This fixer was clever. His street-level office's back wall stopped ten feet short of the exterior wall and created a hidden space, accessible only through the basement. It would take one resolute search team to find the hidden cache.

Shelves and wall hooks displayed pistols, shotguns, and rifles. A decent selection from a variety of countries, with the lion's share military grade. I considered picking up a higher-caliber pistol but settled on known versus unknown reliability. The 9mm Townsend provided would fire every time I pulled the trigger. No such guarantees with the pistols displayed before me. On a lower shelf, unloaded rifle magazines sat stacked. My rifle, a standard NATO caliber, would accept a variety of 5.56mm magazines. I plucked three from the shelf and, from a higher shelf, collected a hundred rounds of ammo.

"Can I help you find a particular weapon?" the fixer asked, hoping for a higher-end sale.

"I think I found it," I replied.

Hanging from a stock strap among webbed belts and battle vests, the big bang I'd hoped for. An old M79 grenade launcher, a Vietnam-era single-shot weapon, with a cut-back stock and sawed-off barrel. No longer a shoulder weapon, it resembled a pirate's old flintlock pistol, but with a major difference. It would send a 40mm grenade downrange. Accuracy diminished with the homemade modifications, it would still ruin someone's day.

"Do you have ammo for this?" I asked, lifting the old weapon from its hanging hook.

The fixer turned and rummaged inside several cardboard boxes on the floor. He produced one, two, then three 40mm grenades, held them up for display, and smiled when I nodded acceptance.

"I'll take the magazines, the ammo, the grenade launcher, and the three grenades. Plus I require a hard-copy Ecuador map and special information."

He rubbed his chin, lips pursed, and worked on a price point.

"Five thousand US."

About what I expected, but we ground through the usual haggling, more for show than effect, and settled on four thousand three hundred. He pulled a canvas grocery bag and loaded it with my selection. Back in the basement, he rifled through several paper stacks and found a decent blueprint-sized topo map of his country. Then back upstairs and into his well-lit office, the goodie bag at my feet as we sat.

One option presented for the great escape—head north, into Colombia. A bit of a skillet-into-the-fire element about it—Colombia, as I well knew, could get as gnarly as anywhere—but no other direction seemed viable. From a strategic perspective, the plan held water. Take out the Norks, rescue Bart, head north, and avoid more spookville outfits than you could shake a stick at. A list that included the CIA, and, God forbid, a Delta Force team. While I used run-of-the-mill brigands, smugglers, thieves, killers, and mercs to bootleg Bart back into the States. Piece of cake.

Chapter 25

"What route would a smuggler use for entering Colombia?"

The fixer opened a desk drawer and retrieved a red pencil. He acted with confidence, a positive sign.

"Here," he said, marking a spot northeast of Quito, deep in the Andes. "And here." He marked the map again. "Here as well." Another spot marked in red.

All were Andean highland locations, and all required a return trip from the coast through Quito. My preference, which I insinuated with a gentle touch, was along the ocean. Not a quicker route, but it avoided a return to the hornet's nest.

"What about this area?" I asked, using a forefinger with broad brushstrokes across the map.

"Access is very limited, and authorities on both sides guard those areas. The mountains, my friend, offer routes unguarded. The ones I have marked. You should cross at night. I will detail these choices for you."

He spent ten minutes redlining what appeared, at best, as trails on the topographic map. Oh, man. I didn't doubt the guy and appreciated the three options for illegal crossings into Colombia. On the flip side, if he exchanged intel for cash with a spy outfit, they'd receive the same three options for my crossing. Not good.

I rolled up the map, shook hands, and headed for my Airbnb in the city's old historic center while checking again for tails. Still clean. The room proved large, clean, and welcoming. I spent the next hour or so perusing my operational areas with Google satellite views and planning stage-one logistics.

A six-hour drive from Quito to the coast. I checked the highway— ugly conditions weaving down from the Andean highlands, then a more sedate path through the foothills and down to the coast. The nearest town where Bart's captors could collect supplies and buy groceries was officially named La Real Santisíma Villa Rica de la Bendita Providencia de San Cayetano de Chone de esta nuestra Nueva Castilla. Or Chone, if you didn't feel like reeling off a grandiose name for a small and gritty town. I'd stop there and scour for signs of a Nork presence in the area.

Adding an hour for mucking around Chone made it a seven-hour fishing village trip. Leaving Quito at four a.m. put me there at eleven a.m., and matched low tide for beach road access.

The Google satellite images of the village revealed little. Two dozen shacks, two small pickups, no electricity unless a local generator provided power. The Norks would have their own small generator, tucked against a shack they'd taken over. Landward from the village, salt-grass-covered dunes. My hiding spot for figuring out a rescue plan—or better put, a battle plan. I guessed four or five Norks. Hardened operators, they'd go down swinging, no doubt about it.

What was in doubt, satellite imagery. Not the Company. They would still have their big bird eyeballing broad swaths of Ecuador. But the Chicoms worried me. They, too, might have a geostationary spy satellite overhead, focused on the fishing village and surrounding area. If not, I could formulate a one-man rescue plan using surprise as the prime tool. If a Chinese satellite was positioned overhead with assured communications to the hostage-takers, life became a lot more difficult. They'd lie in wait, any surprise elements out the window. I'd make the best of it and use my arrival's confirmation as a way to suck them away from the village, away from Bart. Not easy, but doable.

I gave myself two hours for the beach operation, then I'd head for Quito, climbing a dangerous winding highway into the Andean clouds for six hours. It would put me back in Quito around seven p.m. Then off for the border. Five hours later, with no hiccups, we'd enter Colombia around midnight. Busy day.

But there were always hiccups. Always. Those known unknowns Marcus often referenced. Was Bart at the location? If so, would the Norks receive an alert from a Chicom big bird about my imminent arrival, a lone vehicle barreling along the beach headed their way? Would the Company's eyes-in-the-sky home in on a beach firefight? Would the Company tap into MSS intel and find out my position? If they did, would they send the Delta team? The last question had a ready answer. If the in-country Delta team engaged me while I had Bart, game over. I wouldn't tangle with those dudes, end of story. And also my quest's end, as subsequent actions would then consist of negotiating with Townsend, getting the Halls the best deal possible. Which would suck. I hit the rack early with what-ifs pinballing inside my head, the pistol under an extra pillow, the rifle leaning against the bedside table. I drifted off to sleep later than I'd wanted.

Four a.m. arrived too early, and I hit the road. The weather remained the same—low, thick, drifting clouds and a light drizzle. The first hour proved easy traveling, the terrain ranging between flat and rolling. Then the drop-off. The two-lane blacktop weaved downhill through mist and fog, with an occasional semitruck either downshifting with harsh gear-grinding or engine roaring, struggling to climb. Passing another vehicle bordered on suicide with visibility poor and drop-offs on either side often a thousand feet down. Guardrails, few and far between, displayed sideswipe scars as vehicles had attempted to negotiate curves while traveling too fast. I gritted my teeth and accepted this was it for the next couple of hours and gave thought to the returning climb. A hairy proposition.

Occasional breakfast fires displayed near the road as tiny villages started the day. I knew from past experience those folks made up Indigenous populations, descendants of the Inca, still speaking Quechua. For many, Spanish was a second language.

Sunrise—a gradual increase in ambient light as clouds remained thick—brought the tension meter down a notch or two. Until, on a short, flat stretch between tight curves with a steep drop into a canyon on my right, my peripheral vision picked up movement. Slow movement, on my left. Decades before, a construction crew had blasted out a mountainside and created a flat football-field-sized staging area for their heavy equipment. Scars from bulldozers and other earthmovers remained. New to the scene, a massive boulder, slowly rolling across the open area and headed for the highway. The size of at least a three-story house, it had released from the sheer mountainside and landed with sufficient momentum to continue rolling. And slow roll it did, at the speed of a person jogging, first across the open area, then across the highway as it cracked and broke up asphalt, then over the side, plummeting at least a thousand feet. Woe be to anyone or anything at the canyon's bottom. It was so surreal I'd watched with wide eyes and an open mouth, a strange and awesome sight. Nature didn't always come at you at a rush. You'd best look out for the slower stuff as well. I eased across the broken asphalt and continued with the drizzle and fog and low light adding to the unreal vibe.

Hours later, as I approached Chone, still fifteen miles from the coast, the heavens cleared, and bright sunshine brought both relief from the gloomy conditions and a concern. If the Chicoms had positioned a satellite over the fishing village and its access, I'd stick out like a sore thumb upon my arrival. Not a thing I could do about it.

Chone was as expected. A few paved roads among dirt paths with ramshackle structures and electrical wiring strewn overhead without pattern or design. Multiple houses and buildings sported fresh paint—bright blue, yellow, green, and tan—while others hadn't seen a paintbrush in decades. The local trucks and sedans and buses eased down bumpy roads as donkey carts hugged sidewalks. Not a bad town, and the locals carried a light and cheerful air with smiles and waves at passersby. I parked near a street with an outdoor market.

I visited several stalls with the same question—had they seen any Asian men in the last few days? At a stall with fresh fruit and vegetables, I received confirmation.

"How many?" I asked.

"Two."

She smiled, expecting a sale. I complied and bought a small bunch of bananas.

"Did they speak any Spanish?"

"No. They pointed and paid, which is sufficient."

"What did they look like?"

"As you asked, Asian."

"How were they dressed?"

"As soldados."

Soldiers. My heartrate bumped up, my nostrils flared, and my adrenaline engine rose past idle. The trail no longer felt hopeful or filled with possibility. Nossir. The trail was now red-hot, and Case Lee Inc. would soon bring down the hammer on those Nork bastards at the fishing village. I thanked the vendor, headed back for the vehicle, and understood her uninterested response toward the visitor's attire. The Chone folks lived a hardscrabble life, and a significant purchase by non-Spanish-speaking visitors far outweighed their attire. Soldiers or ballerinas or astronauts—make the sale, ease life's weight a little bit.

I punched it outside Chone, behind schedule, behind the travel window offered with the tides. A dozen miles later I left hard-top and took a sandy two-track road for the last miles. Out of sight, I stopped and prepped. Off with the jeans and sneakers, on with fatigues and boots and battle vest. I donned a holster and inserted the Beretta pistol, shoved two full rifle ammo magazines into my vest, and ensured a round was chambered in the rifle. As a last act I slung the pirate-pistol-appearing 40mm grenade launcher across a shoulder, still with the long lanyard it had hung from at the fixer's armory, and popped a grenade into the single-shot breech-loading barrel. Party time.

Chapter 26

The two-track road ended at the shore where I stopped, hidden among low dunes. With low tide and sand and sunlight, a thirty-foot-wide smooth and semifirm beach awaited. The salt air blew crisp and fresh as the engine idled and waves lapped at the tidal shore. An isolated serene and contemplative place, soon to be shattered with ugliness and death. The entire job had come to this. A couple miles away, Bart Hall and his North Korean abductors. A job, a quest, taken on because I'd given my word to a nice scientist back in Stanley, Idaho. And because, all ifs and buts aside, it meant doing the right thing.

A puffed-cheek exhale, and I dismissed all rationales and reasons and ramifications. A singular goal lay ahead—all else was static, white noise. From deep recesses, I dusted off a too-often-used on-or-off switch. Kill or be killed time, and the latter held no sway over immediate events. Not this day. With absolute determination and ice-cold commitment, I threw the kill switch.

The beach highway allowed speedy passage with few tidal speed bump irregularities. Half a mile, and I squinted through the windshield. A vehicle headed toward me, taking advantage of the now open passage. Damn. A local in a pickup, maybe, bringing fish into town. Or an SUV with Norks intent on blowing me away, alerted by their Chicom overlords with real-time satellite imagery. I stopped and sought clarity as options flashed by, lifted the field binoculars, and cranked up the magnification.

Not an old pickup. An SUV. But something off-kilter about their approach, with no knife-between-the-teeth aggression. They cruised, not in a rush, and as they approached within a quarter-mile, small, white intermittent smoke signals from both open windows. Two Norks, having a smoke, lollygagged along. With the beach passage now open, these guys headed into Chone for more food, other supplies, a liquor purchase, a stop at the local bordello.

Sure, they'd stop and prevent my passage using hand signals and, maybe, flashing weapons, sussing me as a tourist or fish buyer. Send me on my way and continue their shopping trip. Fine. Let's meet, boys. I rolled again at a casual speed, shrugged off my battle vest and the sawed-off grenade launcher, and placed them on the passenger seat. If they considered me a tourist, I'd comply.

Distance plus ambient sounds around the fishing village—villagers talked, waves lapped, wind blew—would likely prevent gunshot noises from reaching the left-behind Norks, but it presented an iffy proposition. And iffy wouldn't cut it in the here and now. I unholstered the Beretta pistol, lifted the silencer from the SUV's console, steered with my knees, and threaded it onto the pistol's barrel.

We both continued our casual progress, Sunday freakin' drivers, as the distance closed. At a hundred yards, the Nork passenger flicked his smoke out the window. At thirty yards, we both slowed as the oncoming driver held up a "stop" hand outside the open window. We both halted, our vehicles' noses seven paces apart.

I performed my best midtown Manhattan hand gestures, waving both hands near the windshield with irritation and indicating room aplenty to pass each other. I tossed in verbal hounding as well, loud enough for the two enemies to hear. They turned their heads and chatted across the front seats. Then the passenger opened his door and began a casual slide out, an assault rifle now evident. The driver remained seated and lit another smoke. I opened the door and began my slide, shaking my head and still verbalizing annoyance, the Beretta in my right hand and still hidden.

The passenger stood, for a quick second, framed with his door's open window. My left foot hit sand, I whipped the pistol up, and delivered two shots into the passenger's chest. Double tap. Poleaxed, he collapsed onto sand. The shock element provided the needed time for sighting on the driver, who, wide-eyed, scrambled for his weapon. Three shots through the windshield, each hitting the target, ended his search. Two down, plenty left.

Clinical, cold, well-versed action. And no regrets. Two hard-bitten North Korean abductors and killers eliminated. I laid the pistol on the front seat and hustled toward the first victim stretched across the sand. I'd perform a minimal cleanup in case eyes-in-the-sky captured this tiny section of turf. After tossing the dead man back into the passenger seat, I slammed the door shut and left their vehicle where it was. A static vehicle on the beach road might draw mild aerial attention, but a sprawled body alongside it would damn sure ring a few bells.

Low odds the Chicoms had a satellite fixated on the area. Had they alerted the fishing village Norks, our beach encounter would have exhibited more aggression. Meanwhile, the Company satellite still worked the entirety of Ecuador as Fischer and his team chased flimsy leads from their field assets. The upcoming conflict at the village would play out in isolation.

I donned the battle gear I'd removed and drove at a normal pace, avoiding attention. At a half mile the village came into view. My plan remained cut-and-dried. Pull into the dunes at a quarter mile, move on foot, and remain hidden among the sand hummocks and dune grass. Approach the village from the rear and assess. Not a time for screwing around, but when bullets flew, the off chance Bart Hall could catch one mandated caution.

At the appropriate distance I nosed the SUV between small dunes, grabbed the rifle and grenade launcher, and kept low while weaving, moving fast. At a hundred yards I plopped belly-flat and scoped through the rifle's sight. Two dozen shacks constructed from plastic tarps, plywood, corrugated tin, and driftwood. A few kids dashed about while several men performed maintenance on small boats with outboard engines. Cooking smoke drifted from several shacks.

The sun high in the sky, bright and squint-worthy, as the ocean breeze swayed the surrounding dune grass. An occasional yelp from a playing kid, a woman's voice called from a shack, and deep in the background a portable generator's low, quiet rumble. I sought it, scoping shack to shack. Frustration mounted until I spotted the power cable laid across the sand. It ran from the farthest shack—the largest one in the village—into the dunes. Bingo.

Crawling backward, I changed direction and headed deeper into the hummocks and salt grass. Opportunity shouted—I could whack at least one if not two as they checked why the generator had stopped working. Fifteen minutes later I halted at the edge of a small rise, the generator out in the open five paces away with two gas cans nearby. Moving at a snail's pace, I inched forward for a clean look at the large shack. No windows on three sides, with the fourth side an open-air affair. An overhead tarp from the open side extended eight paces over sand, supported with wooden posts along its length. Beneath the tarp, a cookfire and firewood pile and pots and pans and four cheap lawn chairs with several hard-sided storage cases now acting as footrests. Multiple wooden boxes, some open and others not, lay scattered about—the outdoor setting's decor. Two Norks lounged in chairs, backs toward me, chatting as they viewed the ocean and smoked, their assault rifles at rest against the hard cases. A third voice called from inside the shack, which prompted responses from the outside two. At least three Norks. No sign of Bart.

I scratched the generator plan. Two targets sat with their backs my way, but inside the large shack remained an unknown, and a full picture was mandatory before my assault. I hustled past the generator and, at a low stoop, hidden among the dunes, worked past the Nork shack. At fifty yards distance, I eased up a slope and sighted inside. One guy stood in profile as he cleaned fish on a makeshift cutting board. Another lay stretched out on a portable cot, hands behind his head. Asleep or just resting, unknown. And between the fish cleaner and me, Dr. Bart Hall.

He sat at a rickety table on a low stool in boxer underwear and owlish eyeglasses and nothing else. His sparse Friar Tuck hair ring moved with the ocean breeze, disheveled, as he stared at small objects on the tabletop. It took a few moments to register. He must have carved or drawn a chessboard on the tabletop and created game pieces. Ruth's husband, my quarry, played chess against himself in his skivvies under the Norks' watchful eyes. The guy defined desolate as his shoulders sagged and head hung, and I felt for him, big time.

If they captured Ruth, they'd jerk him from here and put the two together in another isolated location, albeit modern, and demand they produced. Inside China or North Korea or some other hidden spot where they'd perform until no longer deemed useful, then killed. Couldn't say it was any different for the US, except they'd get tucked away in Maryland or Virginia, with the ultimate outcome the same. It remained unclear if even Marilyn Townsend could alter the inevitable equation. But the Chicoms and Norks held an advantage. They had half the equation in hand and would fight like hell to keep it.

The good news—I could take out the shack's two occupants. Start with the cook-of-the-day, and if Bart remained at the table or, better yet, dropped to the ground, I could then engage the two guys sitting outside. It would make for a firefight—the two outside would hear the bullets bee-buzz past them as I took out the interior two. They'd grab their weapons and engage. Couldn't avoid it. The two inside posed immediate danger with their proximity to Bart and would go first. So be it.

I visualized the scenario and embraced movement as part of the success formula. The two under the tarp, operators from a North Korean special forces outfit, could shoot. Crack shots? Unknown. Their training could have included an emphasis on full automatic fire, peppering an enemy with lead. Regardless, the tarp twins would send bullets in my direction once I'd begun firing. So, after whacking the two inside the shack, I'd reposition, moving fast, and prevent them from using Bart as a shield. I sighted in, finger on the trigger. It would work out if Dr. Bart stayed put. He didn't.

Chapter 27

The enemy acting as the day's cook received a headshot, my rifle's sharp crack wildly incongruous against an otherwise peaceful setting. The distinctive sound kicked off frantic activity, with the guy stretched out on the cot bolting upright and signing his death warrant. His new position, static for a spit second, ensured headshot number two. In my peripheral vision the tarp enemies dropped, grabbed weapons, and positioned—one behind the firewood stack, the other behind a hard-sided case. The firewood guy didn't wait to acquire a target—me—and instead ripped a seven-shot burst toward my general position. The village men, women, and children screamed and dashed for protection while Bart stood, baffled, and shifted position. You'd expect a guy in his position to perform a ground drop or frantic scramble for cover, not a wide-eyed adjustment of the glasses, a slow head scratch, and a meander out into the line of fire in his underwear. Gimme a break, Bart.

I bailed on my position and performed the world's fastest low-stooped dash, stayed below the dune tops, and traveled much farther than first intended, ensuring Bart wouldn't receive an inadvertent hot round. Back near the generator and belly-flat, I crawled up a dune. Bart had exited, stage right, his whereabouts unknown. But I had a clean side shot at firewood guy, squeezed the trigger, and nailed two bullets into his upper torso. Then the enemy behind the case joined the fray as he popped up and ripped fire. As I ducked, angry buzzes overhead and lead-on-sand slaps and flying grit said he'd sighted me. The grenade launcher option flashed past. Take the bastard out and be done with it, but I dismissed the idea knowing artifacts—including Bart's laptop—could get damaged.

I slid down the dune and rolled left three times and crawled back up, seeking my target. He'd shifted as well, now hunkered down at the angled intersection of two hard cases, presenting poor target opportunities. I flipped fire select to full auto and blasted his position with three- and four-shot bursts, which sent him scurrying toward what he perceived as a more protected position. Bad move. Switching back into single-shot mode, I'd sight body glimpses as he shifted between scattered cases and wooden boxes, until a half-second torso shot presented itself. My weapon barked three times, punching lead into him with each trigger pull.

Over. Over and done. Death delivered, the outcome expected. My adrenaline meter lowered, the aftermath still and quiet, backdropped with the generator's low hum and an ocean breeze. No jubilation, no self-exultations—just relief over ugly business attended to and now dismissed. Acts performed, tucked away and, while not forgotten, shoved into a dark recess already filled with too much of the same.

I strode toward the tarp area, rifle shouldered, and picked up another sound, which in close proximity carried over the ocean breeze. A voice. An Asian voice. At my last victim's original position behind a hard case, a satellite phone lay on the sand. The dead Nork had placed a call when I attacked. Besides English, I spoke Spanish, Portuguese, and Arabic. No Asiatic languages. But I could discern between Chinese and Korean as up-and-down tones filled the former. Korean lacked tonal emphasis. And the frantic voice coming through the phone's speaker was Chinese. Oh, man. Red alert time among the Chicom MSS operators in Quito. Decent odds they wouldn't have a chopper available—China, unlike the States, avoided overt displays—but still. They'd received an alert from an active firefight, and they wouldn't sit still.

And where the hell was Bart? I called his name while standing among four dead men. Silence. Then jogged into the village's center and called again. Nothing, nada. I stopped and hollered in Spanish toward the surrounding shacks, asking where the gringo had headed. A lone voice, a woman, replied from inside her home.

"Quitado." Gone.

"Donde?" Where?

"La Playa."

The beach. Yeah, he's on the beach. I got it. Rather than play a back-and-forth *Where's Waldo?* a quick dash past the shacks found him. The lady was right. Several hundred yards away and still making headway, Bart Hall. His arms made forceful swings, but his legs moved at a brisk walk, at best. He'd decided his best bet was booking it down the beach. I called after him with no effect, so I jogged, fast, and caught up, calling his name the entire time. The last thing I needed was him having a freakin' heart attack.

As I drew alongside, he glanced at me, a guy in battle fatigues toting weapons, and continued trucking, eyes on some perceived destination. But at least he talked.

"You work for a government. Yes, a government. I do not wish to talk with you."

"No, sir, I'm not with any government. I'm Case Lee."

"I will not tell you where Ruth is."

He'd worked up a sweat—the boxers stuck against his skin; his bare feet picked up sand.

"I know where Ruth is. My friends and I rescued her."

He halted, wearing a severe frown and sucking air.

"You work for a government. Ruth did not require rescuing."

"I'm afraid she did. Government people had converged on your cabin in Stanley."

He blinked twice and placed both hands on his ample belly, standing a good six or eight inches shorter than me.

"Your friends?"

"Yeah, my friends. We got her before the others could."

"At the cabin in Stanley?"

"Not exactly. We found her in a hot pool on the Salmon River near the cabin."

He leaned in, the sea breeze lifting thin tufts of side-hair.

"Where is she now?"

"A safe place, with my friends."

"Why did you do this?"

The job's persistent question, one writ large on the chalkboard as MSS scrambled and the Company searched, while a Delta team itched to get into the game. Stir in MI6 and Mossad and the Russians, plus six dead Norks. And now I stood on an isolated Ecuadorian beach convincing the guy I'd come to rescue I was legit. Marcus had a point—dumbass pills by the handful.

"Why? I wonder about that myself. Let's just say you and Ruth were in distress. My friends and I figured a helping hand was the right thing to do."

I wouldn't get into contracts and specific players or the motivations of others. It lent no clarity to the immediate. This hadn't gone as expected, with the firefight's aftermath filled with Bart's relief and appreciation and enquiries about next steps.

"What organization are you and your friends associated with?"

"No organization."

He turned back toward the horizon and took off again, arms pumping, legs less so. I'd failed some litmus test and he was having none of it. Couldn't say I blamed him as my explanation, once I'd heard it out loud, was filled to the brim with crazy. Oh, man. I jogged past him and made the parked SUV tucked into the dunes. Haul it time, and pronto.

I fired the engine, backed out, rolled toward Bart, stopped as he approached, and said out the open window, "Get in, Bart. We gotta go. Let's get you back with Ruth."

He halted and stood at the window.

"Ruthie is safe?"

"She's fine. I'm taking you back to her."

Tears welled. He remained standing and blinked, sending tears down his unshaven cheeks. I got it. The poor guy's journey—hair-raising and terrorizing and filled with uncertainty. Now this, out of the blue. A rescue. Potential relief.

"Ruth knows I came for you," I continued. "You can call her soon. My name is Case Lee. I'm one of the good guys. Please get in."

Maybe it was the "please," but he nodded back, opened the door, inspected the interior, and climbed inside. I punched it toward the fishing village.

Bart sobbed once while staring at the floorboard, wiped his nose with the back of a hand, and said, "I am afraid I have placed sand in your vehicle."

"Don't sweat the sand."

"Is Ruthie well? We talk often because the men who took me wished to learn her location. They insisted on limited conversations. Limited."

"She's fine. Promise. I listened in on one conversation. You did a great job dropping clues in those."

"There was little else to think about while here." He twisted his head and addressed me. "Good guy. I most certainly hope you are."

"I try. You can call Ruth once we gather your stuff and haul ass. It's a long drive to Quito."

At the shack, he averted his eyes from the two dead men under the tarp and tried, without success, to avoid acknowledgment of the two inside.

"This is a grotesque scene. You must be an excellent shot."

"I know, it's a mess. Where're your clothes?"

"I have only what I wore in Palo Alto. When they took me."

He retrieved folded clothes and pulled on khakis and a long-sleeve shirt and slipped into white socks and black walking shoes.

"That one," he said, pointing toward the Nork in the cot, "spoke a little English. He struck me once when I mentioned seafood."

"Let's focus on the here and now. Where's your laptop and phone?"

He found and lifted a well-worn brown leather shoulder satchel, checked the contents, and nodded.

"This is everything."

"Are you sure? We don't want anything left behind."

He addressed the etched tabletop chessboard and gently swept the handmade playing pieces into the open satchel, buckled it closed, and nodded toward me. Then he refused to leave the village until he'd

218

thanked the woman who'd washed and dried and folded his clothes. Not knowing any Spanish, he repeated, "Gracias," over and over while she peeked from inside her shack. Concluding the exchange, she edged outside, glanced around, took his head in both hands, and kissed him on the forehead. The act sealed the intended gratitude, and I slipped her a Benjamin and reiterated the thanks. Then we mounted up and tore down the beach.

"May I call Ruthie?"

I asked for his phone, powered it up, and confirmed the GPS function was disabled. Then handed it back. An awkward ten minutes ensued—while I negotiated the two-track away from the beach, he spoke and cried and repeated the cycle multiple times. No doubt Ruth mirrored his pattern. He referenced me as "good guy" several times. It came across as so personal, so touching, I almost stopped and allowed him privacy. But our progress was behind schedule, and even though we had built-in leeway, movement ruled the day. He asked me several questions for Ruth's sake—all involved next steps, each danced around without answers.

"Let's keep things between ourselves. Just in case."

An answer he, and Ruth, would fail to grasp, but loose lips remained an ever-present danger. Bart handed me the still-active phone.

"Your friend wishes to speak with you."

Marcus.

"Status?" he asked, voice no-nonsense.

"Cleaned the Norks, but they alerted MSS."

"Do they have a chopper in-country?"

"Unknown, but I doubt it. Not their style."

"They'll head downhill as we speak."

"Roger that."

"What if you hid for the day? They won't make you out through a windshield at night."

"Gotta cross the Colombian border at night, and it's a five- or six-hour run getting there from Quito. If I delay on this leg, we won't make the opportunity window."

He mulled over my reality and fell back on his standard concern.

"Do you have sufficient firepower if they engage?"

"Solid kit, Marcus. Plus a sawed-off Thumper."

The chopped-down grenade launcher would get his attention. Added firepower in the form of a big bang.

"Excellent. Tell me about the Company."

"Mighty pissed, I would imagine. Which is fine. It's not them I'm worried about."

"Explain."

"A Delta team arrived with me. They're on standby, tugging on the leash."

He sighed and muttered, "Shit."

"Yeah. Exactly."

"Did you meet with them?"

"A brief conversation at the DC hangar before departure."

"They know your background?"

"Yep."

"What do you think?"

He'd asked the sixty-four-dollar question. I damn sure wouldn't squeeze a trigger pointed in their direction. Hands up, hand over Bart, gave it the old college try. Would they reciprocate? Or send lead downrange in my direction? Unknown. Mission-oriented in the extreme, their eye on the prize focus might eclipse my background.

"Don't know."

He remained silent for several seconds.

"If push comes to shove, drop the package and walk away. Chance nothing."

"Yeah, I know."

"Let's say you make daylight tomorrow with package in hand. Then what?"

"Working on it."

"Right. The Case Lee standard operating procedure."

"How's Ruth?"

"Fine. Better now that she's talked with her husband. How can I help with current events?"

"Don't know, bud. But I'll sure give you a holler if need be."

"You do that. And don't hesitate. Meanwhile, stay low, move fast, aim sure."

We signed off. Ahead, unknowns out the wazoo. Yeah, well, not the first time I'd waded those waters.

THE SAWTOOTH JOB

Chapter 28

Bart remained silent as we hit hard-top and sped toward Chone. Mental wheels churned, played odds, leveraged assets. I pulled the satellite phone Fischer had given me from the console and fired it up. Thirteen messages. Sufficient so if things didn't work out on Fischer's end, he'd cover his ass telling the bosses he'd left over a dozen voice mails. I listened to them, windows rolled up, vents open so we wouldn't sweat.

They started with flat demands. He asked where I was and what I was doing. After four or five messages, his voice became more strident, his irritation clear. The last several voice mails communicated direct threats. Yada, yada. I turned the phone back off with plans for its use later down the road.

I checked my personal phone, relieved to find it without texts or missed calls or voice mails. Marilyn Townsend lurked in the background, but my disappearance's time frame remained short, and she wouldn't attempt to contact me until our situation bubbled to the surface. I was one of a hundred items on her plate. A Case Lee shift into incognito mode wasn't new and wouldn't shoot any red flares. Yet.

We flew past Chone. I'd visited once, and twice increased the odds I'd get remembered. Bart stared out the window and said, "Chocolates."

We'd driven past many cacao groves.

"What about chocolate?"

"Ruthie would appreciate some Ecuadorian chocolate."

"Maybe when we stop for gas. I also need to get you some clothes. It'll get chilly at night in the mountains."

"I overheard you say Colombia. What will we do in Colombia?"

"Make our way north. Back toward the States."

Since Bart appeared amenable for a chat, I pressed for answers. Answers that would both satiate my curiosity and, perhaps, reframe our movement forward.

"If you would, please, tell me about the discovery you and Ruth made. In layman's terms."

I sought either a different take than Ruth's, or at least concurrence. He remained silent, stared out the windshield, and muttered, "Oh, dear."

I didn't press as several miles rolled past, but "Oh, dear," wouldn't cut it. Whether or not Bart understood it, a quid pro quo element remained in play. I'd retrieved him from a lethal situation, and he owed me honest answers. Ruth had emphasized their discovery's theoretical nature, and had intimated that the physics side, Bart's bailiwick, held stumbling blocks. All I wanted was big picture—would their head-scrambling technology work?

"Hubris." He spoke with a soft tone to himself. "Yes. Hubris."

"Would you mind elaborating?"

"Such a wonderful collaboration." His head turned as he addressed me. "All these years and we had never faced such an opportunity."

"For a major discovery?"

"No. No, not discovery. An opportunity to work together."

He went on about their collaboration and the incumbent excitement and the scuttlebutt that grew around their work. Heady stuff, I supposed, although he dipped into the technology with terminology that left me in the dust.

"When we presented a research paper at a conference in DC, it created overwhelming experiences."

"I'm sure."

"Overwhelming experiences for us both."

"Right."

"There were obstacles, of course."

"I bet."

"Our findings presented those obstacles, as any honest assessment would."

"Sure."

"I discussed those challenges with fellow scientists and was quite open about them."

"So, we're talking technical challenges, right?"

"Oh, my, yes. I should note Ruth's work remained spot on. The physics portion, the engineered physical actualization, presented barriers. Barriers I could not overcome."

Somewhere within his ramble nested truth, and it showed signs of leaking out like a bike tire going flat. My goal—don't hinder Bart's stream of consciousness.

"You mentioned hubris. How did hubris play into all this?"

He delivered a loud sniff and wiped his nose with a shirt sleeve. I fished in the console and pulled a semiclean rag and handed it over. "Use this."

"Thank you. We had never experienced such treatment."

"What treatment, Bart?"

"People from all over the world had such keen interest in our presentation."

"At the DC conference?"

"Yes. At the DC conference. My goodness."

Under other circumstances, I'd fight to restrain myself and not throttle the guy. But we had a long trip ahead so I played along and allowed the slow air leak to continue.

"My goodness what?"

"A weather change ahead."

As we climbed, gained elevation, thick clouds sat as a wet blanket on the horizon. Good. I wished for low light conditions and rain. Those MSS cats would haul it our way at some point. Given the Chicom system, they first worked through layers of approval. Then assembled their team and headed out. Best guess for our intersection—Santo Domingo, a midsized city. I'd exit there and purchase Bart's clothing and hope the enemy would stay on the highway and bypass us. I was flying on a wing and a prayer, but a diversion was well worth a shot. Meanwhile, oncoming semitrucks would appear around every seventh or eighth curve, the painted dividing line a mere suggestion. It would become worse as we neared the highway's steepest parts.

"It'll get cloudy and rainy. We're climbing. Tell me about the DC conference."

"It was quite something."

"I'm sure. Out of curiosity, Bart, did the white paper you and Ruth submitted imply any military application?"

"Oh, no! None whatsoever. We simply explored a unique niche. You might say a novel blending of biomedical science and engineering physics. Its intended application, if successful, would improve lives."

That's not how others viewed it, bud.

"So you garnered a great deal of interest?"

"Oh, yes. A scientist from England appeared very interested."

MI6. A British spook.

"And a scientist from Israel, and China, and even Russia. It was quite exhilarating."

Israel's Mossad, check. China's MSS, check. Russia's SVR, check.

"I'm sure. Anyone else?"

"Anyone else?"

"Did anyone else show keen interest in the presentation?"

"Two men from the US government. They took Ruthie and me out for dinner."

DIA spooks.

"Was one named William Barrett?"

"I am afraid I do not remember their names. But we saw them again after Ruthie and I returned to Stanford."

"What did they talk about then?"

"I must say they were much less friendly."

No shit, Sherlock.

"How so?"

"They insisted we consider moving to a new location and complete our research. Yes. Very insistent."

"What happened after you met the second time?"

"The North Koreans kidnapped me the next day."

"And Ruth then fled to Idaho?"

"Yes. I know how she accomplished it without being followed. We have a friend with an airplane."

Man, a big miss by US intelligence. Maybe they assumed the Halls didn't have friends.

"About the hubris, Bart. What did you mean?"

He sighed.

"There are limits, you see. Limits on our knowledge."

"Okay."

"You are familiar with quantum mechanics?"

Hoo, boy. Off the deep end. I tried pulling him back.

"Not really. I wasn't a science guy at school."

"Ah. But you are familiar with Newtonian physics?"

"At somewhere around fifty-thousand-feet. Like Newton's three laws of motion, right?"

"Correct. They do not apply, or at least do not add value to the realm we were theorizing."

"Okay."

"Newtonian physics does not describe accurately object behaviors traveling near the speed of light, or interacting as subatomic particles."

"Gotcha."

I didn't have jack, but the slow leak continued.

"Relativity and quantum physics are required in those non-Newtonian realms. And there are limits with those theories."

"And you ran into those limits?"

"Goodness, yes. I ran into those limits. I should add this is nothing new and is the reason we made such theoretical exercises public. Perhaps other minds, whether in collaboration or in isolation, could explore and find a solution."

A picture developed. Ruth and Bart treated, for the first time in their lives, like rock stars. Swept up in the adulation, they—or at least Bart—exaggerated their findings and sidestepped the limits he'd run into. Pride and vanity. Hubris. He'd lit the spookville fuse and they'd circled, drooling at the prospects of a new superweapon. Not the first time, and for sure not the last.

"I want you to do something for me, Bart."

"I had no idea such a fuss would occur. Then they kidnapped me."

"Yes, and we're not out of the woods yet."

"And they went after my Ruthie!"

The waterworks started again as his shoulders shook. He used the dirty rag to wipe tears and blow his nose. I left him alone, figuring there was little I could say to cushion reality. And I cut the guy slack as he recovered from a harrowing experience.

Five minutes later, he asked, "We cannot return to Stanford, can we? Or Stanley?"

"Not now. Maybe later, over time."

The waterworks showed signs of firing up again, so I said, "I want you to write another white paper. An addendum for the one you and Ruth submitted at the conference. It won't kill the fire, but it will sure turn down the heat."

"Why?"

"Admit the issues you encountered are insurmountable. Not everyone will buy it, but it'll force a second look at your theoretical application. It's your best shot at you and Ruth someday having a normal life."

"I would wish for nothing more. Are you quite sure she is safe?"

"Quite sure. Is your laptop charged? You can start on it now."

As he pulled the device from his satchel, I added another safety feature. We'd arrive in Santo Domingo within the hour, and any oncoming vehicle could contain unfriendlies. If MSS operators appeared, I'd cut loose on them in a heartbeat.

"If I tell you to duck, don't screw around. This is important. Please pay attention."

"Duck?"

"Hunker down. Duck out of sight below the dashboard."

"Why?"

"It may keep you from another kidnapping. Understood?"

"Yes. Yes, I understand. How will I know when to duck?"

"When I tell you. Okay?"

He replied with a serious nod and fired his laptop. The white paper creation would keep him busy while I focused on maintaining his freedom. And maintaining a healthy and vertical position for Case Lee Inc.'s lone employee.

Chapter 29

I gave every oncoming vehicle other than a semitruck a hard inspection when sighted. Not much traffic headed in either direction on the highway, which helped. All the tight curves didn't. On the short straights, I maintained a decent shot at recognizing the enemy. They'd come after us with late-model vehicles, and high odds multiple SUVs. This winnowed ninety percent of oncoming traffic from the equation. As a newer-model vehicle approached, I focused on glimpsing an Asian face or two behind the windshield. If sighted, I'd stomp the accelerator. The road, narrow and winding and treacherous, had few turnouts, which left the enemy two options. Continue driving until they could safely pull over and reverse course, or perform a high-speed one-eighty in the road's center. With the occasional semitruck roaring past, and fog and mist and MSS's tendency toward caution, I'd put money on the first option, but you never knew.

We made Santo Domingo, and I exited as the worry meter backed off. I gave us forty-five minutes or so to futz around in the city, a sweet window of time where our pursuers could shoot past on the highway. I bought Bart socks, underwear, pants, shirts, toiletries, a duffel bag, and a waterproof jacket. I also grabbed several blankets—when we hit Colombia it made for a twenty-four-hour day, and we'd require shut-eye. Plus a box of chocolates, at Bart's insistence. Once we filled up with gas, I reviewed the current situation.

"The Chinese are after us."

He had pulled his laptop from the satchel.

"Thank you for the purchases. Goodness, it is nice having those items. Quite nice. Thank you. The Chinese? What happened with the North Koreans?"

"You saw what happened with the North Koreans. I doubt any more are in pursuit. It's been kicked upstairs."

"What has been kicked upstairs?"

His rabbit hole showed no termination point, so I kept things simple.

"The Chinese sent the North Koreans after you and Ruth. The North Koreans failed. Now the Chinese are in the States, looking for Ruth. And they're here in Ecuador, chasing us. Right now. Guaranteed."

They may have hired proxies for the US pursuit, but I left it unsaid. Too much geopolitical wrangling for Bart. The Chinese may have sent more Norks into the US. Kept their hands clean with their largest trading partner and the country that owed them over a trillion dollars in national debt servicing. Don't piss off your best customer when they buy so much of your stuff and owe you a massive chunk of change. Outside the US, on turf foreign for both, it remained Wild West time, with MSS not hesitant to pull figurative and literal triggers.

"They wish to kidnap me again?"

"Yes. And kill me. Understood?"

He nodded at the windshield several times.

"This is most serious business."

"Yes, it is. Now, when I yell duck, what will you do?"

"I will lower my body in this seat."

"Good, Bart. Good."

We took off. With dusk a couple hours away, the weather had worsened, and high odds it wouldn't improve as we climbed into the Andes Mountains. Drifting fog patches joined the low clouds and misty rain. Our route along the narrow and treacherous highway represented a "been there, done that, and won't do it again" experience. Tight curves, thousand-foot drops, few guardrails, and no road shoulder. The traffic remained light, and those of us traveling turned on headlights. Bart continued tapping away at his laptop.

I hadn't lied about the Chicoms painting a bull's-eye on my back. I'd run into them multiple times around the world. They knew my name and face—the latter a disconcerting turn as facial recognition software became more ubiquitous within the clandestine world. Even unrecognized, they'd sure know, if they spotted Bart, that I was the guy who carried the prize. They wouldn't hesitate to blow me away.

"An excellent approach writing this. Yes. An excellent approach. Our work's reality should have been an open book. I failed to make it so." He twisted his head in my direction as I white-knuckled uphill. "You are a good guy."

"Thanks."

I picked at operational logistics while focused on the road and oncoming traffic. MSS wouldn't have the required flying equipment for this weather, this terrain. It took a specialty chopper with all-weather capabilities. Yeah, the Chicoms had helicopters and planes and vehicles and boats in Ecuador, no doubt. But an all-weather chopper for battle operations like the Little Bird chopper US Special Ops used wouldn't sit in China's Ecuadorian infrastructure. As a military tool, high odds the US wouldn't have one in place either, because of political optics. In contested geographical areas around the world—war zones, revolutions, conflicted areas—sure. But not Ecuador, and especially on such a short notice ops like this one. So my gut said Delta, too, would use vehicular travel.

The big unknown—would US ops have tapped into MSS. Yeah, both sides would play plant-the-bug on vehicles at their respective embassies and any operational houses or offices around Quito. Bugs with GPS trackers. And both sides would perform regular electronic sniffing sweeps, finding and removing most if not all the bugs. Electronic three-card monte, ongoing and less than effective. But they'd both have human assets, watchers, assigned to the embassies and in-country ops centers who'd hit the alarm if a pile of MSS or Delta operators scrambled and hit the road. And MSS had damn sure scrambled when the Nork called from the beach shack, with appropriate upstairs channels satisfied by now. Instinct and prior experience told me Delta would have scrambled as well with MSS's movement. Both now barreled down the Andes. Toward me. What a freakin' hair ball. A chance existed they'd both passed along the highway while I shopped in Santo Domingo. I had no feel, none, on the odds of such an occurrence.

I drafted behind a large semitruck as it struggled uphill. No passing lanes, wet pavement, with constant mist and fog drifts as sunset approached. Combined, it prohibited sane passing opportunities, restricted to those rare straight sections. Even then, a dangerous maneuver as an oncoming vehicle or, God forbid, a semitruck approached without their headlights on ensured a horrific crash. And dead travelers. So I limped along behind the truck and waited for a decent passing opportunity.

One of life's double takes presented as I took another curve and recognized the football-field-sized cleared area on my right where the massive boulder had landed and slow-walked across the road and down the steep ravine. Ahead, at the clearing's end, and just before another curve, an Indigenous man squatted in the downhill lane's center. He wore only shorts, no shoes, his long hair stringing in the icy drizzle. Arms upraised, eyes closed, mouth wide open and moving as he delivered a chant. A death chant. The next downhill vehicle rounding the nearby curve either wouldn't see him in time to swerve or couldn't avoid him because of oncoming traffic. This guy wanted to die. Perhaps he had taken a local hallucinogenic or drank too much local booze. Or maybe the enormous boulder I'd watched had taken out his village, his family, far below, and he'd had enough. Or a combination of all three. Hard to say. What wasn't hard to say was I couldn't let the poor bastard become a mangled mess on the highway.

Such a surreal vignette. I swerved onto the large dirt-and-gravel cleared area, slammed the brakes, and skidded to a stop. As in an amphitheater, sheer rock walls over a thousand feet high surrounded the area. At their base, rubble and rocks and smaller boulders—dozens the size of my vehicle—stood sentinel. Across the highway, a thousand-foot drop into an Andean green dripping ravine. Draped with drizzle and fog and impending darkness, an uphill vehicle appeared as a mechanical ghost, visible for a few moments, then gone, lost, in the otherworldly environment.

"Stay put, Bart."

I sprinted toward the soaked, squatting man; his arms were upraised, and his beseeching death wails sounded loud. But not as loud as the

235

semitruck's downshifted grinding gears as it rounded the curve, headlights appearing as two ghostly eyes. Its air horn blared at the sudden sight of the asphalt-planted man with arms reaching skyward. No time, no time, gotta move.

Five sprinted steps made the highway, three more and I swept up the man, the speeding semi's presence already in my peripheral vision. No time, no time. Still at a sprint and cradling the guy, I dived over the highway's edge, tumbling, as the truck sped past with horn still blaring. Eight or nine tumbles across wet vegetation and biting stones, stopping with an extended slide. Below, more of the same, the ravine's bottom lost within the drizzle and fog. Oh man, close one. A trail existed somewhere for this cat to have climbed up from his village, but I focused on not sliding any farther. The Indigenous man continued his wail, limp, lying on his side, unengaged with immediate events. His inner demons or abject grief left him disconnected from material reality.

Scooting side hill, I laid him against a larger boulder's uphill side and ensured he wouldn't tumble down the ravine. Then I began a foot-and-hand-grab ascent, sliding one measure for every three gained, and unclear on my next steps: leave him to battle his torment or carry him back into the SUV and seek the nearest town—while weighing the ramifications on our great escape. Another vehicle passed above me, headed uphill. I climbed until head-level with the no-shoulder highway and captured Bart as he stood between our vehicle and the asphalt, concerned, staring my way without his jacket, soaked.

"Tell me what I must do to help," he called. "I have no familiarity with such situations."

"It's okay. Get back in the vehicle."

Bo would claim cosmic convergence. I'd call it raw and shitty luck. On my left, rounding the curve and emerging from the mist headed downhill, three red SUVs traveled near bumper-to-bumper and hauled ass. Until they came abreast of Bart and my protruding prairie dog head at hard-top level. I didn't draw their attention. But Bart sure as hell did. The occupants of the three vehicles reacted instantly, excited and pointing. I saw hand gestures. And Chinese faces. Oh, man.

One razor-thin silver lining—with wet pavement and zero room for error, they traveled too fast to jerk the steering wheel left and enter the large, flat pullout area. The nearest turnaround pullout past us? No telling. I hadn't logged those small indentations against the looming mountains or those spots overlooking steep ravines. A half mile? Mile? Oh, man. Either way, their passage signaled exit time, and right freakin' then.

Scrambling like a mad man, I pulled onto the asphalt and dashed toward Bart.

"Get in now!"

He blinked as reply. No time, gotta move. I grabbed his arm and pulled him toward his open passenger door.

"Those were the bad guys, Bart! Get in!"

He did, eyes now wide and fearful. I fired the engine, rolled to the open area's edge, and waited for an uphill-headed sedan's passing. I'd haul it like a bat out of hell on a road that defined dangerous under the best of conditions. Wet, slick, with poor visibility and perhaps stuck behind a slow-moving semi—those MSS cats would arrive on my butt in short order. Then what? A mad car chase up the Andes?

Screw that noise. Enough. A job, a commitment, boiled down to the here and now. A quest I'd stumbled into for reasons simple and without nuance. Right and wrong. Those bastards now seeking a place for a course reversal somewhere down the mountain belonged with a group, an organization, which had sent proxies to kidnap the guy sitting beside me. Then sent more after Ruth. All on US turf. My turf. And now it had come to this, here on neutral ground. They'd shown their hand. Ten or twelve well-armed MSS agents committed to recapturing Bart. And killing me. Enough.

The sheer rock wall's base, a rough half-circle, sat littered with rubble and rocks and boulders. The boulders varied from waist- to head-high and even larger. I threw it into reverse, backed into the killing field, and edged alongside a vehicle-sized chunk of mountain, staying visible when the three MSS vehicles approached the area. No point hiding. Time to end it.

Alright, you SOBs. You want to tangle with Case Lee? Bring it.

Chapter 30

"Get your jacket on, Bart."

I exited the SUV, threw on my battle vest, strapped on the pistol holster, snatched up three extra magazines for the M4A1 rifle and two extra 40mm grenades, then looped the pirate pistol grenade launcher around my neck. I holstered the 9mm pistol without the silencer—nothing subtle about upcoming actions—and adjusted the rifle's sight magnification to 4X. Then ensured I'd racked a rifle round. Good to go.

"What are we doing?"

"Get your jacket on. Hurry."

"I do not understand."

I circled the SUV, opened the passenger door, grabbed his jacket, took his elbow, and led his exit from the vehicle.

"The Chinese whipped past us headed downhill. They spotted you, so they'll return any minute. Not your fault, Bart. Simple bad luck."

As he slid his jacket on, he asked, wide-eyed, "You intend to fight them?"

"Yes. And wipe them out. Don't worry. C'mon." He remained frozen. "I'll find you a safe spot. They won't shoot at you. They'll shoot at me."

With a firm grip on his arm, I led him into the rubble and boulders at the rock wall's base. Twenty paces from the parked SUV, I found a tight spot with sufficient protection. An enormous boulder three feet from the wall's base.

"Lay down here."

239

"I believe we should discuss this approach to our dilemma."

"Talking's over. Lay down."

He did. I sympathized with the guy, thrust into another live-fire situation hours after the beach firefight. Which prompted my final instructions.

"When you hear gunshots—and you will hear gunshots—stay put. Do not get up and walk away. Do not leave this spot. Hug the ground until I come and get you. Understood?"

Wide eyes behind owlish glasses stared back, unblinking.

"Bart?"

"Yes. Yes, I understand. However, there is but one of you and many, I assume, of them."

"Not an issue. Stay put. It'll be okay."

I hustled farther into the half-circle, kept an eye on the highway, and sought an advantageous tactical area. Another sedan whisked past, headed downhill, followed by a semitruck. Then silence again. The Indigenous guy I'd tumbled down the canyon with had stopped his wailing. A change of heart, maybe. Didn't matter now.

I found a large, jumbled area filled with rocks and boulders that extended eight or nine paces from the wall's base and provided both excellent cover and premium firing positions. On one knee, I waited. Ten or twelve hardened MSS operators in three vehicles. They'd face deep shit if Bart was killed or injured, so caution would rule their assault. Good. They'd find out soon enough my operational position, yet remain unsure about his. I'd use their uncertainty as a tactical advantage.

One item stood clear—no negotiations, no ifs, no sidestepping reality. Men would live or die and no middle ground. I'd strike first and establish those ground rules. The wall opposite my position, a hundred yards away, loomed vertical and dark, its top lost in the clouds. Highway to the half-circle's back wall, fifty yards. The killing floor, with boulders and rocks aplenty for fire and maneuver. I shoved all noncombat thoughts and considerations away as mental white noise, and waited.

Ninety seconds later, they approached at breakneck speed, my vehicle on full display at the open area's far side. They flew into the arena, braked, and all three red SUVs made a hard right turn, headed for the area opposite my vehicle where they'd dismount and hunt. I had other plans.

The lead vehicle turned sideways to me as tires skidded and kicked up wet gravel. I sent a bullet through the driver's window. A headshot, which also sounded the starter's pistol for this little fandango. With an instant reaction the front seat passenger ducked, grabbed the wheel, and kept the vehicle's turn active. These were pros. The lone back seat passenger dropped from sight as well. I shifted aim toward the other two SUVs. They'd completed their skidding turn and roared straight for the protective boulders on their side of the amphitheater with all MSS operators' heads now low, not offering a target. Definitely pros.

The first SUV continued its roll forward as the passenger seat operator steered, unable to touch the brakes. He headed straight toward a large boulder collection a quarter-way along the rock face and, just before impact, bailed. Along with the back seat operator. They both tumbled, the front seat guy protected by the now-crashed vehicle. The back seat hitter popped up and started a wild and final dash across the few yards of open area before accessing protective stone. He didn't make it. The first shot cut him down, the second finished him. Two down, nine or ten left.

As I swung back toward the other two SUVs, they both entered another tight turn, drifted on the wet gravel, and stopped alongside another massive boulder patch. They opened the doors on their vehicles' wall-facing side and bailed. Their SUVs protected them and left me without a shot. Damn. They were good. I ducked back down and repositioned several yards away, sighting through a two-inch slit between small, slick boulders. The drizzle increased, the light grew dimmer, the environment somehow haunting, alien, as vast mountains, covered in green, stood lost in the overcast.

Silence. They gathered their resources, sent hand signals, planned an attack. I knew the routine well.

"Is it over?"

Bart's call sounded across the arena. I eased back and hunkered down, hidden. Delivering a verbal admonishment from my position guaranteed return fire, with some likely directed at my two-inch sighting crack. Shit.

"Bart! Listen up. No more talking. Remain silent. Please."

He did. But they now knew his and my general location and assault rifle crosshairs would now scour the rocks and metals around me. They'd also assume the man who called the question was the scientist. An operator—they understood at this point I fit the bill—wouldn't have given up an unknown position's advantage unless an admonition required delivery. Move time. They'd send several men around the cirque's perimeter, try and outflank me. The surviving MSS operator from the first SUV already positioned a quarter-way around and would join with another two or three as they worked their way toward me. The key—greet them as they made their move. It would leave Bart alone but not exposed, and if one or all the remaining enemy decided a mad dash toward the scientist across a hundred yards of open ground was a sound approach, fine. I'd cut them down before they made it twenty paces.

The ones who worked their flanking maneuver shifted positions, hidden behind their wall-ensconced boulder fields. The battle now presented us all with whack-a-mole tactics. Focused on my own quick hidden movement, glued against the perimeter, I headed toward the cirque's back wall. Take out the two, three, or four intent on flanking me as they made their way in my direction. With a big difference. Me headed for them was the last thing they'd expect. A more standard effort on my part was hunker down, wait for darkness, attempt an escape. Not gonna happen, boys.

A sedan headed downhill slowed as it passed the open area containing one wrecked SUV, two others parked nearby, and a third, mine, nestled against the opposite side. Then a semitruck followed suit as it slowed and sounded its air horn. I kept moving. Rapid low crouch progress when larger boulders allowed it, a fast crawl when small stone chunks provided two or three feet of cover. One MSS operator, perhaps the team lead, hollered in Chinese toward the back wall, toward his flanking team, with orders or directions. Then silence.

With all sensory input redlined, breath low and quiet, adrenaline meter near-pegged from anticipation rather than concern, I halted progress a quarter-way through the back wall's curve, belly-flat, weapon aimed ahead. They were nearby—a sense, a feel. I kept one eye focused through the scope while the other took in the larger picture. One minute passed, then two. Nothing. Nada.

The situational lighting dimmed as dusk wrapped the area, the drizzle cold and steady as low fog patches drifted past. Soon. The trigger point where I had a view of the bastards. I picked up movement noise thirty paces away, cloth against stone, combat boots on broken rock and gravel. But still no sighting. They remained glued against wet stone, protected, as they progressed toward me.

Then the wailing started. The Indigenous guy kicked off his death chant, still below the highway, somewhere down the ravine. The lamentations, haunting, drifted into the dark cirque and added a surreal mood to the killing vignette. Eerie enough that a flanking opponent showed his head and searched for the lament's source. Big mistake. Another headshot canceled his birth certificate, which brought a wall of automatic fire in my general direction with no effect other than identifying relative positions for the flanking team's three remainders. My shot also brought the attention of the operators who'd remained across the open space from Bart, evidenced with a few potshots toward me from their position.

If more daylight remained, I'd have worked the guys at my front, picked them off, then continued my path forward, circling and flanking the gang hunkered down across from Bart. A deadly, methodical stalk. But for someone this outnumbered, darkness threw too many variables into the battle. But I owned a tool for accelerating events.

It remained slung around my neck and at my side. The sawed-off grenade launcher. A finger-over-finger retrieval along the weapon's lanyard placed it in my left hand while I remained focused through the rifle's scope. Then a slight head-lift, using both eyes to isolate the best location for the grenade's strike, and a quick weapon shift into my right hand. Hammer cocked, trigger pulled, and hell sent downrange.

The chopped weapon—four or five pounds heavier with a full stock and barrel—kicked like a mule as the flying grenade struck as intended, against the massive stone wall and near their position. The blast: deafening. The effect: immediate, killing all three. The aftereffect: unintended and a son of a bitch. Like a glacier calving, a monstrous slice from the carved-out mountain wall separated and fell. Toward the three dead men. And toward me.

THE SAWTOOTH JOB

Chapter 31

The explosive rock-splitting crack from high above freaked me. A thousand-ton stone slice emerged through the fog and drizzle far up the mountainside, headed straight toward me, kicking my adrenaline meter into overdrive. I didn't remember the leap up and mad dash with every fiber of my being, but would recall that time slowed, floated. A half-second became ten seconds with speed and movement the lone lifeboat available. The ground impact behind me lifted my body midstride and popped me higher during the crazed sprint. At my mental periphery, fired shots struck rock and stone as I flew, angry bee-buzz sounds as bullets whipped past, inches away. Dim awareness that cargo-container-sized boulders landed, bounced, within the immediate surroundings. A kitchen-stove-sized rock slammed into my path, half a pace ahead. I tried leaping it, caught my toe, and flew forward, tumbling. The acrobatic act likely saved my life.

The remaining Chicom operators went after me like in a carnival shooting gallery. Eventually they'd have struck gold. The forward tumble sent me behind protective rocks and boulders and away from their line of fire. Smaller stones, basketball-sized, continued raining down as I pressed against my protective boulder shield and prayed one didn't land a direct hit. The deadly deluge lasted five or six seconds. I edged away from my tucked-in position and searched forward, toward Bart. No sign any huge stones had landed on his area, although I didn't have a direct view. I crawled forward and sought a shooting position. At least five enemy operators remained across the littered-with-rocks battlefield.

Then the cavalry arrived. They would have felt the avalanche's impact, even in their vehicle and a half-mile away, causing them to slow down. A single black SUV rolled past the area, a rapid assessment was made, and they pulled off the highway into the battle area just past the MSS operators' positions and behind a protective stone shield of boulders. The Delta team. Five operators leapt out in full battle gear, spread out, and went to work doing what they do best. Clean house.

Whether they'd followed the MSS operators with an overhead big bird—three MSS SUVs running bumper-to-bumper in tight formation would have created a distinctive thermal signature—or whether a planted GPS tracker on one of the red SUVs had led them here, I'd never know. And didn't care. I was just happy to see them. And the added opportunity they presented.

Delta came at the MSS operators from their flank, along the wall near the highway. Fire and maneuver, overwhelming firepower, always on the attack. An awe-inspiring exhibition as they swarmed, moving as one. An immutable creature, terrifying, with a deadly efficiency unmatched on the planet.

I could have stretched out and observed with admiration and pleasure, but a slim window of opportunity had opened, and I formulated a plan. The two operable MSS SUVs faced perpendicular—perfect for a tire sidewall shot. Across from me, the Delta team's assault delivered sharp cracks, both single shot and full automatic, which echoed off the cirque's walls. Time was short as Delta would wipe them out in seconds. I put a bullet through one red SUV's front tire, then the other. Scrambling up and ignoring the chaos a hundred paces across from me, I hauled it toward Bart and found the poor guy huddled where I'd told him to stay, shaking.

"Get up, Bart. Get up now, please. We gotta go."

He remained frozen.

"C'mon bud. We gotta move fast. Take my hand."

"There is still gunfire."

"It's okay. Here."

I extended my hand. He stared at it several seconds as wheels turned, and then took a weak grip. I hauled him upright and hustled him over to our vehicle, shoving the scientist inside. As I hustled around the SUV, the ultraviolence wound down across the way. A single shot, then another. Delta operators delivered the last coups de grace. Then silence. No wails from my down-ravine guy—he'd tumbled farther down or settled with his demons. I'd never know.

What I did know was the next twenty seconds held a dead-man coin flip. I counted on special ops brotherhood status, but times change. Braced against the SUV, I sighted on the Delta team's vehicle. The front tires pointed straight at me and afforded a tread shot.

"Don't do it, Lee!"

The team leader I'd met at the hangar in DC glommed on to my intent. I squeezed the trigger, and the rifle's crack signified a twenty-minute lead while they changed the tire. Or would cause a received headshot from an active Delta operator.

I lowered the weapon. Five hardened operators started at me across the almost-dark misty killing field. Not a one raised their weapon. I shrugged and lifted a single hand, palm up, signaling an apology. Then climbed behind the wheel. Whether they'd risk knocking me out with a tire shot, unknown. They didn't. I stomped the accelerator, gravel and small stones flew, and we headed farther into the Andes Mountains.

"Is the shooting over?" Bart asked as he twisted in his seat for a rear window view.

"For now."

He absorbed the statement, and said, "A good guy. Thank you. But I must say, your directives can be contradictory. Do not move. Then move fast. Are the Chinese who pursued us now dead?"

"Yes."

"Who were those other men?"

"US special forces."

"Did they wish to capture me?"

"Yes."

"Ah. Thank you again. From both Ruthie and me. Thank you."

"No worries. On to Quito."

Bart pulled his laptop more from habit than intent. He stared out the windshield, silent, as we wound our way through the mountains and exited onto the somewhat flat stretch leading into Quito. I punched it when the highway changed into four lanes and attempted to ease the lingering disquiet from the firefight. Not the battle itself. Yeah, a helluva firefight, and I acknowledged luck had played a part in saving my rear end. But something wasn't right.

Organizational brotherhood goes only so far, and those Delta operators had had ample opportunity to place a bullet or three in my tires, stopping me in my tracks. Then take Bart and leave my sorry butt behind. It didn't jibe. I suspected behind-the-curtain string pulling—nothing unusual given the crowd I associated with. And contracted with.

On Quito's outskirts a truck stop offered added assurance for a clean backtrail. I filled up with gas, took the satellite phone Fischer had given me, turned it on, and reenabled the GPS. Wandering over toward refueling semitrucks, I addressed a guy beside his rig as the diesel pump dinged.

"Where're you headed?" I asked, delivered with a friendly smile.

"Cuenca."

An Ecuadorian city far south. Opposite my intended direction.

"Long drive. Are you doing it tonight?"

"Yes."

It opened the floodgates for a long grievance list about his job, wife, and life in general.

"I have a side job for you. Maybe it will help your situation."

Fischer's satellite phone exchanged hands. The trucker stared at it, then me, unsure. I pulled a Benjamin from my pocket and explained.

"Place it in your truck's cab. The passenger seat works fine. And do nothing other than drive it to Cuenca. If it rings, don't answer it. In Cuenca, throw it away or keep it. I don't care."

I extended the Benjamin.

"That is all?"

"That's all."

"Issues with a woman?" he asked, smiling.

"Exactly. Will you do what I ask?"

"What does she look like?" His smile widened. "I may talk with her."

"Looks aren't everything."

He pursed his lips, nodded, and said, "True. True. I will do what you ask. Since I have my own women troubles, it would be best if I did not talk with her."

"A sound strategy, my friend."

He pocketed the cash. After purchasing road food and water, we took off and wove through tiny streets and back alleys, losing, if it existed, any thermal satellite tracking of my SUV. Behind schedule, we'd make the Colombian border past midnight. Our next hurdle. My Quito fixer may have compromised us and, for sufficient cash, detailed my plans with the Company or MSS or both. Even without him spilling the beans, both organizations might assume we'd head north and place assets at the smuggler bypass roads. One slight advantage—my fixer had pointed out multiple routes, and I doubted either the Company or Chicoms had sufficient resources for covering all the bases. But you never freakin' knew.

An hour into our drive Bart snored, woke, and asked if he could call Ruth. No issues, except I explained he shouldn't mention guns, or gunfire, or men with guns, or explosions, or massive rock avalanches. It would worry her. And for God's sake, don't mention dead bodies.

"These things are behind us now," he said, confused. "We have escaped."

"Maybe. Just don't mention those items. Understand?"

"Why did you say maybe?"

"Everything remains a maybe until you're back with Ruth. Sorry. That's just the way it is."

He stared at me for several seconds, then laid his left hand on my shoulder and squeezed.

"Variables, good guy. I understand. On the call, I will mention you have shown remarkable ability when handling the variables."

Their conversation lasted fifteen minutes and contained a lightness, a relief, missing from previous chats. I wore a wry smile listening to Bart's half, pleased with the change and positive perspective. A feel-good moment, and more than sufficient reward instead of kudos or accolades. A sweet couple, swept up, shaken like a dog with a rag doll, and now with a light at the tunnel's end. Wonderful stuff.

"Your friend wishes to speak with you," Bart said, handing me the phone after he and Ruth exchanged goodbyes.

"Well done, you," Marcus said, cutting to the chase. "I'll assume your activities included a payback element."

"Two. Norks and Chicoms. The latter engaged a team of hombres you and I once belonged with."

"They didn't claim the prize?"

Bart Hall, the prize.

"A weird situation, that."

"Weird squats right in your wheelhouse. What's the future hold?"

"Working on it."

"Once again, I admire a man with a solid plan. Don't sweat events here. Everything's copacetic."

"I appreciate it, bud. And I'll let you know our status over the next twenty-four hours."

"Roger that. Watch your topknot, Case. Don't get yourself killed over a goodwill mission."

"Such thoughts top my priority list."

We signed off. Four hours on a decent highway, through Ibarra, and we approached the border with no issues. During the drive I squeezed and twisted and wrung out plausible scenarios until dry. It didn't relieve the unease. But I stuck with the plan and figured the Colombian city of Pasto, sixty miles across the border, a decent reconnoiter location. From there, I hoped to get the hell out of Dodge via aircraft. Maybe not make it stateside, but at least depart Colombia and head farther north. Keep moving. Lose any remnant tails on my butt. I considered shooting the Clubhouse a fixer request but even Jules, who never ceased to amaze, wouldn't have tendrils into a small isolated western Colombian city like Pasto.

Miles clicked past, the drive uneventful, and the night sky cleared. And Bart, reflective, chose our calm interlude as an appropriate time for personal exchanges.

"Have you ever been in love?" he asked.

"I have."

Rae, my murdered wife. Thoughts and remembrances would still bubble up from years past. Memories embraced then tucked away, locked, for private consumption. My relationship with Jess hadn't reached the same level, but the possibility existed.

"It is a peculiar thing. Love."

"It can be, I suppose."

"It overrides all else—food, shelter, creature comforts. It runs contrary to basic needs. It is, I am afraid, beyond my comprehension."

"Maybe it's beyond anyone's comprehension."

We remained silent for a while.

"Comfort," he said, speaking toward the windshield. "Comfort and consideration and familiarity. But more than that. Much more."

"Yeah. It is."

"Ruthie and I are partners. You are familiar with the expression 'more than the sum of the parts'?"

"I am."

"Together, she and I create a larger human dimension. A yet unidentified energy, perhaps."

"Perhaps."

Several more miles clicked past in silence.

"Case."

"Yes?"

"Your name. I am very poor with names, and I apologize. It remains a challenging condition."

"It's okay."

"Tell me again your full name, please."

"Case Lee."

"Case Lee. Case Lee. May I address you as Case?"

I smiled wide. The awkward genius sitting next to me was, to his credit, trying.

"That works fine. Tell me about soaking in natural hot springs. What's the big deal?"

"Goodness. Well, they are best experienced nude."

"That right?"

"Oh, my, yes. The hydraulic flow one encounters, and full-body sensory immersion is enhanced when nude."

"How 'bout that."

I wouldn't review my soak with Ruth, leaving that up to her. We left the highway before hitting Tulcan, an Ecuadorian border town. I pulled over and consulted the Quito fixer's red-line-marked map. Bart, sleeping again, woke up when we stopped. A dark night, no town or village lights, and Andean Mountains—their massive outlines against a partly cloudy sky—greeted him as he stepped out and peed.

"It is quite cold out there," he said, returning. "Where are we?"

"We're at ten-thousand-feet elevation. Let's just be happy the mist and drizzle have left us. We're about four miles from the Colombian border."

I picked a route, less direct than the others, and began rolling.

"As a data point, you should know your headlights are off."

"Yeah, it's best they stay off for a while."

The dirt-and-gravel road narrowed, split, and split again. My route, more a track than a road, hugged mountainsides and pressed against fallen boulders. Drop-offs with the bottoms too far down in the darkness for sighting, on-and-off moonlight, a steady ten-to-fifteen miles per hour. And white-knuckle awareness that either a careless driving mistake or a run-in with the enemy spelled adios. Eyes adjusted to no-headlight darkness as intermittent moon- and starlight peeked from behind clouds, I peered forward and sought anomalies. Movement, a moonlight glint reflected off a vehicle, anything other than daunting mountains and vertical terrain. Well past midnight, fellow smugglers were the only other travelers I expected on this goat track. Bone-tired, grenade launcher on the dashboard, rifle between my legs, I was not in the mood to mess with anyone or anything.

"I believe Ecuador stares at us from our rearview mirror, Bart. Welcome to Colombia."

Relief? Yeah, to a degree. But I needed a break, a bit of luck, while moving forward. Everything ahead lacked definition, and our current isolation in the middle of nowhere didn't lend itself to comfort. Still, we'd made it this far, and in anyone's book that was no small shakes.

A mile or so later, on a long and gradual quarter-mile curve with vertical mountain on my right and a dark abyss on the left, moonlight reflected off an oncoming vehicle. Several hundred yards later, when a cloud break allowed full illumination from the moon, it became clear my new neighbor drove an old minivan. Couldn't see MSS in such a vehicle. A Delta team for sure could occupy such transport. Blend in with the environment, take on a plain Jane smuggler's appearance. Not a lot I could do other than continue a slow roll. No hiding spots, no turnouts, no option other than squeeze past each other if the approaching vehicle's occupants behaved. Not a given. If a Delta team, I stared at game, set, match. The best I could hope for under such a scenario was hitching a ride back stateside while they took Bart. And if the minivan held smugglers, no assurances they'd pass in peace. Whack two gringos, toss the bodies down the canyon, take the shiny new SUV, continue on their merry way. I lowered Bart's window.

"Pull your side mirror in as far as it will go."

He did, while asking a legit question.

"Do we now enter another dangerous situation?"

"Maybe. We'll see."

He sighed.

"Another Case maybe. My goodness."

With the vehicle's right side an inch or two away from the near-vertical mountainside, I pulled my side mirror in as well, draped the grenade launcher's lanyard over my head, killed the engine, and turned off the interior lights so they wouldn't shine when the door opened, and exited with assault rifle in hand.

"If shooting starts, duck. Okay?"

"I most certainly hope there is no more shooting."

"Me, too, bud. Me, too."

I stood at the SUV's rear, not hidden, but in a position for a quick protective sidestep if required. Then waited. The approaching vehicle had stopped when I climbed out, gaming their own assessment, and now again rolled our way. I could make out the driver and passenger silhouettes, along with piled boxes filling their van's interior. They eased up, the driver's window down as he, too, pulled in his sideview mirror. I stood with rifle butt on hip pointed skyward, finger on trigger. Not a direct threat, but a don't-mess-with-me posture. The front seat passenger held a sawed-off double barrel shotgun, the weapon's stock between his legs, barrels pointed at the van's ceiling as he mimicked my pose. Inches from my SUV, they performed a slow crawl past. The lone sounds within the dark, vast, and isolated environment—my vehicle's engine ticking as it cooled and their van's protesting squeaks from an overused chassis. The driver halted as he pulled even with me. I stood three feet from his window.

"Buenas noches."

Good evening. He fired a cigarette after addressing me.

"Buenas noches," I replied.

"American?"

My conversational Spanish held an unavoidable gringo accent. Couldn't be helped.

"Yes. And you two? Colombian or Ecuadorian?"

"This would depend on the situation and who asked."

He and the passenger both chuckled. I remained silent.

"A good night for travel," he continued. "You will find the way ahead clear."

"As will you."

Our confab over, information shared, he nodded, eased off the brakes, and rolled forward.

"Vaya con Dios," he said.

Go with God.

"You as well."

I waited until they'd traveled another hundred yards, progress slow, as an insignificant vignette played out in the awesome isolation of the Andes Mountains. Fatigue and a weird lost feeling washed over me. Adrift, lacking definitive direction—driven, I supposed, through weariness and jumbled events and an adrenaline meter pegged too often over the last eighteen hours. I lifted my head and cast a prayer of gratitude for making it this far. And asked for sevens or elevens on the next roll of the operational dice.

THE SAWTOOTH JOB

Chapter 32

The world's most powerful spook called past daybreak. We'd made a legit paved road without incident and traveled for another five miles before I pulled off onto a dirt track and traveled another mile, parking at a tumbledown shed. Seat backs reclined, blankets layered, windows cracked, we both grabbed five hours of shut-eye. At sunrise, the air cold and sky clear, we used bottled water to wash up. Dead brush provided sufficient firewood to heat water, and the instant coffee tasted better than fine.

Using my satellite-enabled laptop with a VPN and encrypted browser, I sussed out Pasto, fifty-odd miles away. At eight thousand feet elevation, the small city had an airport twenty miles north of town. Flat ground for a runway, I supposed, remained at a premium. The airport handled a few domestic flights and cargo planes. Cargo carriers piqued my interest. Those cats, with sufficient Benjamins waved around as incentive, often flew less than legal routes, loaded with much less than legal cargo.

I answered the phone when Marilyn Townsend called, having considered during the night's drive how to handle the inevitable. Thin ice, for sure, but the Company had played me like a marionette multiple times in the past, and I was in no mood for having my strings pulled again. I spoke first, as always.

"Morning, Director."

"I am most displeased, Mr. Lee."

"Me, too."

"Oh? And the source of your displeasure? I can assure you it pales in comparison to mine."

I considered the teeth-gnashing from the Company's Ecuador operations, placing me high on their, and Townsend's, shitlist.

"Something is going on I'm not privy to. You want to fill me in?"

The morning hadn't brought a lessening of spookville angst. Slim odds she'd add clarity, but worth a shot.

"I have neither the time nor inclination to tolerate your flights of fancy. Where are you?"

"Colombia."

She paused, not expecting such a direct answer.

"Do you travel with the package?"

Bart Hall, the package.

"Yep."

Another pause as her three-dimensional chess pieces moved about.

"Provide me a location. I will send a plane."

"No, thanks."

Silence. I listened for teeth grinding.

"You walk a razor's edge, Mr. Lee."

"Understood."

"I expect the package delivered safe and sound."

She didn't specify a delivery location, a bridge too far within the context of the current conversation. She'd damn sure broach the subject later as this passion play played out.

"That's my intention."

She hung up. The call had gone as well as expected. Two dogs, hackles raised, circling. Oh, well. I wouldn't lose any sleep over it.

An hour later we stopped in Pasto for a quick breakfast and more coffee. Rice, beans, chorizo, and a fried egg fit the bill. The coffee, amazing. Our scruffy and foreign appearance drew stares from the other dozen patrons.

"Case, please do not infer my questioning as a lack of confidence. But I must ask you. What might be our next steps?"

"There's an airport twenty miles away." As I spoke, a small jet aircraft passed on the horizon, visible through the diner's window. Heartening, as it reflected air traffic. I'd feared the Colombian version of tumbleweeds rolling down a runway at the Pasto airport. "We'll try and catch a flight north."

"Once again, please do not take umbrage at my questions. It is remarkable that we sit here, consuming breakfast, after such an adventurous trip."

"No offense taken."

"Goodness, I would hope so. When you say north, I gather you speak of a general direction. Would it not be preferable having a specific destination?"

"Yeah, it would. But right now, our best bet is leaving Colombia. Put miles between us and the folks after you. And after me."

"Is it possible to rent a private plane?"

"I'll give it a shot if we come up empty at the airport. The charter flight we'd require comes with several caveats. First, will anyone service the Pasto airport? We're way out in the boonies."

He chewed on my statement and the rice and beans. I asked the proprietor for ají picante, their Colombian hot sauce. I'd eaten rice and beans the world over, and most times they filled your belly with little flavor. Local hot sauce helped.

"When you say come up empty, is there a reference point I would understand?"

"Cargo planes come and go here, like at any remote commercial airfield. And cargo planes offer anonymity. And sometimes added features such as bypassing customs and immigration at their destination. Remember, we don't want your name as a fresh entry on any databases. The bad guys can access those."

"Ah. We will travel incognito, then."

"Yep."

"And how might you see north as a destination?"

"Central America or the Caribbean. Someplace where we can charter a flight that would sneak us back into the States. Under the radar, both figurative and literal."

"Ah. What about Mexico?"

"I've recently burned a few major bridges in Mexico. It's best we avoid it."

Boy howdy, had I burned bridges. Several recent jobs entailed dealing with Mexican cartels. "Dealing with" translated into bullets flying as dead cartel members bobbed in my wake. I'd sidestep Mexico for the foreseeable future.

"Back in the US, Ruth and I should remain incognito. Is this correct?"

"Afraid so, and I know it's a pain in the ass, and I'm sorry. But, yeah, this whole thing won't blow over for a year or two. How's the white paper coming along?"

He explained progress and lost me, but it made up his comfort zone, so I nodded and acted interested. Good seeing Bart perk up a bit.

264

As we approached the small airport, ensuring no one followed us, the scene presented possibilities. I discounted the lone small passenger aircraft with a Colombian airline paint job and focused on a plane near what appeared as a cargo area. As we approached the tiny cargo warehouse, with not a security detail in sight, two pilots and two workers loaded a relic from the past. A C-47 Skytrain, the venerable DC-3's military version. Perhaps the most famous aircraft in history, it had dropped paratroopers in Normandy on D-Day, supplied Berlin during the airlift, and performed a million other remarkable duties during and after World War II. Old as the hills, they quit manufacturing them in the nineteen-forties. I recalled a couple hundred still flew, working gigs such as the one before us. It offered perfect cover—an old semidilapidated plane, with little attention paid toward it among modern cargo carriers.

"Stay in the car, please, Bart. I'll try and make arrangements."

"I wish you the best of luck. Would such an antiquated airplane offer sufficient safety?"

"No worries. It's just what we're looking for."

The day was clear and cool with massive mountains across the horizon. A fine day for a flight. A fine day for fleeing a hot zone. I strolled onto the tarmac and addressed the two pilots. One presented as the classic milk run cargo pilot. Thin, with clear signs of a hangover, company shirt and epaulets disheveled, cig hanging from his lips as he instructed the two-man loading crew who placed cardboard boxes and wooden crates inside the plane and tied them down. The other pilot stood to the side, fit, his shirt pressed, wearing aviators even though the day had yet gained the brightness fitting for such eyewear. He remained detached from the loading process.

"Good morning. Where are you guys headed?"

Again, my American-accented Spanish drew special attention.

"Colón," the thin one said, his tone friendly. "Colón, Panama."

He smelled opportunity. A gringo had appeared on the tarmac and asked a destination question. Over the years, he'd learned to sniff a side hustle. The other pilot remained silent, expressionless.

Colón as a destination offered escape in the right direction and a seamy side I well knew from past Panama experiences. The city sat at the Panama Canal's entrance on the Atlantic side and carried the well-deserved reputation as a place with a Wild West atmosphere. Perfect. Once there, opportunity abounded for a bootleg flight into the States, avoiding US customs and immigration. Luck had rolled our way.

"My friend and I could use a ride."

"I am afraid we are a cargo carrier only. No passengers."

The thin pilot's statement kicked off negotiations. He shrugged, retrieved the cig from his mouth, flicked it onto the tarmac—disregarding the area's position as a refueling station—and turned back toward the loading crew.

"I'll pay cash. US dollars."

"Such a payment would be quite large," he said over his shoulder, feigning indifference.

"Let's discuss how large."

The standard act, well honed, played out. He waited several beats, dismissive, and turned. He approached with a languid stride, lighting another smoke on the way. Standing near me, he surveyed the horizon, nonchalant. The other pilot stood at a distance, unengaged.

"More than you have," he said, a conversational marker with a tinge of insult meant to rile my macho side.

"Let's find out. How much?"

Still staring into the distance, he said, "Twenty thousand."

"Five thousand for us both. Or I could drive to Cali where such an amount would assure a flight."

Cali, a major Colombian city, sat two hundred miles away. A bluff, but genuine enough as an alternative. The thin pilot sighed.

"You are most fortunate our cargo weight allows for two passengers. Otherwise, I could not do this for such a small sum. I will fly you to Colón and drop you at Panamanian customs and immigration near the passenger terminal."

Round two negotiations. This cat knew the game like the back of his hand. So did I. A fifty-fifty chance he'd offload his cargo at a Colón airport location where Panamanian officials were few and far between, and likely paid off. A partial bluff on his part. He knew it. I knew it.

"No customs," I said. "No immigration. No Panamanian officials."

He locked eyes with me.

"Such an act is most illegal. And, therefore, very expensive."

"I have an exceptional weapon. One you could find handy during your travels."

He raised one eyebrow and waited for details. Colón's streets, regardless of how seedy, didn't afford the opportunity for toting an assault rifle. I'd keep the 9mm pistol and silencer. And the small handheld grenade launcher. Just in case. But the rifle, once there, became untenable.

"A rifle with a fine scope. US military grade," I continued.

"Full automatic?" he asked.

"Either automatic or semiautomatic. Your choice with the flip of a switch."

"Ammunition?"

"Three full magazines. Thirty rounds each."

He puffed his smoke and again stared into the distance, considering the offer.

"Such a weapon would fit inside a hidden space in my cockpit. I will take you and your friend. Payment, full payment, is due before takeoff. We depart in thirty minutes."

"Fine. Be aware I will still carry another weapon."

A stake driven into the ground just so we understood each other. He'd receive the rifle before takeoff. I'd remain armed with another weapon. Logistics and ground rules and payments clarified, time to buckle in. And thank you for flying black market airways.

Back at the vehicle I explained our good fortune.

"Panama. Goodness. And once there?"

"A flight back to the States. I'm beginning to smell the barn, bud."

I texted the Clubhouse as Bart collected his things.

Colón fixer.

Jules would respond by the time we landed. The Panamanian city held sufficient grim underground activities to ensure her spiderweb tendrils extended there. I reengaged the rental vehicle's GPS and texted the company their SUV's location along with a lie it had engine troubles. They'd get plenty irritated, not for the first time. On board, I handed over the Benjamins and assault rifle and extra ammo mags. The pilot admired the weapon, smiled, and tucked it into a tiny closet inside the cockpit. I kept the pistol on full display, tucked into my waistband. Promises made, gifts exchanged, good to go.

We sat at the plane's forward section where two small benches folded down from the fuselage, facing each other. Sheet aluminum bench backs and seat padding long ago compressed down to a quarter-inch thick. No seatbelts. I helped Bart get situated, assured him all remained okay, and the twin engines fired. The starboard engine blew black smoke before it settled into solid rhythm with the other. We rumbled down the runway, the old C-47's tail lifted, and soon the plane took off. The pilot set a northern heading, between two mountain peaks, and in short order Colombia disappeared behind us, the Pacific Ocean below. But the irritating small voice continued sounding. A feral feel something wasn't right.

THE SAWTOOTH JOB

Chapter 33

With no door on the cockpit, I opted for the left-hand side bench with an unobstructed view of the copilot. Mr. Ray-Bans with pressed shirt and silent manner. He never touched an aircraft control, instead sitting silent and grim with arms crossed. A position and attitude that failed the legit test. Not good. And the morning's call with Townsend still stuck in my craw. Not the expected hard-nosed back-and-forth, par for the current course. But she'd dropped the hand-over-Bart gambit too quickly, without layering on more abrasive exchanges. Weird. My situational awareness remained in flux, and my gut roiled over the possibilities.

For two hours the old plane lumbered along, then circled Colón for its final approach. I stood and viewed out a tiny hatch window the city and Panama Canal and massive cargo docks and infrastructure construction. The sight set off more unconsidered alarms. It wasn't unusual for air shipments to fly back-and-forth between other Latin American countries and Panama—the Colón Free Zone was the largest free-trade zone in the Western Hemisphere. But underlying geopolitical currents below me also held sway.

The US built the Panama Canal over a century ago and returned it to Panama's government in 1999. It opened the door for foreign investment, financial ties, political ties. And influence. China stepped into a prominent role. The US, without stating so, still clung to the two-hundred-year-old Monroe Doctrine—the Western Hemisphere was under America's sphere of influence. China's response—yeah, whatever. A 'tude reinforced as we came in with flaps lowered for landing.

China had built massive port facilities on both the canal's Pacific and Atlantic side as well as other infrastructure projects. Enormous bridges and roads and industry, all on full display as we descended into Colón. Investments worth billions. China had also built close political ties with the Panamanian government. You couldn't blame the Panamanians—China poured in the bucks and integrated top-to-bottom into Panama's economic future. The US government's perspective—pushed through policy wonks, elected officials, bureaucrats, intelligence agencies—still claimed Panama as their turf, not China's. Which set up some interesting dynamics. Dynamics I didn't want a thing to do with.

The antique aircraft touched down, bounced, touched again. Then the back landing gear settled onto the tarmac, and we taxied toward a vast warehouse complex. Our warehouse, like our plane, had seen better days. While we taxied, I took off my jacket and stuffed it into the rucksack. Panama greeted us with a rising eighty-something degrees and high humidity.

"Bart, I'll carry the rucksack and your small duffel. You tote your satchel."

"It would appear we have left cool weather. Would you please place my jacket in the duffel as well?"

The "as well" referenced the pistol with now-attached silencer and hand-fired grenade launcher. Both nested among his meager possessions in the small duffel. I'd leave it unzipped for ready access.

The pilot killed the engines, opened the door hatch, and pointed toward the outside. Trip over. I helped Bart down the steps and waited for a private chat with the pilot. It didn't take long. The copilot exited, nodded our way, and headed toward a small chain-link gate alongside the old warehouse. The gate's rusty hinges squeaked as he opened and closed it. Then he disappeared on a path behind the warehouse. Mental claxons sounded as my unease roared. Operational fog, misdirection, lies and deceit—or personal paranoia in overdrive? I went with my gut and viewed the copilot's actions as a potent signal it was time to develop a backup plan. A Plan B.

Yeah, I'd still use Jules's fixer for our escape's next leg. Maybe. But the copilot's conduct, spooklike, triggered an experience-driven desire for alternatives. My Colón fixer might occupy a spot on an espionage outfit's payroll. Time for Case Lee's own misdirection and fog. Man, I hated wading through this mess.

The pilot climbed down, lit a smoke, tucked errant shirttails back in, and explained the same chain-link gate would work for us, that it led to a road with decent traffic. No customs, no immigration. I thanked him and asked a few questions as the tarmac radiated heat and the still Atlantic air hung thick and steamy.

"What's the deal with your copilot?"

The pilot shrugged, uninterested, and said, "New to our company. I do not know him. I wish you safe travels, wherever it might be."

This cat's reticence stunk to high heavens and justified my suspicions.

"Where are you going next?"

"Colombia. Tomorrow, of course. If not tomorrow, the next day or the next."

"Do you ever fly into the States?"

"No."

"Would you?"

"No. We have plenty of business between here and Colombia."

"Ah. Well, thank you for the ride. We flew in a major piece of history. There can't be many C-47 Skytrains still in service."

"She is a fine aircraft. Forgiving and durable."

We chatted about spare parts, maintenance, and the plane's history. Then I worked on Plan B.

"Where do you drink? A bar nearby?"

Pilots, cops, and a few other professions collected at their own drinking establishments. Shop talk, gossip, job opportunities. This guy returned a wry smile, hawked, spit, and lit another smoke.

"Rosalinda's. You may find what you seek there." His smile widened. "Or you may not. Either way, I wish you luck."

We shook hands as sweat stuck shirt material against my back. I checked electronic messages. The Clubhouse had delivered, as always, with a fixer's phone number. A person I'd contact after a bar visit. Bart stood, sweating more than me, with a "what's next?" look. No doubt he considered the last twenty-four hours an otherworldly experience. A firefight on an Ecuador beach, a mad dash escape, another firefight in the Andes Mountains—with players he did not know existed—plus a dead-of-night illegal border crossing. Now this. Standing on a steaming tarmac in Panama with a man who'd pulled him along for one helluva ride.

"Okay, Bart. We're at the end game. I'll do everything I can to smuggle you back into the States and reunite you with Ruth."

"I must tell you, without reservation and with the utmost sincerity, thank you. Thank you. I do not hug others, except for Ruthie, but if you would like I could hug you."

"That's okay. I appreciate the thanks. Now, let's leave this area."

"Goodness. I feel as if I am inside a thriller novel. It is a strange sensation. Most strange."

"C'mon, Bart."

I started toward the small latched gate and ensured he followed. I was less concerned with Panamanian officials and more focused on shadow players. Were we being watched? And if so, by who? Rucksack shouldered and gripping the small duffel with my left hand, I reached into it with my right and ensured pistol access remained unhindered. A habit, a security blanket, and one fitting for the time and place.

Through the gate—the rusty hinges squeaked again—and a path appeared through tall weeds and wild growth and tall trees. Ahead, a hundred yards distant, traffic noises. A public refuge where I could flag a taxi.

I pulled the pistol and addressed Bart.

"Stick with me like glue. Understand?"

Wide-eyed, he stared at the weapon, then me, and nodded affirmation. A locked and loaded hundred-yard stroll along a fine ambush-potential pathway. Rationale enough for pulling the weapon, sure. But it was more than that. We'd made the home stretch, and I'd had enough. I'd taken on a mission with a cut-and-dried objective, now polluted with shadows and hidden strings from players who had no business messing with Bart and Ruth. Or me. Maybe I'd been stupid, an altruistic bridge too far, attempting this whole deal. Yeah, I'd committed to Ruth, but folks back away or fail or stumble every freakin' day of the week with commitments. But I wouldn't waffle on the job's goal, and the entire effort was now buttressed with an undeniable element of pushback, a hardwired feistiness. The Company, the Chicoms, the Norks and

Russians and Brits and Israelis—they all, each and every one, could kiss my ass. I was Case freakin' Lee. 'Nuff said.

"We'll be okay. Stay close. Don't talk with anyone other than me. That's important. You can do this, Bart. I've got confidence in you."

He took a deep breath, removed his glasses, wiped his sweaty face with his shirttail, and said, "Yes. Yes, let us move forward. And let it be known, I have confidence in *you*, Case."

We hustled through the urban jungle, pistol with silencer leading the way, and emerged on a gritty avenue lined with more warehouses. With the pistol back in the small duffel and relief at standing within an open urban area, we waited for a passing taxi. Five long minutes later, I flagged one down.

"Where to?" the driver asked as we crawled into the back seat, my rucksack between us.

"Rosalinda's. Do you know this place?"

"Yes, of course. It is not far."

I paid him an extra twenty up front to drive there on back roads and through alleyways while I monitored my backtrail. All clear. The drive also emphasized the haves and have-nots in Colón. Well-kept high-end condos and palatial houses within gated communities, pressed against shacks and abject poverty. No middle-class transition, just a stark juxtaposition. I supposed folks become inured to such disparity. Not me. On the flip side, such seedy areas held folks I dealt with on a regular basis, with fixers the prime example.

Fifteen minutes later we pulled into a small parking area—dirt with deep tire tracks from navigating across the area during rainstorms—and stopped at a ramshackle tin-roofed establishment and piecemeal-constructed front porch occupied by three young but hard-bitten working girls, who smoked and eyeballed our arrival. A hand-painted sign declared we'd arrive at Rosalinda's.

THE SAWTOOTH JOB

Chapter 34

The taxi driver agreed forty bucks bought a twenty- or thirty-minute standby time. Rucksack shouldered, duffel in hand, I approached the entrance, Bart a step behind. I delivered the universal "leave me alone" signal for the three working girls—a grim expression and brief forefinger wag which spelled out no thanks. Two girls attached themselves to Bart, one on each side, hands on his shoulders and arms.

"Goodness. These are awfully friendly ladies."

"They'll get a lot more friendly for twenty bucks."

"Forty," one replied, in English.

"I stand corrected. C'mon, Bart."

I tugged his shirt front and pulled him inside. Rosalinda's displayed interior Christmas lights strung across the ceiling, an old large wooden airplane propeller hung on a wall, a dozen tables and chairs, and a sizeable half-polished wooden bar. The barkeep, a large and florid-faced man with a pleasant expression, waited for our approach.

"I'll have a light beer."

He nodded and looked toward Bart, who leaned close and, whispering, asked, "What should I have?"

"Beer or soda."

"Do they have a diet soda?"

"Is that what you'd like?"

"Yes. A cold one, please. It is quite hot and humid. Might you have noticed the Christmas lights?"

"Common decor, bud."

He'd taken the "don't talk with anyone but me" edict to heart. Good for him. I ordered him a Diet Coke and surveyed the room. Our C-47 pilot had provided the right place. Four tables held groups of pilots. Freight haulers. Several wore once-pressed company shirts, now wrinkled and showcasing stains from sweat and spilled coffee and cocktail mishaps and fallen ashes from drooping cigarettes. A few wore polo-type shirts with company insignias. All enjoyed either pre- or post-flight beers and cocktails as their casual banter filled the place. At one table, my objective.

The table held two company shirt guys and one man, in his thirties, who had potential out the wazoo. Dressed in jeans and a plain faded-blue T-shirt, long hair in a ponytail, a neck tat, and dark-inked tribal tattoos along both arms. His left ear displayed a dangling earring with a symbol I wasn't familiar with. It swayed as he engaged the other two in conversation.

"C'mon, Bart."

We approached the table. The two freight pilots looked our way with pleasant expressions. The third dude stared with a blank expression. I returned a friendly smile toward the two pilots and asked the pony-tailed cat in Spanish, "Are you a pilot?"

He replied, in English, "Maybe."

Good answer. An American, he held his cards close.

"Could we talk?"

He stood and carried his beer to a nearby table. The three of us sat.

"I'm in the market for a charter flight."

He sipped beer and waited.

"A stateside flight. Under the radar. Me and my friend."

He eyeballed Bart first, then me.

"I might know someone who could help."

Another appropriate answer. Low odds his comment referenced someone else.

"A nighttime run. Remote airstrip. No shipments in the plane. Just us two."

Panama was known as a transit point for cocaine. A Colombia-Panama-US supply chain. I would insist on a clean ride. If busted, we'd be guilty of two US citizens entering the US without a pass through customs and immigration. Not trafficking drugs.

"That's a pricey charter."

"How pricey?"

"Forty large."

"Twenty. With a clean plane it's a low-risk excursion."

The same smuggling penalty would apply for him. Two guys making an illegal entry. Plus, he could claim engine trouble and a forced landing at a remote airstrip as cover. If caught. But this dude, clearly a multiflavored contraband smuggler, knew the ropes, and our chance of a bust remained small. The forty-thousand bucks he'd quoted was high. How he viewed my counteroffer, unknown.

"Well, you're lucky," he said. "The someone who might do it isn't busy now. Thirty large."

A working girl approached the table, waved away by the smuggler who sucked down half his beer, waiting for my response.

"Where's the landing?" I asked.

"South Florida."

Expected and all good. He'd have several isolated airstrips available.

"What aircraft does this someone fly?"

"Beechcraft King Air."

A popular twin-engine prop plane with over five thousand manufactured. For a good reason—reliable, fast, with a long range. And in common use among smugglers for those attributes. I nodded back an agreement and added, "Alright."

Thirty grand wasn't too bad for such an operation.

"Cash?" he asked.

"Bank transfer."

"Where's the bank?"

"Caymans."

"The same place as someone's account."

He named a particular Cayman bank. It was the one I used in the Caymans. Oh, what a feeling, rubbing physical and financial elbows with the likes of this cat. For the umpteenth time, I considered a career change.

"We good to go?" I asked. "Depart after dark tonight?"

"Maybe. The aircraft is undergoing a minor repair. Could be tomorrow. The bank transfer would happen before takeoff, right?"

"Right. If we depart tonight. Any delay is a deal-breaker."

He finished his beer, belched, and said, "Well, I'd best check on the King Air and see how it's going. You got a number I can contact?"

We exchanged phone numbers.

"One last thing," I said. "After I make the bank transfer with a certain someone, we'd best not find out the aircraft repairs didn't do the trick. If that happens, there'll be a major problem. A problem I'll handle on the spot."

We locked eyes for several seconds. Then he nodded, the message crystal clear with no gray areas. He stood, said goodbye to his buddies at the other table, and left.

"I must ask. Was your exchange a positive one?" Bart whispered.

"Maybe. He's part of a backup plan in case things don't work out with my primary contact."

"Who is your primary contact?"

"A person we'll meet next."

I stood beside the taxi and called the number Jules had texted me. A woman answered.

"I require special services," I said. "Services I understand you might provide."

"Of course. I offer both goods and services. What might you require?"

"I'd rather speak face-to-face."

"Understandable. I am Angelique. And you are?"

"Joe."

"Joe. A unique name, Joe. American?"

"Yes."

"Of course. I look forward meeting you, Joe."

Angelique gave me an address, we signed off, and I passed the location onto the taxi driver.

"You should not go into this area," he said, shaking his head. "For someone such as yourself and your friend, it is a dangerous place. A very dangerous place."

"Thank you for your concern. We'll be fine."

The driver shook his head with mild disgust and started driving.

"What did he say?" Bart asked.

"We're headed into a bad neighborhood. It'll be fine."

"Goodness gracious. I cannot wait to inform Ruthie about our adventures."

"You two will have a lot to talk about."

As we drove along, and minutes later, he tossed into the ether, "I miss her terribly."

"I know, bud."

Again, I asked the driver for a roundabout route, checking for tails. We remained clean. Twenty minutes later we wove through an area best described as a large slum. A mixture of tumbledown shacks, corner bodegas with iron bars on windows and doors, two- and three-story concrete buildings in disrepair and once painted in green, blue, yellow, and pink hues—the paint now peeled and faded as concrete's gray showed through. Tin roofs abounded, and electrical wiring hung everywhere, strewn in bundles under balconies and across narrow alleys. Trash lined sidewalks and curbs, the entire scene accented with graffiti from spray-paint artists galore. Several narrow alleys contained laundry drying on thin clotheslines stretched across and high above the walkways. People kept their heads down and neither waved nor chatted with neighbors except at the bodegas and outside the tucked-away bars. Rough trade, and expected.

The driver stopped at a substantial structure well past its prime. Once an aqua-green, the concrete now displayed the original color with only mottled remnants. The street-facing first floor contained four closed doors with varied wooden construction. Each showed haphazard repairs. An open narrow alleyway split the lower floor and led toward the building's rear. Two young thugs stood at the open alley, staring. Above them, a long, rotted wooden balcony, supported with timbers of varying grades and age, showing two doors and two windows, all but one window shut and boarded up. The porch's length was protected from the regular rain with rusted metal corrugated roofing. Above it, the main roof consisted of more metal roofing, some rusted, other pieces with the original paint still intact. Our fixer's abode and place of business.

THE SAWTOOTH JOB

Chapter 35

I paid the driver, who pocketed the cash and said, "Vaya con Dios," and sped away. Lingering wasn't in his game plan. I shouldered the rucksack, held the small duffel, and helped Bart sling his leather satchel strap over his head rather than resting it on a shoulder.

"People will have a harder time snatching it if you carry it this way."

"Who in the world would wish to steal it?"

"Everyone you see. Stay close."

He did. We approached the young thug guards at the building's cut-through alleyway.

"We have an appointment with Angelique."

Covered in indigo tats, they wore off-white baggy cargo pants and sleeveless bright white undershirts. The day's uniform. One nodded and indicated we should follow him. The other trailed us. Through the narrow passageway, up rickety wooden stairs at the building's rear, and halting before we reached an open second-floor doorway. The lead thug signaled we should wait as he entered the room and held a brief conversation. The entire environment reeked of garbage, sewage, and desperation. With another head signal, he showed we could enter.

The wooden floor protested as Bart and I entered the large, dim room with light provided through one glass window and the open door. A couch, two leather chairs, several throw rugs, and a large modern wooden desk adorned the place. Behind the desk was a fortyish fit-looking umber-colored woman wearing a bright tie-dye sleeveless shirt. She'd shaved her head on the sides and the remaining strip, dyed a turquoise hue, formed a three-inch-high mohawk. Her left eyebrow displayed a large silver stud.

A young woman, also in cargo pants and white undershirt and, unlike the two thugs, unsteady on her feet, hunched over and whispered in her ear as Angelique stared at us, not unfriendly, and rubbed the younger woman's butt. Behind Angelique a seventies Keep On Truckin' poster adorned the wall, and a lava lamp—pink globules doing their slow-motion float—perched on a cluttered bookshelf. A cocaine bullet-shaped sniffer and semiautomatic pistol occupied the desktop. Angelique gave small nods as the young woman delivered her report. Finished, our fixer plucked the cocaine sniffer from the desk and lifted it toward the young woman who smiled, retrieved it, and took two hits, one in each nostril. Angelique slapped her ass as she left, eyes lit.

"Hello, Joe. Would you like a toot?" she asked, holding out the sniffer.

"Hello, Angelique. No, thanks."

"It is the highest quality. Straight from the cooking sheds in Colombia."

"No, thanks."

She cocked her head, and with a tight smile snorted a hit up each nostril.

"Who is your friend?" she asked, giving her nose a vigorous wipe.

"Just a friend."

"I don't do business with people unless I know their name. You can understand that, can't you, Joe?"

I eyeballed Bart and said, "Angelique wants to know your name. I've told her mine is Joe."

Delivered with a play-the-game look, which had a fifty-fifty shot at Bart absorption.

"Yes." Angelique switched into heavily accented English. "I wish to know your name. You don't mind telling me your name, do you?"

"Atticus Finch."

A blurted pronouncement delivered with surety. Bart was into his adventure. Fine, as long as he understood calamity and dire consequences perched on our shoulders like buzzards.

"Hello, Atticus. Sit, please. Both of you."

She extended a hand toward the two large leather chairs across from her desk.

I sat across from her, rucksack on the floor, unzipped duffel in my lap. Switching back to Spanish cut Bart out of the conversation.

"I require two things."

She chuckled and brushed a hand along the top of the turquoise hair strip ensuring, I supposed, it remained upright.

"I take it we will not learn more about each other. Straight to business. How do I know you are not with your government?"

"Do I look like I'm with my government?"

Angelique performed a quick lean-back in her leather office chair and scratched a forearm, clearly buzzed.

"No, you do not. I can spot those people."

"How's that?"

"They try too hard. You do not try too hard, but you are a hard man. Your older friend is not a hard man. You make a curious pair."

I had no clue where she headed with her assessment, so I dived into business.

"We require a flight. Panama to the US. Tonight. No government officials on either end."

"Are you criminals fleeing justice?" she asked with a wide smile. "Or simple tourists who wish to avoid inspection?"

"Simple tourists."

Hands over head, Angelique stretched. Light conversation mixed with laughter filtered through the open door and window from the downstairs crew. The lava lamp kept circulating its ever-changing globules, casting eerie shadows. I acknowledged that most folks, Bart included, would view the immediate environment as more than peculiar. In my world, it was business as usual.

"I do not believe any flights are scheduled until tomorrow, at the earliest."

She placed her forearms on the desk and leaned forward. Her hands began a light rhythmic bongo beat. She'd assumed we wanted a ride on a regular cocaine run.

"Not a scheduled run. A private charter. No other contraband. No coke. No anything but us, two simple tourists. Landing somewhere in the western US would work. Colorado, for instance."

Angelique and I referenced small jets. Aircraft capable of a Panama to Colorado flight, using an airstrip owned by an amenable and paid off rancher. New Mexico, Arizona, Colorado—take your pick, they'd all work. I planned on enlisting Bo's help when we landed for transporting Bart to Marcus's place.

Drug flights, especially those packed with high-value cocaine, landed across the US in the dead of night on a regular basis. As in every night. Whatever cartel Angelique dealt with would have their own private airstrip network. The pilots—highly specialized. I'd heard some, on longer flights, would air draft on commercial airliners' tails partway, avoiding radar detection. Others used sophisticated radar-scrambling gear. But tried and true still worked best—use topography. Haul ass at treetop level, hugging canyons and buttes and any geographic anomaly that would block radar. They'd have the routes nailed down pat.

"You must have a great deal of money," she said, "or are quite desperate. Or both. A combination flight with cargo and you two as passengers is much less expensive. Why do you not wait for the next scheduled flight? If you fear for your safety, I can provide help with this as well."

She lifted the semiauto from the desk as an example. Before the weapon left the desktop, my hand slid into the open duffel and gripped my 9mm. Just in case. She held her pistol up as a display item.

"I can provide you with a wide variety of weapons. Anything you might desire."

"No, thanks, but I appreciate the offer. Is it possible for a flight out tonight?"

She shrugged.

"Anything is possible. I will make enquiries."

"That would be great. Thanks. Which leads into my second request. Sanctuary. A place where my friend and I can stay, unseen and unknown, until the flight."

I'd considered this request long and hard. We'd landed in enemy turf. Colón had a large Chinese population—commensurate with their massive financial investments—and, no doubt, also had a large MSS presence. Same as the US and the Company, who now didn't fall into the friendly bucket. We sat in Panama at the largest free trade port in the western hemisphere with enormous geopolitical and financial changes underway. Spookville central, bees to honey. Public visibility—a high-end or modest hotel for example—afforded little cover. Here, smack dab in a slum's center, was our best bet.

"Of course. There is such a place not far from here. My people can take you there. Would you enjoy entertainment while you wait? Girls? Grade A coke?"

She held up the coke sniffer as another display item.

"No, thanks. When will you know about the plane?"

"Soon. Late afternoon arrives, so we must move fast."

I provided her my phone number, unavailable when I'd called her because of encryption technology.

"Let me know as soon as possible, please," I said. "Let's work out costs for the flight and sanctuary."

She waved a dismissive hand.

"We will settle everything later."

She called out for a crewmember while my unease meter went from zero to sixty. Fixers were prone to collect at the moment. No wait time, no settlement later. Nossir. Angelique could have employed a different business model, but I doubted it. And such doubt spurred major concerns.

Chapter 36

I asked the cargo-pants thug for, first, a bodega where we purchased water and snacks. Then off into the jungle. The streets narrowed so much that two oncoming vehicles couldn't squeeze past each other without both jumping the low curb and setting tires on the narrow sidewalks. The alleys narrowed as well, and more concrete slab structures appeared empty, abandoned. Electrical lines, rat's nests, wove under roof beams, their tendrils shooting off toward empty apartments or dangling down above streets and alleyways. Moss, mildew, and mold nested on deep shade surfaces. The people count decreased as even the hardscrabble folks we'd seen avoided the immediate area.

"Where are we going?" Bart asked. "Please do not construe this as complaining, but I am quite uncomfortable here."

"Sorry, bud. But we need a hideout for several hours until the flight situation gets straightened out."

We stopped at a three-story concrete structure, once painted red but now faded to a rusty pink with concrete gray splotches. Door openings without doors, window openings without glass. We stepped inside—the interior design courtesy of graffiti, trash, and broken plastic furniture.

"Goodness."

"I've seen worse."

Cargo pants led us up open concrete stairs to the third floor. End of the line. A dank narrow hallway revealed two doorways. The first opened into a room with a stout wooden high-backed chair. Water pooled in a corner from a roof leak as cut rope segments and ground-out smokes and dark dried stains covered the concrete floor around the chair. Dried blood. The place where Angelique's henchmen, or perhaps Angelique herself, tortured and killed competitors or perceived business threats.

The second doorway opened onto home, sweet home. A ragged card table and four serviceable plastic chairs and litter from snack bags and crushed cigarette packs occupied the front room. It displayed two windows, one overlooking the narrow street below while the other stared at the next empty building fifteen feet away across an alley. The two back rooms, empty. The bathroom had lost its toilet, plumbing, and sink, although the toilet hole remained and had been used since the toilet's removal.

"Goodness!"

"I know. Pretty gross. But we're here for just a few hours, okay?"

"It must be said, I am unsure of our situation. Very unsure."

"Yeah, I'm not rock solid on it either. But we'll work through it. Why don't you get back on your white paper?"

We set up shop at the card table. Outside, a light rain began falling and brought mild relief from the fetid heat. Cargo pants watched for a while, smoking.

"Stay here," he said as a new Adidas sneaker ground out his smoke. "Do not leave. Angelique will contact you."

I nodded his way as he turned and headed down the stairs. I logged the sound signature—one flight, walk across the second-floor access, another flight, and out the doorless entry. At the window, I pressed against the filthy wall and watched his progress along the street as he made a phone call. Bart pulled his laptop while I paced, avoiding visibility from the two windows with a stop and peek outside at regular intervals.

On the street side, two young toughs wandered past, chatting. Along the narrow alleyway an addict shuffled along, mumbling to himself.

Pace, view, pace, with brief breaks for snacking on mashed then refried plantains and deep-fried leavened bread, washed down with bottled water. Bart, hungry, availed himself and appeared satisfied. Neither snack did much for me. I again assessed our interior layout, checking the torture room down the hallway and a steel rebar ladder bolted into the concrete where the rainwater pooled. Above the ladder, a corrugated steel hatch, the leak's source, which opened onto the roof. I climbed the narrow rough ladder and pushed against the hatch. It wouldn't budge. Climbing higher afforded my back full contact with the hatch's wooden frame. A quick strain and the entire hatch popped off. Like a ground squirrel checking for coyotes, I stuck my head up. The roof was almost-flat concrete, as were many other structures. Our building's ends sat spaced apart from similar structures with an eight- or ten-foot gap. A three-sixty perspective displayed an architectural mishmash with similar buildings, two-story abandoned tumbledown houses, and far distant high-rise exclusive condos and office buildings. Dark clouds roiled overhead, promising more rain.

An hour and a half passed as I paced back and forth while Bart worked on his scientific paper. I wracked my brain, reviewing events and context, with context the most bothersome. I couldn't shake the bad wrong feeling, starting with Townsend's morning conversation in Colombia. My last encounter with a player, Angelique, did nothing but ladle more discomfort over this entire mess. In the home stretch, yeah, but Jules's one big thing wrapped me tight—nothing was ever as it seemed. Man, I just didn't know.

Glimpses out the windows revealed little. A small electric company van pulled up, one set of tires on the sidewalk, and parked. Three young men and two young women strolled past below, engaged in animated conversation. My phone registered an incoming call. Marcus.

"Tell me," he said, straight to business.

"In Panama, holed up in an abandoned building's third floor. It's not a friendly neighborhood."

"What's your condition?"

"Worried."

"The package?"

"He's fine."

"Back to your condition. What's going on?"

"Waiting on a treetop flight for the States."

I summarized the two flight options. During my download, his Zippo clacked, a cigar lit.

"What's your armament status?"

Classic Marcus. If a knife fight brewed, bring a full-auto rifle.

"9mm with silencer and sawed-off thumper with two grenades."

"What else?"

"That's it."

"Why didn't you snag a decent rifle from your fixer? If nothing else, added insurance during your wait time."

Solid point. I should have. It would have helped shove down my disquiet. If Marcus had been in my boots, he would have loaded up with an assault rifle, extra loaded magazines, grenades, and an extra pistol.

"Because I'm a dumbass."

"We established that a long time ago. What's your gut say?"

I continued pacing, checking the windows. Outside the alley window, another drug addict, filthy, long hair stringy with rain and grease, shuffled along with his possessions in a black plastic garbage bag slung over a shoulder.

"I'm leaning toward the bar smuggler and Florida. Not for any tactical reasons. More a feel. This fixer didn't give me any warm fuzzies."

"What if you broke from your current position now and met the Florida guy later?"

"He might not enact repairs on his plane in time. Then what?"

"Then you're away from your current uneasy position and looking for another option. Not such a bad thing if your gut alarm is sounding."

"Don't think it's reached that point yet. It's nothing I can put my finger on, but it started with the flight from Colombia and hasn't gotten any better."

"Then bail. Grab the package and haul it."

I checked the street window again. Two scruffy workmen in their electric company overalls exited the parked van.

"An option, Marcus, for sure. I gotta go. My phone battery is running low."

We signed off. My phone battery was fine.

I hustled toward Bart and said, "Grab your satchel and laptop. Now. Right now."

He did, without question. I snagged a plastic chair and led him into an empty room, windowless, and set the chair in a corner.

"Sit here. Do not get up until I tell you to."

"It is apparent something is happening. What might it be?"

"The shit's hitting the fan soon. It'll be alright. Stay here."

Back in the main room I pulled the pistol and draped the grenade launcher's lanyard around my neck. A quick glance out the alley window provided confirmation.

The two workmen who'd exited their electric company van were Delta. I recognized them from the airplane hangar in DC and the shootout along the highway in Ecuador. No uncertainty about it. I hustled over and checked out the alleyway addict. He paused and performed a sloppy drug-addled lean against the opposite building's outer wall, then fired a quick glance at his back trail and the alley path forward. The hair of his former ponytail now displayed greasy and bedraggled and hanging around his face. The black plastic garbage bag over his shoulder indicated clothes or bedding, but tucked within sat an assault rifle and extra ammo mags. Guaran-freakin'-teed. And without any doubt, two more Delta operators lurked nearby. I dashed back for the street window. The two overall-wearing operators now stood in the rain at the small van's back, doors open. One operator played with electrical wire. Inside the van and within reach, two more assault rifles. Again, guaranteed.

Angelique had sold me out. Sold my sorry butt's location to the Company, who passed the word on to the enemy. Delta hadn't arrived to capture Bart. At least not yet. No, they'd set up a classic operator ambush. Not for me. For the next group's arrival. Absolute clarity descended and highlighted a key point with bright neon letters.

You really are a dumbass, Lee. A world class dumbass.

Chapter 37

Bait. Dangling bait. That was Bart's role. My job—keep the bait alive.

I shifted from the room and dashed into the hallway, stood at the staircase and listened, 9mm at the ready. Not for use against Delta. That game was over. If they came for Bart, they got Bart. I'd never fight them. The 9mm stood at the ready for MSS operators.

Bart's voice carried down the hallway.

"I must ask, what is happening?"

I entered his sanctuary after a quick dash back into the empty apartment, ducking below the window openings.

"You gotta keep still and keep quiet, bud. The quiet part is really important."

He nodded back, grim, acknowledging—perhaps through my facial set—the situation's gravity. Another firefight headed our way.

"Who are the combatants?"

"The US and China. And I've gotta tell you, I'm not fighting the US contingent. And they're going to win."

"I can assume this would mean they will capture me?"

"Yeah, maybe." I searched for words and came up near empty. "I'm so sorry. So, so sorry."

He let out a slow exhale, then shocked me with a wry grin, and said, "'Show me a hero and I'll write you a tragedy.'"

"Not the most uplifting quote for the moment, Bart. Who's it from?"

"F. Scott Fitzgerald."

"You're going to like my friend Bo. But don't start writing a tragedy just yet." He raised both eyebrows, still and stoic. "Know this. It isn't over. We've still got a chance at escaping from both sides. So hang in there. And stay quiet."

I repositioned by the street window, out of sight, and waited. My mind worked in overdrive and plucked floating jigsaw pieces from the ether, building a picture.

The first contract stood legit. Find Ruth. Mossad or the Brits or a defense contractor, US or otherwise, had contacted my client in Zurich, with a slim chance China had also contacted them. But the Chicoms knew I worked through Zurich and, given MSS and I had run into each other several times in the past, they wouldn't risk engaging me. I represented an asset too close to the Company, with too much opportunity for counterintelligence directed their way. So smart money lay with the Russians or Mossad or the Brits or a defense contractor. When Ruth turned on her GPS in Stanley, all bets, and contracts, were off. Fair enough.

One, two, three, and then four vehicle doors closed somewhere nearby. Down the street and around a tight corner, the doors not slammed shut but still discernible. There'd be more as kickoff approached. And I'd brought a pistol to a full-automatic rifle battle. Crap.

Thoughts about the Chicoms brought more concern. Did MSS know Case Lee had the prize? The Norks left on the beach sure as hell didn't have the time for a photo shoot, uploading my image for their overlords. Same with the MSS operators at the highway shootout. And I gave it high odds I wasn't exposed to them in Colón. Still, a slim chance existed that back in China, at the Ministry of State Security offices, they'd somehow connected dots. I'd run into MSS far too often in the past. They knew my face and name. The last thing I needed was MSS on my tail for the foreseeable future. But the immediate held no mystery. MSS's intent— capture Bart. And kill his handler.

A Delta operator in overalls sidled away from the electric company van and slid into my building through a window. He carried an M4A1 Carbine against his leg as he slipped through the opening. The same weapon I'd traded with the cargo pilot in Pasto, Colombia. Except this operator had a noise suppressor attached to the barrel. All the players for this upcoming soirée would use suppressors, silencers. The device wouldn't silence the rifles' loud cracks but reduce them to a spit-crack at much lower decibels. It wouldn't sound past a two- or three-block radius, and within that limited area nobody would give a damn. The operator who'd climbed through the window wasn't after Bart. At least not yet. Nossir. He'd set up an ambush for the new attendees.

I remained at the window and waited, scooting once over to the alley window for a look-see. The fake addict operator had disappeared, likely into an adjoining structure. Delta would position using the element of surprise coupled with the best firing angles.

The second contract with the Company had kicked off events in Ecuador and every bloody thing since then. I felt it in my bones. Townsend had faith I'd find and eliminate the Norks. She wouldn't have any problem with me pulling a solo act for her phase one. And she didn't have any problem with me avoiding, or thinking I'd avoided, her people. Why the Delta team she'd engaged hadn't taken a tire shot at me after the highway shootout became clear. More work lay ahead for both the bait and bait-keeper. Had to be.

I was a blue-collar grunt in Townsend's larger picture. And the larger picture had geopolitical gamesmanship stamped all over it. The western hemisphere, the Monroe Doctrine, the still-our-turf certainty. Kicked off when China's henchmen, the Norks, carried out ops on US turf, captured Bart, and later killed a DIA agent. A big red flag and a call to battle within shadowland. So Townsend figured let's dangle Bart, draw MSS in, and deliver a clear message. Once I'd taken out the Norks on the beach, the highway shootout fell smack dab into her action plan. So did the here and now. Whack another bundle of MSS operators in Panama. Send another simple message—enter our turf at your own peril.

I'd played my role well. Man, I was an idiot. The Company-provided phone ploy in Quito—flip on the GPS and have the truck driver take it with him to Cuenca—should have thrown them. It didn't. My Quito fixer had squealed, they'd positioned a big bird above the Colombian border the night of my passage, and tracked me the entire way. Son of a bitch. The call from Townsend early a.m. after we'd crossed into Colombia deserved an Academy Award. She'd delivered the pissed-off and threatening persona with an actor's aplomb.

The reality—she'd known exactly where I was and had helped facilitate my movement. Movement toward Panama, the stage set for act two of the hit play "Not on Our Turf, China." The silent copilot on the old freight carrier from Pasto, the guy who'd disappeared through the small gate once we landed, was a Company spook. I'd bet big money on it. He'd likely flown in on the small jet headed for Pasto's airport I'd seen out the restaurant's window while Bart and I ate breakfast. Sent to help lead ol' Case by the nose. Great. Just freakin' great.

The grand plan's next act came across crystal clear. After Townsend delivered a Colón statement, haul Bart stateside and leverage him to bring in Ruth. Set them up in northern Virginia's woods, near to Langley, and expect results. As I wouldn't put up a fight when Delta climbed the stairs—something Townsend knew—Bart's capture was a given. Then they'd leave me alone to fend for myself. Maybe.

More vehicle doors sounded, this time a litany in succession. At least three vehicles, bringing the enemy count somewhere around a dozen. With five Delta operators already in place. Plus one fed up ex-Delta operator with the prize. But this fed up operator hadn't finished. I called the bar pilot with the Beechcraft who offered Florida as a destination. He answered after three rings.

"How's someone's plane?" I asked.

"Just wrapped up repairs. Someone took it along a taxiway for several dry runs, and it's good to go."

"Let's do it. What time?"

"Eight works."

About three-and-a-half-hours travel time put us wheels-down in Florida at eleven-thirty or midnight.

"Eight does work. Where?"

He provided an address near the airport.

"Bank transfer, right?" he asked.

"Roger. Bank transfer. We'll be there."

Townsend contracted me for a specific purpose. For specific skill sets. Yeah, well, she shouldn't expect those skills turned off because her grand plan had worked up till now. No, ma'am. So, all you SOBs up and down the line, buckle up. I had no intention of waving a white flag. Not by a long shot.

Chapter 38

I still had a hole card. They say the fog of war is the situational uncertainty manifested in military operations. Maybe so. For sure, the fog of *battle* held uncertainty in spades. I'd experienced it multiple times, and my current environment offered leverage, advantages. But first things first—don't get killed.

Pressed against the interior wall by the street window, I caught a quick glimpse of an enemy contingent. Four hardened MSS operators dashed across the street a block away as their combat boots splashed through rain puddles. They failed the undercover test, with full battle fatigues, kneepads, helmets with built-in comms, and armed to the teeth. Subtle. The Chinese held heavy sway over local dynamics and had come in full bore. They would recognize Bart from available images on the internet. Anyone who didn't fit his description became fair game. Did they suspect Delta lay in wait? Unknown. But they'd head straight for me and Bart via Angelique's intel, courtesy of the Company. At street level, the Delta team realized it as well.

The operator two floors below represented ground zero. The other four Delta members would occupy the nearby area in ambush and tactical fighting positions. Take on the enemy before they reached their aim. Interacting with the operator below had no upside, his response sure. Shut up and lay low.

It began at the empty structure on our south. Two three-round rips, two MSS operators taken out. At least ten left. I laid low and waited until the heat cranked up, the battle at a boil. More shots fired from both sides, the Chinese assault rifles cracking different than the US weapons. Everyone used suppressors, and the spit/cracks sounded from a two-seventy-degree radius, all within a half-block. The one area without battle sounds lay north and defined our exit route.

I slid up the wall and peeked out the street-side window, then ducked back as a 5.8mm rifle bullet plastered the window's concrete edge with a glancing blow and splattered against the room's opposite wall. The shot had landed an inch from where my head had been. Not good. The MSS operator had positioned for a specific shot—eliminate the scientist's protection. I dropped onto the floor intent on a quick crawl under the room's window opening, on accessing the hallway and seeking a decent firing angle. The body drop saved my life. A five-bullet rip, each chunk of lead with my name on it, pounded against the concrete where I'd stood a half second before. At the third floor across the alleyway, a different shooter had positioned for a kill shot. A pincer move, with one enemy on the third floor across the narrow street and this latest guy across the narrow alley at the building's back side. I thanked my lucky stars he'd missed as the alleyway only separated us by six or seven paces, plus the distance within my room. Maybe the darkening day and thick clouds and rain had reduced the shooter's visibility inside my room. I'd never know. Spread below me, the battle raged in close-quarters combat. The two third-floor MSS shooters would remain in place until the Delta operators went after them. Or I did.

"Do you remain well, Case?"

"Hanging in there. Stay quiet, Bart. And don't move."

I pressed against the room's interior wall, hidden from visibility through either window, and scooted along the littered floor past the old card table and plastic chairs. Exiting the room for hallway access wasn't on the menu. Both my shooters would have clean shots. I was screwed, and after lifting an extra pistol magazine and last extra grenade from the small duffel by the card table, I squatted on my haunches and aimed the pistol at my room's entrance in case an enemy took out the Delta operator below and ascended the concrete stairs. The street battle cycled with typical savage engagement—mad firing bursts, combatants repositioned with intermittent rifle cracks, then another hot firefight engagement lasting fifteen or twenty seconds. I heard one, then two, then three empty ammo magazines hit concrete as the fighters reloaded.

Then my luck changed as Delta hammered home a familiar message—mess with us and die. The window shooter across the street fired a useless burst into my room, his last act on this earth. After his shots pounded my room's interior concrete walls, a three-shot burst from a US weapon sounded from his position. A Delta operator had ascended the stairs and taken him out.

Situational awareness alarms screamed. The Delta operator would approach his newly gained window position, exposed. The MSS alleyway shooter would sight him through the two opposite windows in my room. A mad hands-and-knees scramble placed me underneath the alleyway window and in plain sight of the Delta operator across the street. Hair stood on my neck and arms. A wing and a prayer moment, placing full faith in Delta's ability to discern me as a friendly. But I couldn't leave the guy hanging, exposed and unaware of the waiting MSS operator across the alley. I reinforced my friendly status, and covered my Delta brother's butt, with my pistol hand placement on the window's ledge, and popped several blind rounds across the alley and, hopefully, through the enemy's window. My pistol's sharp cracks sounded inadequate, puny, as automatic rifle fire continued cutting loose at street level.

My maneuver worked. Rifle fire from across the street began zipping through the street-side window, crossed the room just over my head, and exited the alleyway window headed for the MSS shooter. The MSS operator returned the favor, and I had a front-row seat as hot lead sizzled at three thousand feet per second through my room from both directions.

Dusk and steady rain added major visibility issues, with my room in dark shadow. As a Delta brother and Chicom hitter blasted away at each other a foot or two over my head, a hard-earned lesson kicked in. Change the dynamics. I jerked on the lanyard and the 40mm grenade pistol plopped up on my belly. With both its stock and barrel cut way back, it fit the current situation well.

I exposed just a few firing-hand fingers, laid the weapon over the window's rim, and aimed, I hoped, for the window across the alley. The trigger pull caused a *pfft* sound and nothing else. A dud. Shit, oh dear. Lowering the weapon, I pushed the locking latch and cracked open the breech, pulled the dud, and shoved in my final grenade as high-velocity bullets continued flying through the room. Deep breath, quick prayer, and the weapon's blind placement on the windowsill again; I pulled the trigger.

Guaranteed the grenade's explosion inside my enemy's room was heard well beyond the ongoing battle sounds around me. An explosion that spelled, more than anything, adios MSS operator. Concrete chunks blew from his room, across the alleyway, and smacked against my exterior wall. Multiple small chunks flew through the window and littered my room's floor.

The Delta operator across the street would assess the situation and move on for attacks at a hot zone below him. As he shifted position and rejoined the ground-level battle, he'd absorb the reality of a former Delta Force warrior who'd brought a grenade launcher to a rifle fight. And smile at the prospect.

Haul ass time. I had no operational trigger for the moment, no surety my chosen route provided escape, but my gut said now or never.

"Bart! Pack your satchel and crawl out here. Fast!"

He did. The leather satchel, hung over one shoulder and around his neck, dragged on concrete below his belly, his eyes wide and wild as round eyeglasses worked their way down his nose.

"My goodness! What on earth was that explosion?"

"Our exit signal. Stay on your hands and knees, and follow me."

I ensured no ammo remained in the small duffel and dragged my rucksack alongside me. Bart followed. Exiting the room, I stood in the windowless hallway, waited for Bart, and we made our way for the other third-level room. The torture room. I'd left the roof hatch open and rain now drizzled in, adding to the room's corner pool.

"Hands and knees again, bud. All the way to the corner ladder."

"Through the water?"

"Afraid so."

I led, stayed below window height, and considered how Angelique and her crew made no attempt to cover the window openings while they worked over some poor bastard. On purpose, I imagined, so his screams would echo through the immediate neighborhood. At the welded rebar ladder's base, I stood, shouldered my rucksack, checked Bart's progress, and climbed. A quick peek at nose level with the flat concrete rooftop confirmed no immediate danger as battle ebbed and flowed far below us.

"You're doing great. Now, follow me up the ladder and stay on your hands and knees when you get on the roof."

Bart stared up at me, licked his lips, and nodded. He was game—I'd give him that. As he climbed, I checked out the northern adjoining building's roof, across a narrow eight-foot gap with a slender walkway at ground level. The walkway could hold combatants, but we'd pass high overhead, unseen.

Our destination's metal-and-wood roof hatch was already open and shoved to the side—whether an act performed in the past or today, unknown. Beggars, choosers, with one direction for potential escape. Once Bart joined me, we began a quick hands-and-knees crawl while the pistol remained in my right hand.

"I must tell you. I have not crawled in many years."

"You're doing fine."

We halted several paces from the edge.

"Okay. There's a short gap between us and the next roof. It's not far."

"Yes, I can see it, and it appears as a substantial distance. Substantial. A gun battle continues below us."

"Let's not worry about the gun battle. It's not far to the next roof. A two-and-a-half-step distance, at most. You can jump two and a half steps, Bart."

"I am not fond of heights."

"Me either. But it's a short gap, and we've got no other options."

"Will this require a running start?"

I lacked confidence a rotund sixtysomething dude would generate much of a run—I flashed back on his beach run-walk in Ecuador—but if he could do it, all the better.

"Wouldn't hurt. Hand me your satchel. If you'd like, we'll do it together. I'll hold your hand."

I didn't advise caution about slipping on the wet concrete or how to land, needing his rear end on the next roof by hook or by crook. He began a backward crawl.

"What are you doing?"

"Establishing a greater runway for achieving momentum."

"Hand me your satchel."

He'd quit listening. He stood with a grunt after crawfishing backward multiple paces with his butt in the air, clenched his fists, and took off for the gap with hard-nosed determination painted across his face. Lips pursed, arms pumping, satchel bouncing against his belly, he hit the rooftop gap and leapt.

THE SAWTOOTH JOB

Chapter 39

No Olympic gold medal forthcoming for the landing, but a hell of an effort nonetheless. Bart hit his target on uneven feet and tumbled forward, rolling, glasses flying. His yelp when he hit concrete and loud grunts when tumbling didn't concern me. Three stories up with a firefight still hot among the streets and alleyways far below, I doubted anyone heard Bart's cries. I was wrong.

As I stood and prepared for the leap, a head poked up through the destination rooftop's hatch. The MSS operator and I locked eyes for a split second. A frozen moment, broken when we both started raising our weapons. Holding the ladder with his left hand, the operator raised his right, with first the barrel and then the whole weapon appearing. A microsecond thought flashed—outgunned again—as the operator shouldered his full-auto rifle. But I had the drop on him, pistol already in hand. A lengthy pistol shot at forty feet, the target small. Bart struggled on the rooftop, still prone as he collected himself, directly between me and the operator.

"Don't move, Bart!"

He froze as I squeezed the trigger. The shot grazed the enemy's head. He didn't flinch or alter his plan to kill me and lowered his cheek onto the weapon's stock. A tough bastard. But not tough enough to withstand my second shot, which drilled into his skull. He disappeared and tumbled down, creating a ruckus when his body struck wooden debris at the ladder's bottom.

Three steps and a leap landed me on the rooftop, then a dash for the hatch, leading with my pistol, and I confirmed the operator dead. He'd landed on rotted and semirotted wooden pallets stacked below. I scrambled back for Bart, retrieved his glasses, which appeared undamaged, and lent a hand so he could continue our escape. A battle crescendo took place at ground level and at our backs, then died down as combatants reloaded and repositioned. Gotta move, man. Gotta fly.

"You're okay, Bart. Nothing broken or sprained. You're good to go."

I didn't know that. He could have sprained an ankle or twisted a knee, but best ignore injuries and focus on forward movement. I handed him the glasses.

"My goodness. I do not wish for such a leap again. Who did you shoot at?"

"A Chinese secret service guy. Crawl with me for the rooftop opening."

"Where is the Chinese secret service guy?" Bart asked as he rolled into a sitting position with a groan and adjusted the satchel.

"He's at the bottom of the ladder. Dead. We gotta keep moving. We're in a narrow window of opportunity. C'mon, let's crawl."

Before I could turn and lead the way, a primal feel, an animalistic sense, kicked in. I was a dead man. At my back, someone close had me sighted in. Might as well see my killer, and a slow kneeling position shift brought me eye-to-eye with the Delta operator who'd masqueraded as an addict. His long, stringy hair draped the assault rifle's stock, his head and shoulders above the roof hatch line, seven paces away, his arrival route clear. He'd occupied a lower floor, heard the MSS operator crash into pallets above him, and came running.

A moment frozen in time, ending when he issued a no-nonsense nod downward and eased away, disappearing back down the hole. The message crystal clear—get your sorry butts down here and stay put. Yeah, bud. Yeah. We'd get our tails down the hole. The stay put part—not so much.

Firing quieted, crescendoed, and quieted again. The cycle continued repeating below us as our Delta operator descended the stairs and joined the fray.

"C'mon, Bart, crawl. Follow me."

"Goodness. Who in the world was that man?"

"A US fighter. C'mon. Time's short."

I descended first on another welded rebar ladder. The dead MSS operator lay crumpled in a heap among shattered wooden pallets. As Bart eased down the ladder, I considered and dismissed picking up the Chicom's weapon. I'd gotten a pass from the Delta operator while armed with a pistol. Spotting me in the heat of battle while I toted a Chinese assault rifle opened the door for a different story. Besides, we planned on exiting, stage north.

I took Bart's hand, pulled him away from the dead body, into the building's hallway, and told him to wait there for just a minute. I scrambled into the back rooms, crawled beneath windows, and found a north-facing window that overlooked the adjacent structure. Not a building as much as a two-story wooden shack, decrepit, with a rusted corrugated metal roof. Two stories high, the roofline sat a good ten feet below my third-floor position, although the gap between structures was closer than the buildings we'd just left. Back in the hallway, still scrambling like a madman, I faced Bart and spoke with a whisper.

"No talking, no noise, okay?"

He nodded in return. Can't say he held full faith and credit in my abilities, but he understood I represented a life raft away from the surrounding maelstrom. We descended one flight of stairs, entered empty rooms filled with trash and debris, crawled across floors, and accessed a second-floor back window overlooking the metal roof next door and across a five-foot gap. Still too far for a Bart leap given he'd start on the window's concrete ledge. Damn, Sam.

"Stay against the wall, and don't look out the window. I'll be back."

I perched on the windowsill for a heartbeat, leapt onto the adjoining metal roof, and aimed for a nail line indicating a wooden framework beneath the tin. With the rucksack, I still weighed less than Bart, but it provided a stability indicator when I landed, half-expecting the sheet metal to collapse when my boots struck. It held, although several boards under the tin cracked. Good enough. Working like a banshee, pistol stuffed into the rucksack, I ripped off several roof sections, slipping once as the rain created slick footing. The good news—the metal sections didn't squeal when pulled off the framework. Below, a dank room and wooden floor with the exterior wall's two-by-twelve horizontal planks creating the interior walls as well. I jumped onto the floor, which also held—not a given—and after removing my rucksack delivered a boot kick that dislodged one wall plank. Hard hand pulls freed three others, the nails protesting a bit, each plank eight feet long. I leaned them underneath the roof hole. Good enough.

A kick on every other wall plank below the roof hole cracked the boards sufficient to create hand- and footholds. Climbing, I pulled one long board and placed the end on the sill of Bart's window and the other end near my poked-up head. Another two-by-twelve joined it, creating a twenty-four-inch-wide bridge. Overlaying the other two planks provided some assurance the makeshift bridge would hold.

"Bart!"

Delivered in a furtive voice loaded with urgency. He peeked out the window at the bridge, then the two-story drop, then me.

"You can do it," I said, locking eyes with him while casting a nod and sure smile—both masking my uncertainty.

He checked the long drop again, took a deep breath, and flung a leg over the sill, dangling it over what he considered a death-defying abyss. His other leg soon joined the first, both feet hanging. I'd expected a walk across, but he started with his hands, which developed into a crawl. Fair enough. He glanced my way, and I returned a thumbs-up. Halfway across, the boards cracked, and he froze as the double-decker bridge delivered a slight bounce. No option but keep forward motion, and I hand-signaled him a keep-coming. Which coincided with an MSS operator turning the alleyway corner and entering the weed-filled narrow gap beneath Bart.

With Bart, thankfully, still frozen and staring at me wide-eyed, I altered hand signals with a palm toward him—stop—and a finger on lips. Then pointed down. The Chicom crept along the narrow pathway with slow high steps, working through thick weeds and piled trash. With the firefight winding down, this cat may have seen the error of his ways and planned on exiting the battleground. Or, committed, he planned on a new firing position to bushwhack a Delta operator. My pistol remained in the rucksack ten feet below me. Oh, man.

Another palm-forward stop signal toward Bart, mouthing, "Don't move." I worked my way down, focused on silence, and retrieved the pistol. Then climbed back up, cautious and expectant. The bogey had progressed toward the narrow passageway's end, near the street, and confirmed his intention to kill with weapon shouldered and targets sought. Another long pistol shot but a much larger target—his back. Arms braced against the wooden framework, I squeezed the trigger. The first shot caught him square in the back. His reflex kicked in as he reached behind and sought the penetrating culprit, then he turned and raised his weapon toward my general area. Two more rapid pistol shots into his upper torso put him down. For good. My pistol's muted shots mixed with another brief firepower exchange down the street, away from us.

"Okay, Bart. Keep coming. It's okay."

I had no clue if "okay" fit his traverse, but no other options presented. Bart, perhaps prompted through the violence he'd just witnessed, continued his forward crawl. The bridge held. As he made the opening, where I remained head-up like a prairie dog, he extended one foot then the other, which I guided onto cracked siding planks so he could climb down. I'd slid the pistol into my waistband—not a long-term carry option with the sound suppressor extended down my leg. At least the rain cooled the barrel and suppressor before I performed my version of holstering.

"Okay. Well done, you. You sure you weren't a special ops guy in the past?" I asked as he made the rotted floorboards.

I shot him a reassuring grin. The older scientist lowered his chin and eyes with a tight smile as his face flushed.

"Goodness gracious. An exhilarating event, Case Lee. To think I watched a gunfight!" he said toward the floor in an excited whisper, then raised his eyes to stare into mine. "Although I dislike the killing. I could do without that."

"Me, too. Just remember. Them or us. Right?" I asked, shouldering the rucksack and pulling the pistol.

He nodded agreement, although internalizing delivered death fell so far from his life's realm it had a potent psychological impact. A small voice wished it still did for me.

"Alright. Stay about two steps behind me. I don't trust this flooring or the stairs."

"Roger that."

He cast a sly grin and pushed his glasses back up his nose. I patted his shoulder, turned, and navigated across the room as several floorboards protested. With extreme caution I descended unstable stairs and acknowledged that if a Delta operator had positioned below, it was game over. The first floor proved empty. Hallelujah.

The firefight died down with at least a dozen MSS operators taken out as single shots, signifying deathblows, rang out. I delivered a quick prayer none of the Delta team had met the same fate. The entire firefight had lasted ten or twelve minutes, uber violence doled out, mission accomplished for the Townsend-sent operators. Now they'd enact the secondary mission. Take Bart. They'd begin their activity within a minute or two and find us gone from the concrete structure we'd just left. The battle had played out south to north, and we'd head east, deeper into the slum. With darkness imminent, we had a chance if we moved fast.

"We have to run. Not far, but run. Can you do it?"

He adjusted his satchel and nodded back. I checked the back alleyway. All clear.

"Now!" I whispered and dashed across the alleyway and into another tight gap between structures, turning for a view of Bart—jaw clenched, arms and legs pumping.

We waded fast through weeds and trash, high-stepping, creating distance from the battlefield, until we crossed one, two, then three intersecting alleyways with our best sprints. Bart began huffing behind me.

"Okay. Breathe deep. We'll walk hard from now on, but we can't stop."

I turned and passed through another narrow passage, turned right for a half-block, and left again, still headed east. Bart stayed on my tail. Keeping the long pistol in my hand as insurance no locals messed with us, we wound our way for another fifteen minutes with pissed-off Delta operators far in our rearview mirror.

Chapter 40

Five young men stood as a gaggle under a plywood awning nailed over the bodega's open door when two dripping wet and bedraggled men approached them. One, a worn-out and hell-bent former operator toting a rucksack and pistol while the other—a rotund sixtysomething academic—gripped a leather satchel at his chest. The pistol represented sufficient authority, although my demeanor or physical state—or, if Bo had a say, aura—radiated I'd had more than enough. An old Toyota sedan beater sat parked nearby.

"Who owns the car?" I asked.

The five glanced at each other until one spoke.

"I do."

"You're going to drive us out of this neighborhood and drop us off at a busy street. I'll pay one hundred US if you move fast enough."

They again exchanged glances among themselves.

"I'll pay ninety if you move fast enough. Or I'll simply take the car."

I lifted the pistol, pointed at the sky. The owner hustled into the street and slid behind the wheel. I rode shotgun, Bart in the back. These kids would report back to Angelique what had transpired, but it didn't matter. We would exit the neighborhood before she could react. Ten minutes later we approached a busy intersection.

"Stop here."

He did. I slid him a Benjamin and told him to turn around and head back for the bodega. As he performed the maneuver, I slid the pistol into a rucksack side pocket and zipped it halfway closed.

"What might our next endeavor entail?"

"A taxi ride and meet our pilot."

"A pilot who will fly us back into the US?"

"Yep. We're close to the last leg. You okay?"

"I am prepared for our next steps. I would hope climbing and running will no longer be required."

His Friar Tuck haircut lay plastered against his head, water dripping down his face. His clothes revealed small rips in several places, and one pants leg stuck against his knee. A dark blood blotch evidenced he'd skinned the kneecap.

"I'm hoping the same thing. We could use a freakin' break."

"A freakin' break. Yes. Yes, I would concur."

I stood at the curb for several minutes, hand in the air, until a taxi pulled alongside, and we entered the cab. The driver accepted the street address with a nod and without comment. Twenty minutes later he pulled up to a small locksmith shop, closed. Next door, a Starbucks. We exited and stood under the shop's front door overhang, out of the drizzle.

"Goodness, wouldn't a nice cup of tea work wonders right now?"

"We'll get tea and coffee and maybe something to eat in a while. Right now, the pilot is sitting inside Starbucks and watching us. He's making sure we didn't arrive with a tail."

"A tail?"

"Someone following us."

"Ah. More James Bond maneuvers. I cannot wait to tell Ruthie."

"She'll be excited to see you."

"And I, her. I hope she has not been too distressed."

We stood silent for several minutes, my rucksack removed, pistol in hand and tucked against my leg and unseen in the darkness. Light traffic continued passing as tires hissed over wet pavement. Man, I was bone-tired but kicked myself in the butt to maintain vigilance. The ordeal was a long way from over.

"I must ask you something, Case Lee."

"Ask away."

"Are you certain you do not mind?"

"I don't mind."

"Is this how you always live?"

Great question. Not always, clearly. But during the all-too-similar moments like this one, standing under an overhang out of the rain while waiting for a smuggler to vet my legitimacy for an illegal flight back into the States, I longed for normalcy. Lounging with Jess at her townhouse after a fine meal. Cruising the Ditch on the *Ace of Spades* without a care in the world. Visits with Mom and CC and, especially, taking CC and Tinker Juarez on excursions on board the *Ace*. Relaxing and communal times spent with Bo, Marcus, and Catch. Stability, tranquility, normalcy.

"No, Bart. Believe it or not, I live a plain vanilla life most times."

"Then I must ask another question. Why do you perform duties such as this?"

"I wish I could give you a cut-and-dried answer. A sense of obligation, embracing commitment, trying to do the right thing. And it's never without shades of gray. I waffle and shift among the gray areas like anyone else."

No point delving into the personal wiring that prompted taking on these gigs. I failed to admit such a personal facet to myself half the time.

"I have reflected on the last two days. A great deal of reflection. And am thankful you have revealed such activities are not your day-to-day existence. I am afraid you would not live long if this were so."

I turned and faced him and patted his ample belly.

"Appreciate the concern, but don't worry about me. Let's get you back with Ruth."

"But consider the immediate past. Starting with the beach conflict in Ecuador."

"Yeah, ugly business."

"Then the dangerous drive up the mountains."

"Yeah, but we made it."

"And the horrible battle near the highway. Goodness, a substantial portion of the mountain rained down."

"I know, I know."

Bart continued elaborating on recent events. The midnight border crossing into Colombia, the Colón flight, dealing with Angelique the fixer, and the recent battle and escape. He reeled off events like a freakin' travelogue.

"The thing is, Bart, we gotta focus on the immediate future. Speaking of which, here comes our pilot."

His ponytail was clear in the lighting provided through the Starbucks window as he approached, long earring dangling.

"It's a fine night for a cup of coffee and a financial transaction," he said, easing under the overhang with a smile. "Any takers?"

"Sure. Let me put my weapon away. They may frown on this accoutrement inside Starbucks."

I stuffed the pistol into the rucksack. The pilot remained silent with reemphasized clarity on ground rules. Inside, Bart consumed tea while I sucked down a large coffee, black. Man, it was fine—a personal respite with an elixir of the gods. We both helped ourselves to several pastries. Laptops open, the pilot and I conducted our bank transfer.

"Done and done," he said. "There's no point waiting. You gents ready to fly?"

"Where are we landing?"

"Just west of Miami."

"The Everglades?"

He chuckled and said, "It's not all swamp. I know a few dry spots."

I bet he did. He drove us toward Colón airport's freight section and parked at a locked entrance next to a small warehouse with no lights and no people. The gate contained multiple padlocks, one of which matched the key he produced. Parked on the tarmac, our magic carpet—a well-kept twin-engine Beechcraft King Air. We didn't futz around as I positioned in the copilot's seat, Bart in one of the two seats aft.

"This aircraft is clean, right?"

"As a whistle," he said as the engines fired.

I gave it fifty-fifty his proclamation rang true. You could hide several cocaine bricks beyond my inspection, no problem. I reached back and pulled the pistol from the rucksack and laid it across my lap.

"What's that for?"

"In case we run into any air pirates."

He shook his head, and we taxied toward the runway. Whatever repairs he'd enacted worked from a layman's perspective as the engines sounded sure and steady, the aircraft fit for use. Pedal to the metal, we roared down the runway and took off, a ton and a half of worry in our wake, and an overwhelming sense of relief ahead. The home stretch. My adrenaline and concern and high alert meters all fell into the low-to-middling range with the physical manifestation of almost nodding off twenty minutes into the flight. Zonking out wouldn't do, so I sat up straight and maintained situational awareness.

We hauled ass at wavetop level across inky Caribbean waters, changing course several times. Skirting west of Cuba, the pilot lifted us to ten thousand feet and set a false heading before dropping us at wavetop level again with another course correction. He'd made this run more than a few times. Not much to say or do during the flight except watch distant ship lights whip past and wonder at the closeup view of the Caribbean and the Gulf of Mexico. As we approached the Florida peninsula's west side, small-town lights appeared. We avoided those and skimmed over the Everglades as still water interspersed with flooded vegetation shimmered in the moonlight. Gators and snakes galore whipped past below us as the two-legged variety of gators and snakes lay ahead.

I'd contact Bo and ask him if he'd meet us in Colorado Springs, a five-hour drive from his home in Albuquerque. Colorado Springs offered a neutral location—too far from Albuquerque or Fishtail, Montana, for connecting dots.

I had one large loose end to tie up with the Company. Whatever Marilyn Townsend's attitude or perspective or grand plans, I'd have my say and level-set our playing field. She understood I had Ruth and Bart and would demand both. Not happening, and teeth-gnashing was guaranteed. Townsend also understood I'd figured out she'd used me as bait protection for her geopolitical statement with the Chicoms. I wore idiot stripes often enough, but with a mobile killing field as my constant companion on this escape she figured my realization switch would flick on in Panama. She'd demand a sit-down within twenty-four hours. I wouldn't heed her finger snap, but our relational field required replowing. Fine by me.

The pilot made a hard, low turn, then another, buzzing a particular area. Miami's lights shone on the horizon as below us two bisected oil drums lit up, their gasoline-induced fires designating the dirt or gravel runway's terminal points. It was all the pilot required as wheels and flaps lowered and we made a smooth landing. A pickup truck waited as we slowed and stopped near a drum fire.

"That's it," he said, without shutting down the engines. "I'll take off in a few minutes. My guy will give you a ride."

We shook hands, and I helped Bart deplane. The truck driver first accessed one wing locker, removed a duffel, and repeated the process with the other wing. He tossed both duffels in the pickup. Great. Just freakin' great. We'd headed toward civilization with twenty kilos of cocaine.

"What's next?" Bart whispered as we approached the truck.

"We'll stay in a motel tonight, then another flight tomorrow. My friend will drive you back to Ruth."

"This is all so difficult to believe. You live in a parallel world."

"Sometimes, bud. Sometimes. Just keep quiet, please, until we're alone again."

As Bart and I slid in the older truck's front bench seat, the driver, a rough thirtysomething who looked like he'd cut your throat while you slept, asked, "Where to?"

"The nearest gas station would work."

"There's one at a crossroads about five miles away. No town, just a gas station."

"Perfect."

No introductions, no name exchanges. I'd never see the guy again. He drove along a dirt road and dropped us off without a word, staring straight ahead through the windshield, then roared away with his two duffels of coke. Insect calls surrounded us, my alert meter backed off, and relief, while not flooding, poured itself a tall one. Bart joined me in celebration.

"I do not dance."

"That right?"

"That is right. However, I could dance with joy at this very moment, Case Lee. With joy."

I got it. And might have joined him, shaking a leg to an insect chorus. The kid at the gas station suggested a taxi company down the road instead of Uber.

"Not a lot of Uber business around here, mister. But Fred runs people home from the bars in Loland."

"Does Loland have a motel?"

"They do. I'm happy to call Fred and the motel for you."

I thanked him and slipped him a Benjamin, emphasizing we traveled incognito. He delivered a knowing smile—not a surprise given the regular treetop aerial activities a few miles away.

We shared a clean room at the local motel and paid cash under a fake name. Bart showered and crashed, knackered, while I arranged the next day's flight through a charter outfit I used often. They operated twenty-four-seven, and a Miami to Colorado Springs jet would take off at ten a.m. A fake passport worked for my passenger name. I used Atticus Finch for Bart's.

After I showered, sleep came slow, barriered because of the weird and now irritating sense it would soon be over. The entire ordeal, finito Benito. Relief? You bet. Sense of accomplishment? Absolutely. A tiny character component wishing it wasn't over, with the adrenaline meter ready, willing, and able to redline? Yeah. Unfortunately, yeah.

THE SAWTOOTH JOB

Chapter 41

"Hi-ho, my goober. Tell me a tale."

I called Bo early a.m. and asked for his help.

"Could use a little backup, Bo."

"Where and when?"

The best. My blood brothers. The absolute best. I could have asked him to join me in a fight against the legions from hell, and his response wouldn't alter. And smart money wouldn't bet on the hell brigade.

"Colorado Springs when you can. We'll land in six hours."

"Which, through the magic of this realm's space and time, matches my drive time from Albuquerque. A gathering, a joining, predestined."

"And a delivery for the cow whisperer."

"Can do easy."

"How's JJ?"

"The universe lifts her day by day and moment by moment. She expresses a keen interest in a return to her institutional labors. They reiterate there's no rush, yet she seeks their companionship. A pull toward law enforcement fellowship, perhaps."

I grinned and considered JJ's recent expressions about Bo's constant ministrations. His Balinese puppet show may have been the final straw.

"Maybe so. Anyway, I appreciate it. You'll have to make the trip without me. Our old field companion will want an immediate sit-down."

"Swords crossed?"

"Kinda. I'd best reset the table with her."

"We've experienced glorious feasts with her."

"Times past."

"You, as usual, remain stuck within a linear time constraint. Tell her hi-ho for me."

"Will do, bud."

We signed off. Bart, standing nearby with hot tea, was desperate to call Ruth. I told him if all went well, he'd see her late tonight, and emphasized things could still go sideways.

"Are you confident this timetable will hold?" he asked.

"Yeah. Pretty confident."

"Then I shall share the glorious news. Case Lee's confidence is a potent salve."

"Just remember, no locations, no travel plans, no details. Right?"

"Right. Or roger that," he said with a wide grin.

While he chatted, I called Marcus. He'd be working on his second coffee, staring out his ranch house picture window at snow-covered hills and mountains, considering the day's chores.

"Are you stateside?" he asked as a greeting.

"Am indeed. How's your special delivery holding out?"

"First, how's yours?"

"All good."

A brief pause as he sipped coffee.

"I suppose I should say you never cease to amaze me, but it wouldn't ring true. I'm at the point where you pulling this type of thing off has become routine. Until it isn't. And that's the point where I'm afraid I'll lose you, Case."

"I appreciate the sentiment, Marcus. I do. This one had more twists than a mongoose with a bad itch. I'll go over it with you once it's done."

"Here's a thought. Learn to sniff out the mission parameters before taking a job."

"Yeah, I'm piss-poor at that. One thing for sure—I'm sick and tired of being played like a freakin' bass drum during the *1812 Overture*."

"Then exit the orchestral business."

"It's what I do."

"Which circles back to my overall point. It's clear you've swallowed your day's dumbass pill ration, so let's talk about my special delivery."

We did. Ruth remained with Marcus while she shopped for a new place out west. Marcus claimed she'd set up a new Nevada corporation, paid for everything with cryptocurrencies, and had found a small property with potential. All good. Ruth waited for Bart's arrival before pulling any triggers on real estate purchases.

"Man, I appreciate your help with all this," I said.

"No big deal. What's the ETA on delivery?"

"I'll meet Bo in Colorado Springs. He'll deliver from there, taking off around noon."

"You're not coming with him?"

"Dollars to doughnuts our former field spook will demand a chitchat in the immediate future."

"She'll be bent out of shape. Although she should expect less than by-the-book behaviors with you."

"I've had it, Marcus. Up to here. There's a facet of this job I'll cover with you later, but right now I'm not in the mood to humor her."

"Don't burn any bridges. If you're hell-bent on your current idiotic career, she can come in damn handy. As we all well know."

We said our goodbyes, and the mission's semifinal leg kicked off. Bart and I were heading for Miami's airport with the same taxi driver when Townsend called. As always, and even though she'd initiated the call, she waited for me to speak first.

"Director."

"Mr. Lee. I will send a plane. Where are you?"

Finger snap expected, so the usual irritation remained below the surface.

"Nowhere near an airfield. I'll call you back."

She hung up as we began seeing signs for the Miami airport. At the private air terminal, we boarded without issue, took off, and landed in Colorado Springs four hours later. Bo greeted us outside the terminal, leaning against his SUV, arms crossed, head lifted and eyes closed, wearing a sedate smile as a light breeze lifted several wild strands of red hair. Man, it was good to see him. The guy who'd take this quest across the finish line while I tied up loose ends. The man I trusted with the mission's completion more than anyone on earth. We hugged, bumped foreheads, and I introduced Bart. They shook.

"I like your wife. You presented a very cool signal with the Chaucer quote," Bo said. "A man of letters, I take it."

Bart looked at the ground and said, "I read quite a bit."

"Plus, a man who delves into physics. We can chat about the metaphysical aspect of your work on the drive. What would you like me to call you? Doctor Hall? Bartholomew?"

Bart, overwhelmed at the attention and questions, continued staring at the ground.

"Bart works," I said. "I checked road conditions. It's all good. Snow aplenty off the asphalt and bitter cold, but no ice issues on hard-top."

"I am afraid I am not very good with names," Bart said, looking up. "Bo. Yes, Bo. I believe I shall remember it. Please call me Bart as Case Lee has done throughout this adventure."

"My Georgia peach is an adventurer extraordinaire. I well imagine you received an ample taste."

"Yes. Yes, I would most certainly say so."

"You guys should hit the road," I said. "Ruth will be waiting."

Bo and I hugged again, tossed choice BS at each other, and he fired the SUV. Bart remained frozen, so I approached him, hand extended.

Snippets, vignettes, come and go within life, and I added the next few seconds to my personal remembrance list. Bart, head down, bypassed my handshake and stood close. Then he lowered his bald pate farther and rested it against my sternum.

"Goodness, Case Lee. My goodness."

I rubbed and patted his back.

"Helluva ride, wasn't it, Bart?"

"Goodness gracious. Weights and measures are not required for what I owe you, because I owe you everything. I shall rejoin my Ruthie tonight because of your efforts."

He pulled his head away a few inches and delivered a series of head-to-chest bumps, each accompanied with a "Thank you" as I continued patting his back.

"You take care, bud. You and Ruth. Be happy for me. That's a big one."

He straightened as tears rolled down his cheeks, nodding several times before turning toward Bo's vehicle. I cast a prayer he and Ruth would find happiness in their new, hidden life. No feelings of exaltation at the delivery, only relief soaked with poignancy and tinged with sadness. Bart and I had traipsed through hell together. I'd miss him, and Ruth, with the two together now tucked away in a special place within my heart.

Inside the private terminal, I helped myself to a coffee, and gave them a thirty-minute head start before contacting Townsend because, well, you never knew.

"Director, I'm in Colorado Springs."

I waited thirty seconds while she muted her phone and ascertained flight availability.

"One hour at the airport, Mr. Lee."

She hung up. The Company already had a plane either here or nearby. No surprise with the defense installations, some secret, scattered across the Rockies. I landed in DC at six, the day already dark, the wind biting and cold.

Chapter 42

My mood matched transient surroundings—a black-painted jet, midnight black SUV with dark-tinted windows, two cats in black suits occupying front seats, and shadowy Langley streets with few streetlights. She'd demand Ruth and Bart. I'd let her know the Case-Lee-as-ragdoll routine wouldn't cut it anymore. The admonition from Marcus not to burn bridges had validity and was fair enough, but she and I went too far back for us to tiptoe around hard realities.

The small bistro cast mellow illumination from several windows—warmth and light a false promise for me. Inside, the usual. Marilyn Townsend sat tucked in a far corner surrounded by dour protection. I stopped at the bar and ordered a double Grey Goose on the rocks while seven hard-ass protectors with automatic submachine guns hidden under jackets watched my every move. Townsend remained focused on her meal and never looked up. The queen waited for her minion's arrival.

Drink in hand, rucksack shouldered, I approached the security detail. The jacket hid the 9mm pistol parked in the waistband of my jeans. A few paces from her entourage, I pulled the jacket's hem aside and ensured the weapon's full display. Yeah, schoolyard childish BS and purposeful antagonism, but a gesture matching my mood. No words were exchanged as I waded through their clenched jaws and intense glares.

"Mr. Lee. You exhibit a hidden talent, with quite the flair for a dramatic entrance. Or do you intend to shoot me?"

She washed down a charred brussels sprout with white wine as I sat beside her.

"Director."

"I'm having the lamb kabob and have ordered you the beef version with french fries. As I recall, you've never appreciated lamb. I remain unclear on your affinity for brussels sprouts."

"Can I assume the food isn't drugged?"

"Shall I summon my official taster?"

"I'd appreciate you summoning all the hunyaks in your inner circle who dreamt up the bullshit I just went through. I might shoot *them*."

She chuckled and forked another sprout. Her 'tude threw me, big time. I expected laserlike glares, terse words, and warnings galore if I didn't spill the beans on the Halls' location. Not dinner and a date. It smelled like another two-step twirl as spookville's big dog provided the music. So I plonked a stake in the ground.

"I won't tell you where the Halls relocated."

"Much ado about nothing. I would recommend a nice cabernet sauvignon with your steak kabob."

She smiled. What the hell? Then I remembered the physics professor Bo and I had run into on the Stanford campus and the same quote. Final, unknown puzzle pieces fell into place. Townsend didn't give a rat's ass about the Halls, knowing Bart laced his research with hyperbole. No phase two, bring in the Halls, existed. The Delta operator who'd delivered a tight nod on the rooftop had offered safety, not confinement. Townsend's current attitude—icing on the clandestine cake.

The entire gig with the Company planted me in the keep-Bart-alive role until their geopolitical play against China was completed. Then, whatever. Take Bart, leave Bart. Don't care. Man, I was an idiot. I sucked down my vodka and stared into the big lost.

"Don't mope, Mr. Lee. It doesn't become you."

My food arrived, and she ordered me red wine, playing the hostess with the mostest. My temperature gauge rocketed.

"You know what else doesn't become me, Marilyn?" I asked once the server left. "Playing the Company's gofer. Hanging my ass on the line so you can play your bullshit one-upmanship. Not one bit of that crap becomes me. Not one damn bit."

"Consider this meal a victory celebration, Case. A very successful mission completed, a field operation wrapped in global impact. And do remember whose side you are on. No man is an island."

"Glad you've got the literary metaphors down pat. What you *don't* have down pat is my role. I'm not your lapdog. Sabe? And I'm not a quick summons away from performing in whatever horseshit chess plays you and your team dream up. No more, no mas, never again. Those were real bullets and real dead bodies and real danger you put both Bart and me in. You ever think about that?"

She sliced up a lamb chunk and said, "It may hearten you knowing no serious injuries befell our players in Panama. There remains a brotherhood bond between all of you, does there not?"

Yeah, there was. I felt relief—serious, heartfelt relief—the Delta team had survived Colón with no deaths. But she continued sidestepping the prime issue.

"Glad to hear it. It was a tough firefight. With live ammo pointed in my direction more than a few times. I'm not bulletproof, Marilyn. No more gigs like this one. I mean it."

"Eat, Case. Your food is getting cold. Those fries look appealing."

I slugged down half the wine and tasted the fries. She was setting me up for something, this sit-down way off the normal rails. I attempted a hard turn back toward matters at hand.

"Are other players still pursuing the Halls?"

"A possibility, I'm afraid. If they would discredit their own research, it would help lower the heat."

"Bart will deliver a white paper and call BS on his own work."

"Excellent. But the Halls should bear in mind other interested parties might construe such a missive as a false flag."

"So they need a new life."

"I would recommend it."

Bad news. I'd hoped for a return to normalcy for them after a cooling-off period. Not in the cards.

"You didn't have a clue the Norks worked our turf in California?"

"We are not perfect."

"They took out a DIA operator in Idaho."

"As I am well aware. A trigger point for our mutual mission."

"Who hired me on the initial contract?"

"Unknown. I might place Mossad at the top of the list, although MI6 or the SVR remain strong possibilities."

"Why the hell would the Russians hire me?"

She paused, placed her fork on the plate, raised her wineglass toward me, and locked eyes.

"Because you excel at what you do. The same reason I hire you. It is not complicated."

How much her statement carried sincerity and how much reeked of BS, unknown. She still played me, an ulterior motive held close and hidden.

"Do the Chicoms know it was me in Ecuador and Panama?"

A biggie. They'd focused on Bart, and I may—a big may—have played a simple role as protector from their perspective. The MSS operators who'd seen me in both countries now lay dead, incapable of telling any tales.

"I would suggest no. Such an opinion comes with no guarantees, however."

Better than nothing, and placement I could live with. Unlike the Russkies, who held grudges big time, the Chicoms exhibited longer perspectives and great pragmatism.

"I've run up heavy expenses on this contract."

"Submit them, and I will pay. As well as your fee. There will be no arguments over invoicing. Which leads us into a discussion on future engagements."

"Quoting an old movie, what we have is a failure to communicate. Those gigs are over, Marilyn."

She sliced more lamb, chewed, and stabbed another brussels sprout.

"I might acquiesce to widening the intel parameters on future endeavors," she said, then sipped more wine.

A carrot dangled before the mule. Better than her wielding a stick, but not by much. She'd proposed grand plan exposure for me next go-round. I held little confidence she'd deliver. Besides, I'd had enough. No bridges burned, no definitive proclamations other than quit using me as an expendable asset. Case Lee Inc. versus the CIA. Lousy odds. She'd already muted my fire with softer words than usual, and now I simply sought a break.

"Let's talk future endeavors in the future. Right now, I want nothing to do with the Company."

"An understandable sentiment, although time may well heal your perceived wounds. Let's not overlook our mutual accomplishments. Missions performed in unison with remarkable outcomes."

"Stop playing me, Marilyn. Our road goes back too far for that."

She chuckled and continued eating. I joined her. In short order she dropped all pretense, we kicked the just-completed job to the curb, halted future work discussions, and reminisced about old times.

"Bo says hi-ho."

His name brought a look of genuine affection.

"His actions in Angola still make me smile. Did you ever find out where he stole a high-end yacht on the Congo River?"

Light chuckles and headshakes and past highlights passed back and forth. I ordered another wine, still acutely aware that the person I supped with had no issue hanging my butt on the line. Had I level-set the playing field? No, not really. She had the full weight of the world's largest spy organization at her fingertips. I lived on a boat. Future work together? Hard to say. Not now, not in the immediate, but the door remained cracked open.

Supper over, she wiped her mouth with the cloth napkin, retrieved her cane, and tapped it twice on the floor. Her protective squad stood as one.

She rose from the table and said, "We will meet again, you and I. For my part, I look forward to it."

"Take care, Director."

"You as well, Mr. Lee. Pass on my best wishes to Atticus Finch and his wife."

Surrounded with black suits, she made her way into the cold DC night.

THE SAWTOOTH JOB

Chapter 43

I slouched in a Clubhouse chair as Jules eyeballed my countenance. I'd driven down to Chesapeake after holing up in a motel outside DC.

Chipper and upbeat should have defined the day, but I couldn't deliver. I'd made a late call with Bo the night before after he'd arrived at Marcus's place. No issues. Ruth and Bart now together, their reunion glorious and touching. I'd chatted with Marcus as well—he'd keep them both for another week until they completed their new home's purchase. Ruth had discovered it in western Montana along the Yellowstone River, where hot springs abounded.

Post-job deflation, a nebulous path forward, and Townsend's meeting had dragged me down. Couldn't put my finger on it. The morning's early call with Jess provided a temporary uplift, but our relationship hadn't developed enough, or I hadn't opened up enough, for her to grasp the messed-up internal mechanics twisting my head.

"How's New Hampshire?" I asked.

"It's winter here, bub. Something you southern lads cannot grasp."

"Had a pretty good grip on it in Idaho. There's this thing called snow you're liable to run into."

"Tell me about it. I rented, as per the general program, a vehicle that scoots when called upon. Turns out, rapid acceleration isn't the best driving habit on ice."

I chuckled and said, "What's a poor girl from North Carolina to do? Maybe you should break out the sled dogs."

"What I am liable to break is my rear end if I slip and fall any more. Where are you?"

"Headed toward Chesapeake."

"Ah, your mysterious information broker. I thought those visits happened before and after a job."

"Yep."

"So, Mr. Effusive, you finished the job?"

"Done and done."

"I don't hear any champagne corks popping in the background, and you don't sound enthused. Did things go sideways?"

"Things, or at least the outcome, ended pretty doggone well. Getting there was messy."

"Are you physically alright?"

Messy implied gunfire, which had appeared in spades. But Jess and I maintained a tacit agreement—no detailing those events.

"No worries."

"No worries isn't the same as no injuries."

"No injuries."

Just grenades and bullets and Norks and Chicom operators and a Delta team. And spooks out the wazoo as added spice.

"So what's the deal, cowboy? Chalk one up for the good guys, which should accompany a satisfied uplift. Are you depressed about something?"

"I'm okay. Miss you. How's Lily doing?"

A gear shift, which Jess noted with a conversational pause. To her credit, she didn't fire up the excavation equipment and address my mental state.

"Pops checks in with her every day, as I do via text message, and so far, so good. I should wrap this engagement in about a week and arrive back in Charlotte. Would someone I know care to join me?"

"You bet. Maybe we should look at a winter trip to the Caribbean."

We talked islands and warmth and sandy beaches for a while before signing off. Our chat, with potential warm-water plans, provided a much needed, albeit brief, positive outlook.

Chesapeake was windy and cold, the salt air biting. When I'd entered the Clubhouse, Jules asked for a full download. I provided it in complete detail, which included the previous night's sit-down with Townsend.

"A potent sleuthing element with this one, Poirot," she said, firing a cigar, "with more than a smidgen of *Mission Impossible*. I am particularly fond of the literary and epicurean references. Your Doctor Hall is a well-read individual, although I cannot speak for a guinea pig's flavor profile."

"He, and Ruth, are good folks. As someone recently said, chalk one up for the good guys."

"Indeed. As for the requested Quito and Colón contacts, you realize the Clubhouse cannot guarantee the efficacy, much less the loyalty, of recommended fixers?"

It brought a smile. Jules tended to an immediate business item. No items under warranty.

"I have no quality or closed-mouth commitment expectations with them, and appreciate, as always, the help."

"Then I shall point out, coinciding with raised hackles, you might have grasped the larger picture much earlier had you better internalized the one big thing."

The one big thing. Nothing is ever as it seems. At least in Jules's world. And, I supposed, mine.

"No hackles raised on my end. You're spot on. I should have picked up on it when I bumped into the Delta team at the DC hangar."

"Regarding your former organization, what assurances might you have carried concerning their actions?"

"Regarding them shooting me?"

"Among other things."

"Pretty doggone assured."

"Ah."

I wouldn't elaborate on the Delta bond, but she'd log my statement into her data bank.

"You exhibit an internal fatigue, Horatio. An unusual sight."

"Can't shake it, Jules."

"How might this withered heart help?"

"Listen. Talk." I sighed. "You're it. The lone person on this good earth who understands, really understands, what I do. And, I suspect, why I do it."

"You are not alone, dear boy. Yes, you have me. In toto and without reservation. But let us count the ways—a loving family, an amour, and friends who would crawl through fire for you. These are not minor items."

"No argument on the externalities. All true enough and appreciated. But it doesn't mitigate the sense that, sometimes, I feel like I'm stranded on an ice floe."

She leaned forward, elbow on desktop, chin planted in palm while the other hand wielded the cigar.

"How much might this be postmortem blues?"

"Some. The usual."

"Might your conversation with her yesterday have triggered a greater malaise?"

Neither Jules nor I used Townsend's name. A Clubhouse protocol, the reason unclear. The Company was a good Clubhouse client, and Townsend's identity was well known to Jules. Still. We always referenced "her" or "she."

"Could have. They have used me before, but somehow this was different. A tool. An expendable tool."

"Yes, you are. The expendable aspect shall remain debatable. But a valued tool for her. I cannot emphasize enough your mission, in her eyes, filled a critical role."

"In her grand scheme."

"Yes. The grand scheme. This is what they do, dear. You might consider she counted on you for both brain and brawn. You discovered where the Asian proxies hid the prize. Her own people failed at such an endeavor."

"I had help."

"Yes, you did. And she both knew and counted on it. Again, an exceptional tool."

"Not exceptional enough for a reveal into the mission. Integration with the larger team. Not used and abused."

"Ah. Back on the ice floe."

"Yeah."

She puffed the cigar. I adjusted in the uncomfortable chair, hands across my belly, legs extended.

"You want to ask me if I'd like some cheese with my whine?"

She chuckled.

"Perhaps a bit. Take heart, brave Ulysses. A man with your unique talents, talents lifted with a heart strong and true, stands rare and cherished. I would advise you to ignore the perceived hurts and isolation with the realization that such is your lot in life. Such is the lot of the precious few who might compare to you."

"You're blowing smoke, Jules."

She laughed outright, a rare event.

"To a minor degree, perhaps. On the ledger's material side, your jobs, I would assume, pay exceptionally well. And speaking of which"— she paused and extended a bony finger toward the abacus, shifting black balls on rails—"two thousand for the Quito and Colón contacts. This comes with a substantial Clubhouse discount as your tale offers this wretched creature the opportunity for both near- and long-term strategic repositioning. Would you care for edification on how this would manifest?"

"Not really."

I pulled Benjamins and peeled off twenty bills, sliding them across the desk where they lingered for a few seconds before disappearing into a desk drawer.

"Perhaps you require a respite. A getaway."

"Jess and I talked about a Caribbean retreat."

"Just what the doctor ordered, I would well imagine."

"And I could ask the Zurich gnomes for an industrial job. Any job other than one neck-deep in spookville."

"A legitimate request."

Jules continued eyeballing me, her expression benign. I reflected on how often we'd met, and her role's criticality.

"When I said you're it, Jules, I meant it. I don't want to fling rose petals in your path, but the fact is you've often represented my lifeline. More than that. A trusted advisor, and those remain scarce as hen's teeth. I've got Marcus and Bo and Catch. And now, Jess. But for insights and admonitions and advice within this shadowed freakin' world I always end up in, you're it. And I can't tell you how much I appreciate it."

"I would be remiss not returning the accolades, but I shall keep it simple. It is your heart, Case Lee. It is what separates you from my other clients. A stout and solid heart, one focused on an often nebulous yet foundational premise. Do right. It is your defining characteristic, dear boy. Now, I shall call our mutual admiration society meeting to an end. Let us address the inevitable."

I knew where she headed because, at the day's end, she got me as well as anyone.

"The itch shall appear soon enough," she said, one eyebrow raised.

The doggone weird and dangerous and makes-little-sense itch to hang it out there again. Acknowledged, semi-accepted, and scratched with jobs the Swiss tossed my way.

"Yeah. I know."

"When it arrives, dear boy, know the Clubhouse remains open for you with support and succor at hand."

"It may be a while this time."

"I doubt it," she said with a smile, puffing the cigar.

I smiled back, an acknowledgment toward reality whether or not I liked it.

"Yeah, so do I, Jules. So do I."

Epilogue

"You are better now," CC said.

"Am I?"

We sat at a picnic table in Valona, Georgia, eating a take-out supper. I'd picked up CC, my mentally challenged younger sister, in Charleston and headed south on the *Ace of Spades*. We'd visited Ossabaw and Sapelo Islands off the Georgia coast and when a northeastern blew in, headed inland, up Blackbeard Creek.

"Yes. Better. You took off your worry hat. Mom says we should take off our worry hat and lift our face to the sky. I'm glad we took Tinker Juarez with us."

Tinker Juarez, a mutt of indeterminate lineage and CC's constant companion. On our trips on board the *Ace*, when underway, Tinker would stand at the bow with nose into the wind. Our bow's canine figurehead. Sometimes I'd leave Tinker belowdecks when CC and I made a town excursion, but for whatever reason, she'd been adamant he accompany us on our Valona supper trip. Hence the takeout and picnic table.

"I'm glad to. He likes your shrimp tails."

"He *loves* shrimp tails," she said, sliding him another under the table from her plate of grilled shrimp and fried grits.

My worry hat *had* come off, and with no shortage of gazing upward and expressing gratitude for all I had. Actions kicked off, perhaps, when Marcus sent me a photo on our boat trip's second night. CC slept belowdecks with Tinker while I relaxed on the duct-tape-repaired throne

353

and nursed a Grey Goose vodka. The photo he texted showed two figures immersed in a hot pool along a river as snow covered the riverside. Expanding the photo, I could make out Ruth and Bart packed into the deepest hole, knees touching, eyeglasses fogged on both, as Bart leaned in and spoke while Ruth smiled. Two happy peas in a pod. Marcus called me after he'd sent the photo.

"Not a storybook ending," he said, "but pretty doggone close."

"Man, it's a great photo. Thank you. Thanks for everything."

"My part of the equation was easy. You shake off the blues yet?"

I smiled. Marcus, straight to the point.

"Working on it. How long did Bo stay with you?"

"It seemed like several months."

Marcus, when not engaged in battle, could take Bo only in small doses.

"Went well, did it?"

"In the evenings, after we'd scouted their new property, he'd lead the Halls down philosophical rabbit holes. Which they seemed to enjoy."

"He's good at it."

"No, he's not. You know I enjoy a solid philosophical discussion. But Bo insists on leading the charge without a tiller and sends the exchange way off course. I can only handle schizophrenic navigation in tiny portions."

"The universe abides."

"Don't you start. Bart Hall told more than a few interesting tales about South American adventures. What the hell did you use to bring the sheer rock wall crashing down?"

"A sawed-off thumper."

"Good for you. Maybe my strictures on never entering a fight under-armed has influenced you."

"Roger on that."

An owl flew past the *Ace*, it's wings silent, hunting. I'd anchored up a slough off the Ogeechee River, the night fleece-jacket cool.

"He's fascinated with the fixer you engaged in Colón. Some coke-snorting lady with a purple mohawk? Son, consider, for me, the company you keep on these jobs."

"Turquoise mohawk. Bart got into the whole deal. Felt it had a James Bond vibe."

"You're ignoring my request."

"Yep. Those types come with the turf. As for Bart, he dug deep and showed real moxie several times. You'd have been proud of him."

"Well, they're happy. I'll move them into their new digs once the sale completes. What's next on your agenda?"

"I'm cruising with CC now. Jess and I might make a Caribbean trip soon. What's the Fishtail, Montana, weather right now?"

"Don't start."

"Blizzard conditions? It's bright and in the eighties down in the Carib."

"Leave it."

"Warm water laps at the beaches. Piña colada days, bud. Of course, you'd miss the gentle lowing of your bovines."

"I like winter weather, you moron. It makes me feel alive."

"Until it kills you."

"Speaking about getting killed, are you insistent with your Swiss client on death-defying jobs? It's your current trend, you know."

"Gotta play to my strengths. Besides, it rolls and it tumbles."

Bo's core philosophy about life. And, yeah, it *did* roll and tumble.

"I swear, Case. I swear."

As CC hummed a song between bites, I finished my whole flounder and hush puppies, both deep-fried. Tinker sat at full attention under the table. I relished these trips with CC. When events swirled and adrenaline meters cranked up, downtime with her provided, above all, grounding. Appreciation of the small miracles around us. We stayed at Valona for the night, headed northward toward Charleston, Mom and CC's home, the next morning. I'd keep within the Intracoastal Waterway, the Ditch, as high winds remained forecasted for the next several days.

I rose early, as usual, and fired first the generator, then the wheelhouse coffeepot. My movements stirred Tinker, who joined me for a brief moment and a head rub before leaping onto the grassy area alongside our tie-up. CC remained asleep, even as I started the old, reliable diesel drive and began our trip north. Once underway, Jess called. I placed her on speaker.

"I've sussed out a place in the BVI I think we'd like," I said, steaming coffee mug in one hand, the other on the wooden wheel, steering us up the Ditch with the wheelhouse windows rolled down. Man, it always felt good on the move. "Are you up for it?"

"It would depend, bub. What is a BVI?"

"British Virgin Islands. Smack dab in the Caribbean."

"Oh, mercy, it sounds better than fine. I won't bore you with a New Hampshire weather report, but nobody is meandering about in T-shirts and flip-flops."

I laughed and we coordinated calendars. Mine, wide open. Then she tiptoed around a subject, unusual for her. Big-time unusual.

"So, I was thinking," she said.

I exchanged lifted coffee mugs with a guy who steered another Ditch cruiser, modern and fiberglass, as we passed each other.

"I'm listening."

"The key here and now, and I mean this from the bottom of my heart, is you can say no without any follow-up argument from me. It would end the idea and no hard feelings. Understood?"

"If you're contemplating a sex change, the answer's no."

"Be serious, please. It seems like I'm pushing a dangerous rock uphill."

"I'm all ears, madam. Shoot."

"What if Lily went with us? It would mean a major highlight for her teenage life. But again, I get it if you're hesitant and no recriminations and we'd have a marvelous time without her. Not another word said."

Her request threw me. I'd visualized romance and romping at the small BVI resort I'd found. Romance with Jess's niece around remained on the table, albeit muted. Romping, not so much.

"You're quiet," Jess said. "Are you perusing dating websites?"

"Of course Lily can come. She's a great kid. Can you pull her out of school?"

"She has a school break coming up, so it works. Are you sure? I'll pay for her and me."

"Nope. It's on me. And she's more than welcome to come along. Pack the sunscreen, Ms. Rossi, and let's do this."

"I owe you, bub."

"No, you don't. No keeping-track stuff. I'm a simple guy. We'll have a hoot, with warm water, snorkeling, sandy beaches, great food. What's not to like?"

We signed off. Later I tied us up along the Ditch for lunch and made sandwiches. CC loved white bread, bologna, mayo, and thin apple slices. Neither Mom nor I knew where she got the idea for slipping apple into a sandwich. I fixed myself pastrami on rye. CC sat sideways in the foredeck hammock, legs dangling with intermittent pushes off the deck as she slow rocked. I perched in the throne. Tinker sat between us and eyeballed the two prizes, with greater attention paid toward CC where odds were highest.

"I think you lost your worry hat," she said, sliding a Cheetos from her plate into the sandwich. "I know how to lose mine, too."

"How's that?"

"How is what?"

"How do you lose your worry hat?"

"Love. Home tomorrow?"

From the mouth of babes. It *was* love. Love of family and friends and a lover and appreciation for all I had. Love of life.

"Yep. Home tomorrow."

"Will you stay or go?"

"I'll stay a few days. Since the wind looks like it will keep blowing, maybe we could go fly a kite."

"Oh, Case!"

"And maybe take Tinker to the dog park."

"Tinker Juarez."

"Right. Tinker Juarez. Would you like that?"

"Oh, yes. I would *love* it!"

"So would I, my CC. So would I."

THE END

THE SAWTOOTH JOB

ABOUT VINCE MILAM – AUTHOR OF THE BESTSELLING CASE LEE SERIES.

I live in Idaho, where wide-open spaces and soaring mountains give a person perspective and room to think. I relish great books, fine trout streams, family, old friends, good dogs, and interacting with my readers.

If you'd like to join my Readers Club with insights, updates, an insider's look at story development, and other fun items, **simply click below.**

http://eepurl.com/cWP0iz

OR visit www.vincemilam.com

You can visit my Author Page on Amazon for a full list of the Case Lee novels. All are stand-alone. You can start anywhere and enjoy the ride. They are also available on Audiobook.

https://www.amazon.com/Vince-Milam/e/B00T6H12BO

As for the Case Lee settings—well, I've lived and worked all over the world, traipsing through places like the Amazon, West Africa, Papua New Guinea, Europe, the Middle East, etc. I have either lived and worked or visited every location incorporated into these novels. And I make a point of capturing unique sights, sounds, and personalities that weave through each of my novels. I want you, dear reader, to feel as though you've been there once you've finished the tale.

Thank you for joining me on these adventures!

All the best, *Vince*

Printed in Great Britain
by Amazon

23215492R00209